OPERATION GOODWOOD

OPERATION GOODWOOD

by

Sara Sheridan

Magna Large Print Books
Long Preston, North Yorkshire,
BD23 4ND, England.

2017

British Library Cataloguing in Publication Data.

A catalogue record of this book is
available from the British Library

ISBN   978-0-7505-4415-3

First published in Great Britain in 2016 by Constable

Cover illustration © John Michaels by arrangement with
Alamy Stock Photo

The moral right of the author has been asserted

Published in Large Print 2017 by arrangement with
Little, Brown Book Group

Magna Large Print is an imprint of Library Magna Books Ltd.

Printed and bound in Great Britain by
T.J. (International) Ltd., Cornwall, PL28 8RW

This book goes out to Jenny Brown,
who is a guiding light and quite extraordinary

Ten people who speak make more
noise than ten thousand who are silent

NAPOLEON BONAPARTE

Prologue

Goodwood Racing Track,
Easter Monday 11 April, 1955

Superintendent McGregor laid out a tartan rug and opened the picnic basket. The grassy bank was dotted with couples relaxing in the blazing sunshine, the men with jackets off and the women lazing amid a sea of sugar-starched underskirts and the layers of bright fabric that overlaid them. On the other side of the track, three drivers in grey overalls were swigging American beer straight from the bottle as they discussed the day's programme and their chances on the track. As if to illustrate whatever point they were making, a racing car whizzed past and pulled in at a pit stop. The buzz and roar of the engines was overwhelming. Mirabelle smiled as the drivers became increasingly animated, one of them pointing at the bend, shouting over the noise of the other cars, conjecturing how to take it at speed.

'It's a good spot,' McGregor said. 'The finish line is just over there.'

'How fast do you think they go?' Mirabelle asked, standing on tiptoes in her high heels, as she strained to see.

'A bit faster than we managed coming up here, anyway.'

McGregor was good humoured but it hadn't

13

been an easy journey. The train had been packed, even in first class. The man sitting opposite them had had to give up reading the *Telegraph* because of the crush, and when he did, Mirabelle had had to give up squinting to make out the stories. The headline was about Africa – Kenya, in fact. Additional troops had been sent to quell what the paper termed 'unrest' but Mirabelle thought should be more accurately described as a nationalist uprising. There was a picture of a white man in a pith helmet sitting astride a bay horse. In the article there had been some discussion about the state of the British Empire, what with India having been lost. She wondered how it had concluded.

McGregor passed her a glass of Vimto. 'You must be thirsty,' he said.

Mirabelle sipped. It was the strangest taste – it occurred to her that children might like it but it was far too sweet.

'Thanks,' she said, noting with relief he'd also packed a thermos flask of tea. She hoped they'd move on to that soon. Then, glass in hand, she settled down on the rug, smoothing her sage-green skirt and drawing her legs elegantly to one side as another racing car took the bend and almost veered out of control. McGregor made a sound that indicated how close a call he considered it to be. Then he strained to keep the car in view as the driver pulled up ahead. 'That's Stirling Moss,' he said, in admiration. 'He's tipped to be the British Champion – they say he'll take the Grand Prix this summer. We've opened a book at the station.'

Mirabelle watched as the driver pulled in and

sprang out of the car to shake hands with a chap in a suit. She closed her eyes, enjoying the warmth of the sun on her skin though she was glad of her plaited straw hat – at least it kept the glare off. When she opened her eyes again, McGregor was staring at her, a smile playing on his lips. She smiled back, meeting his gaze. It was pleasant to come out like this, together for the day.

'Ah, it's starting,' he said.

Ahead several stewards with flags took their places and a line of cars formed, jostling like anxious horses. They made a colourful collection. Two Dutch vehicles were painted in orange livery and one Italian in red, but mostly the cars were British racing green. The engines roared intermittently as the drivers revved furiously. In response, the crowd bristled as people jostled to find a place from which to view the race. As far as Mirabelle could make out in both directions, there were rugs and picnic baskets along the grassy bank and beyond them an undulating crowd that moved as one, straining to catch a glimpse of the line-up. The tang of engine fuel thickened the hot air and over at the grandstand everyone turned towards the starting line.

Mirabelle sat up. In the pit stop opposite them a crowd of young men were shoving each other out of the way to get the best view of the starting line. Then, as she turned in the other direction, she caught a glimpse of something that was wrong. Among all the thousands of people in the crowd directing themselves towards the track, she spotted a girl moving smoothly away from it. As far as the eye could see people were closely packed

15

but the girl was wearing a distinctive mauve hat constructed of starched cotton roses, so Mirabelle found it easy to pick her out. As she slipped past one fellow, Mirabelle watched her bump into him, quite on purpose, slip her hand into his pocket and remove a clip of banknotes. Mirabelle put down her Vimto as the flag behind her flourished and the cars took off in a concerted roar. The noise worked up to a crescendo. Immediately one of the Dutch vehicles pulled ahead. With everyone else transfixed by that, Mirabelle took off after the girl, who was slipping away through the tightly packed bodies. A couple of people tutted loudly as Mirabelle pushed past. For a moment she lost sight of the mauve hat, but then it appeared again to the left and she used her handbag like an oar cutting through water, pushing it ahead to part the crush of bodies. The buzz of the engines lassoed everyone's attention as the cars raced by. A hundred yards from the track the crowd began to ease and Mirabelle managed to catch up. She laid a hand on the girl's shoulder.

'I saw what you did,' she said. 'I saw you pick his pocket.' The girl tried to pull away. Up close, Mirabelle could see her dress was patched at the hem and her shoes were worn. 'I'm sorry but you have to give back the money.' She nodded towards the girl's bag. 'I won't report you, but you can't keep it.'

'How about I gave you a quid or two, eh?' The accent was pure cockney. 'Split it with you.'

Mirabelle shook her head. 'I'm sorry.'

The girl paused as if considering this. Then she pulled away and took off again, fast as a shot.

16

Mirabelle ran in pursuit, dodging an ice-cream stall with a tight-pressed queue of eager children and following the line of bunting hoisted overhead as the crowd eased. Fast even in heels, she tackled the girl, bringing her down. Several spectators stared but nobody cut in.

'I mean it,' Mirabelle hissed. 'Do you want me to fetch a policeman? I'm giving you a chance to do the right thing.'

The girl scrambled around to face her. 'You hurt my knee,' she said, indicating a graze on her pale skin.

'I'm sorry, but you can't go around thieving.'

The girl reached into her handbag and thrust the clip of notes into Mirabelle's hand. 'You take it back, if you're so keen,' she spat, getting to her feet and walking away smartly.

Mirabelle brushed the dust off her skirt. There was at least ten pounds in her hand. She sighed, staring in the direction she'd come. If she retraced her steps she'd recognise the fellow, she supposed. She made her way back past the Shell Oil stand and the kids queuing for ices and from there she cut into the crowd exactly where she'd emerged. Within sight of McGregor she laid a hand on the man's arm. He was wearing a light linen jacket and his hat was finished with a blue and red ribbon, not dissimilar in pattern to the bunting overhead.

'Here,' she said, holding out the money. 'I think you dropped this.'

The man glanced at her, clearly more interested in what was happening on the tarmac. 'Oh yes. Thanks, love.' He put his hand into his inside pocket to check it, and fumbled, feeling it empty.

'That's very decent of you.'

The woman beside him gave Mirabelle a dirty look as if this could only be some kind of ploy. She clasped the man's elbow as if she was claiming him.

'You got money on this race, do you?' He was trying to be civil.

'No. Just watching,' Mirabelle said.

There was a screech of tyres as three cars rounded the corner in unison, jostling for pole position. The orange vehicle had not kept its lead. Several people jumped up and down and there was a cheer as they whizzed past.

'Come on Beaumont!' someone shouted. 'Come on!'

'I like these shorter races,' the man confided. 'They do an eight hour, you know. But you got to have stamina for that.' He grinned. 'Can I buy you a drink, love? After?'

'Thanks,' Mirabelle said, 'but I'm with a friend.'

As she slipped back next to McGregor, he put his arm around her. 'Are you all right? You just dodged off there.'

'I had to powder my nose.' She picked up her glass.

'See that car? That one.' McGregor pointed to a long vehicle painted green. It had the number '26' on the side. 'That's Dougie Beaumont's engine. Look at him. He rounded that corner and I thought he was going to take off. Fantastic driving.' He sucked air through his teeth as the long car zoomed past. Ahead, an attendant stepped on to the track and waved a huge flag on a pole, cutting through the thick air as if he was mixing it.

18

The crowd gasped. 'Last lap,' McGregor said, squeezing her shoulder.

The clutch of green and white cars pulsed ahead of the trailing red and orange ones but it was close – only a second or two between them. Mirabelle wondered if Beaumont was going to come in ahead of Moss – after all, if he beat the man tipped to win the Grand Prix, it would be exciting. They were travelling at such speed, too. As the cars appeared again the crowd froze and then a grumble started – like a roar in the belly of a giant. Beaumont and Moss were neck and neck as they rounded that last bend and then Beaumont pulled ahead, managing to wring just a little more power out of the engine when he needed it. McGregor shouted, 'Yes! That's some driving.' And the crowd erupted as Beaumont's car crossed the finish line only inches in the lead. Beside Mirabelle a pretty girl in a yellow frock spilled her champagne with excitement, scattering it on to the grass as she jumped up and down. Everyone was screaming. McGregor punched the air and Mirabelle grinned, floating on the cheers. It felt good to be part of something like this – everyone enjoying themselves together. Everyone celebrating.

The cars pulled in and the drivers slid out, removing their helmets in a smooth movement. Beaumont was surrounded immediately though he was tall so Mirabelle could still make him out. He was young and very handsome – his jaw chiselled like a film star's. He was grinning as if he hadn't expected to win – it was most endearing.

'That was a great race. Fantastic!' McGregor enthused.

Mirabelle watched as Beaumont flung his arms around his crew. He looked as if he might burst with pride – the widest smile she had ever seen. And then he spotted the woman – an older lady in a pink dress with a matching hat, loitering around the garage. The woman gave a curious little wave – only a flutter of her fingers – and Beaumont scrambled towards her, hesitating before he picked her up and spun her around. She laughed, hitting him lightly with her handbag and then wrapped her arms around him. His mother, Mirabelle thought. Well, that's nice. From behind, Stirling Moss came to add his congratulations. He reached out a hand and Beaumont put down his mother and shook it. Someone appeared with a bottle of champagne and the crew moved in a jumble until the cork was popped. The crowd began to settle down, picnic baskets were opened again, people animatedly discussed the race and money changed hands. Mirabelle sank on to the tartan rug and McGregor dug out a bottle of beer. He reached over and kissed her lightly.

'Would you like one of these?' he asked, thinking he really ought to have brought bubbly.

Mirabelle grinned. 'Why not?' she said. 'Let's get stuck in, shall we?'

McGregor flipped open the bottle. She could smell the yeast and the barley even before she sipped it.

'I don't know how those lads manage it. Can you imagine the pressure and then the excitement? They must live on adrenalin.' McGregor opened a bottle for himself.

'Like you when you're assigned a murder case?'

Mirabelle teased. 'A juicy one?'

'Me? You're just as bad and you know it,' he batted back. 'And it's not even your job!'

And then the crowd moved again – a ripple pulsing across as a white car set off on a practice run and people's attention was immediately caught. Mirabelle got to her feet and strained to see who was driving. It was quite addictive, really. She wouldn't have thought she'd get so drawn in.

Chapter 1

The path that leads on is lighted by one fire

**Five months later
Brighton, 3.25 a.m.,
Sunday 25 September, 1955**

Mirabelle awoke coughing and in confusion. The room was full of thick smoke. Panicked, she scrambled out of bed and opened the window to let in some fresh air. The smoke streamed out, funnelled through the void at the bottom of the frame. Her eyes stinging, she wasn't convinced that opening the window had helped. She couldn't even see as far as the pavement, never mind the seascape beyond. It took a moment to take in the seriousness of the situation. A fire. Here. At home. She lingered for a moment, woozy, before her training kicked in. Fires in the night had been common during the Blitz. She pulled a blanket off the mattress, flung the glass of water from her bedside over one corner of the material and then with her shoulders covered and the damp part of the blanket over her mouth, she dropped on to all fours and, wheezing, crawled into the living room. Immediately she toppled a pile of newspapers that was stacked by the sofa and blindly clambered over the detritus in the direction of the hallway. Her eyes were streaming now but she was afraid to close them and she knew rubbing would only make it worse. There was no sign of live flames here, not in the bedroom – not anywhere. She wondered momentarily where the blaze had started. This puzzle stopped her, as if she was frozen by indecision. She considered saving something – grabbing some of her possessions, but she couldn't think where to start. Then there was a loud bang as the front door crashed open and the vague silhouette of a fireman appeared on the threshold.

'Here,' she shouted. 'I'm here!'

The man grabbed her firmly by the arms and slung her efficiently over his shoulder, before carrying her into the entrance hall and down the main stairs. As the open door above receded, Mirabelle strained to keep her eyes open. Through painful lids, she could just make out tiny tongues of flame licking the banister on the second floor.

Outside, she gasped for breath in the cold night air as the man laid her gently on the pavement and a medic rushed forwards with a blanket. Her cough was rapid as machine gun fire. Behind her, a team of firemen unrolled a hose along the Lawns and she could just make out residents from further along the terrace congregated on the other side of the street in a dim huddle of pyjamas and velvet slippers. Someone was handing around mugs of tea.

'Thank you,' Mirabelle managed as she caught her breath. Her eyes were stinging.

'We didn't realise you were inside,' the fireman said. 'Thank God you opened that window. Do you know if there's anyone else in the building?'

'Mr Evans downstairs mostly stays in London – he works there. I don't know if he's in,' Mirabelle spluttered. 'And above, the flat was sold earlier this year. I've never seen anyone go in or out.'

The medic's and the fireman's eyes met as she began to breathe more easily. She lay back, the cold night air soothing her dry, gritty lids like a balm. Turning on her side, the blanket felt scratchy. She could just make out the shape of a body on a stretcher further along the pavement. Another medic was bent over it.

'Who's that?' she asked, propping herself up. Perhaps Evans had been in after all.

'That's the fellow from upstairs, miss. You sure you don't know his name?'

Mirabelle shook her head. 'I didn't know there was anyone up there. How awful.'

Mirabelle's rescuer turned away as the men flocked round the engine to help jet a stream of water across the Lawns. He fell in as they moved into position to douse the flames. To the side, the other medic stood back from the man's body. He shook his head. Mirabelle squinted to make out the corpse on the stretcher in the amber street-

23

light. His head was turned towards her. The eyes were glazed and she could just make out a shadow – a wide red welt around his neck. To one side the medic retrieved a piece of rope.

'The police will want that, I expect,' he said.

'Did he hang himself?' Mirabelle asked, as she tried to sit up further.

'Now, now, miss,' the man fussed. 'There's no point in getting worked up.'

He nodded at his friend to lay a sheet over the body. Mirabelle paused. It was odd but she could swear she had seen the man somewhere. Her bare feet were getting cold now and she tucked them under the thick fabric, drawing the blanket around her. Then she gave an involuntary shudder.

'Don't trouble yourself,' the medic continued. 'There's nothing anyone could've done.'

'But I didn't even know he was there.'

'People these days don't always know their neighbours, miss. It's not like before the war.'

'Please,' she insisted. 'Let me see him again.'

The medic hesitated, then nodded at the other man who removed the sheet from the dead man's face. Then it came to her. It was the racing driver – the young man with the strong jaw. With the mother.

'I do know him,' she said. 'Well, I've seen him. He's a driver. Beaumont? Is that the name?'

'Blow me, she's right. It's Dougie Beaumont,' the medic said. 'That's a tragedy.'

'Why would he kill himself?' Mirabelle kept her eyes steady on the welt round Dougie Beaumont's neck. 'I don't understand.'

24

'Now, now, miss. No point in getting exercised. You've identified the poor fellow. That's a help.'

Two black Marias pulled up behind the fire engine and three uniformed policemen emerged to control the crowd that was forming along the pavement. Then Superintendent McGregor appeared beside Mirabelle. He crouched down and took her hand. She felt curiously detached from what was going on but she was glad to see a familiar face.

'Are you all right? I came as soon as I heard. Can I take you to hospital?' McGregor's concern was evident.

The medic smiled indulgently. 'She's fine, sir. Though we'll keep an eye on her for another few minutes. You were lucky, miss.'

'The fire was upstairs, Alan,' Mirabelle found herself explaining with some urgency, 'and the poor man is dead. It's Dougie Beaumont – do you remember? He won the first race when we went to Goodwood at Easter? It looks like he hanged himself.'

'You leave that to me.' McGregor squeezed her fingers gently and cast a glance over his shoulder at the dead man. 'The boys will take care of it. Right now, you've had a shock and it seems you're out of digs. Why don't you come and stay at my place till we get all this sorted out?'

Chapter 2

There is nothing permanent except change

When Mirabelle woke it took a good ten seconds before she remembered where she was and what had happened. The autumn sunshine blazed around the edges of the patterned curtains and she realised it must be later than she usually rose. Somewhere in the distance she could hear church bells. Turning, she noticed a clock beside the bed. The hands stood just after ten o'clock. She coughed as she sat up too suddenly, prevented from jumping out of bed to get dressed by a sudden heaviness in her chest. As the feeling subsided there was a knock at the door and she pulled up the covers, protectively.

'Yes?'

The door swung open to reveal a woman in her sixties carrying a steaming cup of tea. She was wearing a floral housecoat over a plain grey dress and her pale hair was pinned in such a complicated construction of folds and curls that Mirabelle found herself transfixed by the detail of it.

'Good morning.' She laid the steaming cup on the bedside table. 'Mr McGregor said you'd probably like a cuppa about this time.' The woman crossed to the window in a trail of violet scent and tobacco, and opened the curtains, revealing the interior of the room. This illuminated what had only been murky detail in the half-light – faded wallpaper with sprigs of daisies at regular intervals and a chair with a thick, white antimacassar. Mirabelle's eyes fell on the sign taped beside the light switch: INSTRUCTIONS TO GUESTS. She tried to remember but the night before was hazy – everything after the fire seemed impossible to piece together. She had tried to talk to McGregor about the dead man but he had refused and instead he had helped her into bed. She couldn't recall much else. The arrangements seemed entirely inappropriate now and she felt herself blush.

Downstairs a shrill bell sounded and the older women turned. 'I wonder who that could be?' she said. 'On a Sunday.'

Mirabelle regarded the cup of tea. There was no doubt this was a guest house. There was a sink in one corner of the room with a scrap of a towel laid beside it. Looking down, she realised she was wearing the nightgown in which she'd been rescued. The edge of her sleeve was ingrained with grit and the lace collar was slightly torn. She lay back on the pillow unable to summon the will to get up, the thought slowly dawning that even if she did so, she had nothing to get dressed in. Not a toothbrush, or anything to wear.

As if reading her thoughts, the woman returned with a Hannington's bag. 'Mr McGregor must have knocked them up. He thinks of everything, doesn't he?' she said, laying it down. 'Would you like me to help you dress, miss? I was a lady's maid before. That's many years ago now.'

Mirabelle shook her head.

27

'Where has McGregor gone?'

'He went into the station, miss. He left you this.' She drew a folded paper from her pocket. Mirabelle fumbled the note open. *Dear Mirabelle. I hope you are feeling better. Brownlee will look after you*, it said. *I will try to pick up fresh clothes and have them sent over. In the meantime, I have arranged for Vesta to be informed. She is coming to help. I suggest, if you're up to it, that you go to the office. She will need to use the telephone. She seemed most keen to make the necessary arrangements. Alan.*

'The superintendent said he was bringing me home,' Mirabelle said. It was the most she could get out, given the jumble of information that was knocking around her head. The idea of 'arrangements' was beyond her.

'Yes, miss. This is Mr McGregor's home.' The woman pulled a navy woollen dress out of the bag, then a packet of stockings and a box which contained a pair of rather sensible shoes. She laid these items on the chair beside the window. 'He's lived here for a while.'

Mirabelle lay back against the pillows. It had been months since she started seeing McGregor on a romantic basis. Or was it more than a year? They shared dinner and a walk now and then. Drinks out and a trip up to London. A day trip or two. They had gone to see the terracottas at the British Museum and afterwards they had kissed. It had been surprisingly passionate – but nothing more. He'd never asked her back to his place. It wouldn't have been seemly. After that day at Goodwood, he had suggested they go away for the weekend but then there had been a murder in

28

Hove and the idea had somehow got lost on the warm summer air.

'He lives in a boarding house?'

'Yes, miss.' The woman's expression softened. 'Mr McGregor made an arrangement with Alfie, my brother. He wanted me well provided for, you see, when he went. He had debts to cover, so he sold this place to Mr McGregor on condition that I could work here. He trusted Mr McGregor to look out for me. As long as I live, he said. He's a nice fellow.'

'Oh, I'm sorry,' Mirabelle stumbled. 'At a time of bereavement ... your brother...'

The woman grinned. 'Alfie's not dead, miss. He's inside and he won't be coming out again. He got fifteen years and he's not a well man. So I run this place for Mr McGregor to earn my keep. He's not bad for a copper – a gentleman, like I said. And the old fella's only up at Lewes so I can visit now and then.'

Mirabelle hesitated. This was a new side to McGregor. She couldn't imagine him making a deal with a criminal even if it helped out this woman, who appeared, after all, perfectly pleasant. Fifteen years was a substantial sentence. She wondered what crime Alfie had committed. 'Did Mr McGregor, well, was he the officer who arrested your brother?'

The woman laughed. 'No, miss. I think Alfie was one of Mr McGregor's informants, if I'm honest. Alfie's not a bloke you'd trust. He's my brother and I love him, but that's the truth. He'd never admit he was a grass, but, well... It was nice of Mr McGregor to help us out, really. Look, if

29

you don't want me to attend you getting dressed, I'll just go back downstairs. The paying guests have gone so I've got rooms to make up and I was hoping to nip up to church later.'

'Sorry. Of course. Go on.'

Mirabelle waited until the woman's steps had receded before she got out of bed to inspect the contents of the Hannington's bag and run hot water into the sink. As she did so she realised she had no idea where she was – she didn't even know Superintendent McGregor's address.

Coming downstairs ten minutes later, Mirabelle felt odd. She didn't have a handbag or a coat to hand, but the clothes fitted perfectly. She caught sight of herself in a mirror by the door – the outfit wasn't what she'd have chosen, but it wasn't too poor a selection. She hovered. The woman reappeared almost immediately.

'I'll wash your nightie, shall I, miss?'

'Yes. I left it on the chair. Thank you. What shall I call you?'

'I'm Brownlee.' The woman smiled. 'Betty Brownlee. Miss Brownlee, I suppose. I never married, what with the war.' She reached into her apron pocket. 'You'll need a key, miss. We have rules for the guests but you and Mr McGregor come and go as you please. Dinner is always at seven.'

'Thank you.' Mirabelle took the key and fumbled as she realised the dress she was wearing didn't have a pocket. Betty Brownlee's eyes lighted on the front door. She opened it, letting in a sliver of fresh autumn air.

'I'll need a hat,' Mirabelle said, absentmindedly

laying a hand on her hair as she hovered at the threshold.

'Oh yes. Of course.' Miss Browlee darted into a room to the side and emerged with a garish blue rayon square. 'There,' she said, handing it over. 'Now it's down to the front, miss. Turn right into town.'

Mirabelle tied the scarf in place, nodded distractedly and set off down the terrace. She could feel it was Sunday on the air – there was something that would have felt too still on any other day. On the street half of the properties had boards advertising rooms to let. Glancing back, she checked what McGregor's was called. The Arundel. She wondered if it was the Arundel she would have picked if she'd come here on holiday. Casting her eyes over the others, it seemed likely. One or two of the boarding houses seemed strangely unwelcoming. Mirabelle pursed her lips. A sign saying NO DOGS NO JEWS NO BLACKS hung on one front door. Another was encased in flaking paint, as if it had a terrible case of dandruff. By contrast, the Arundel was in good repair, the small front garden was tidy and there was a substantial laurel in a terracotta pot at the entrance. She decided McGregor had brokered a good arrangement for a bachelor. He'd needed looking after and, now she thought about it, the last few months he'd seemed more presentable than when she first met him. Recently his coats had not been missing buttons and he'd appeared marginally more rested and well fed. Betty Brownlee had done a decent job. Still, he might have told her.

It was a bright morning with a chill on the air.

Along the front there were a few day trippers arrived from London, strolling along the promenade, but most of Brighton had yet to wake up. A couple of locals, keen but late, hurried past her on their way to Sunday service.

Mirabelle was pink cheeked when she arrived at McGuigan & McGuigan Debt Recovery, her mind racing as she ran through the last few hours. She climbed the stairs, realising how eager she was to see Vesta and talk about what had happened. She managed to control her disappointment when she opened the office door and the girl was nowhere to be seen. Instead, Bill Turpin was at his desk. An ex-policeman, Bill was sandy-haired and reliable in all things. He had worked at McGuigan & McGuigan for two years now and this was the first time he'd ever surprised her.

He sprang to his feet as Mirabelle entered and Panther, the office dog, Bill's almost constant companion, came to attention at his heel like a low black shadow. At rest Bill always appeared to be smiling but now his features shifted into an expression of concern.

'Are you all right?' he said, coming forward.

'You heard about what happened then?'

'Yes. Vesta called one of the neighbours. She asked me to come in and help. I've been trying to get hold of a locksmith but no one is answering the telephone. I think I might have to go and knock one up. Out of hours,' he said.

Mirabelle cast her eyes round the office. 'Where is Vesta?'

'She got on to it straight away.' Bill smiled.

'Oh?'

'The insurance.'

'Insurance?'

Bill pulled out Mirabelle's chair and she found herself almost falling into it. It was possible she was suffering from some kind of shock, she thought. She still felt like an observer, as if she couldn't quite grasp what had happened. Everyone was being so kind.

Bill didn't skip a beat. 'Vesta saw to it last year. Don't you remember? The larger-than-expected profit?'

Mirabelle nodded slowly. The previous year – 1954 – had been their busiest since they had taken over the business, and a bumper profit had ensued. Vesta had arranged to spend some of the money. She'd talked about investment and, as Mirabelle recalled, they had bought another typewriter, ordered a brass plaque for the door and had the place painted. They had also treated themselves to a slap-up office meal on Christmas Eve at the Grand.

'We've all got insurance now. Life insurance. Personal insurance. Household insurance. The lot.' Bill grinned. 'Just as well, eh? Don't worry. Vesta is seeing to it. You know what she's like – she's got her head screwed on.'

Vesta had spent the first eighteen months of her working life in Brighton, at Halley Insurances, down the hall from McGuigan & McGuigan. That's how the women had first met. It was four years since she joined the company, though these days Mirabelle couldn't imagine being without her. Vesta brought the office to life and she was meticulous about contracts. Comprehensive insurance was exactly the kind of thing Vesta would arrange given some extra money.

'She's gone over to your place to take an inventory,' Bill said. 'For the assessor. They'll send someone down tomorrow, see. Would you like a cuppa?'

Bill, like most men, rarely made tea but today, it seemed, almost anything might happen. He checked the kettle was filled and plugged it in.

'Did you hear about the poor fellow upstairs?' she asked.

Bill clattered as he sorted out the cups and saucers.

'Tragic,' he said. 'Another year and he'd have been on the Jaguar team. They'd have brought him round. Nothing surer.'

Mirabelle leant forward slightly.

'The Jaguar team?' The words tumbled from her lips as if she had dropped them.

Bill spooned sugar into the cups. 'I expect you'll want it sweet today,' he said. 'He was a hell of a driver, Dougie Beaumont. He stuck to the track like glue.'

'So it was him? It really was?'

'Oh yes. Seems he bought the flat over the summer.' Steam rose as Bill poured boiling water into the teapot. Then with no time to let it brew he poured it into a cup, added milk and laid the resulting cupful of liquid proudly on Mirabelle's desk. The contents were almost completely white. 'Suicide too,' he said. 'A crying shame.'

Mirabelle eyed the pale liquid. She was about to pick up the cup when something stopped her. Weak sweet tea was not what she'd choose, even if it was nice of Bill to pitch in. It wasn't only the tea that was perturbing her. She didn't seem able to control her thoughts. On top of her inbox there was a large debt to be processed – a complex web of missed hire purchase payments. It should be first on her list for tomorrow and suddenly it felt impossible. Overwhelming, even. Everything seemed irregular this morning. Mirabelle glanced at the hook by the door and was grateful to see her green tweed overcoat. She'd left it in the office after Vesta had picked it up the week before from the laundry on Conway Place.

'Perhaps I'll pop over to the Lawns, just to have a look. I still don't know where the fire started, you see. Or how. Last night is rather a blur.'

'Oh the brigade will be looking into that. It's only natural, you can't remember much,' Bill said cheerily.

Mirabelle got to her feet and pulled the coat over her shoulders. There was a pair of dark leather gloves in the pocket in a pristine brown paper bag. A happy discovery. She must have left them there by mistake and the laundry had cleaned them too.

'Vesta might need a hand,' she said, doing up the buttons and thinking that now, if she could only find a hat, rather than this horrible scarf, at least she'd be respectably arrayed.

'Right-o,' said Bill, slurping his tea. 'I'll get a locksmith over as soon as I can knock one up. Superintendent McGregor told Vesta the front door is open – stoved in by the brigade. First things first, eh?'

Panther rubbed against Mirabelle's leg and she felt suddenly intensely fond of the little dog. She leaned down to pat him and he wagged his tail, keeping a steady eye on Bill. There was no question where Panther's loyalty really lay.

'Do you want to take the little fella with you?' Bill offered.

Mirabelle shook her head.

'Go on. He might help you feel better.' Bill pulled the lead from his pocket and Panther's tail picked up its pace. He dashed back to Bill's desk to present himself for tethering. 'He'll be disappointed if you don't.'

Mirabelle relented. Perhaps it would be comforting to have Panther at her heel. Just for today.

'Thanks Bill,' she said, reaching out to take the lead. 'I don't suppose I'll be long.'

Chapter 3

The true mystery of the world lies in what's visible

Mirabelle had lived in her flat on the Lawns for almost eight years. Today, as she approached it, the sight of the building was horrifying. Panther sat at her heel patiently as she halted on the pavement outside. Vesta's bike was leaning against the railings and Mirabelle laid a hand on it to steady herself. She took a moment to try to gather her thoughts. Ahead of her the white stucco was smeared with charcoal as if a modernist had sketched abstract shapes around the windows. Her bedroom window remained open and below it, a particularly thick shadow stained the plaster – a ghostly reminder of the smoke that had almost killed her. On the floors above, a couple of the windows were smashed as if the building had been punched in the face. It didn't look or feel like home any more. Slowly, Mirabelle's eyes fell to the water that pooled at the front door in a shallow grey puddle. Beyond it, the door was ajar, the lock hanging useless just as Bill had said. Feeling surprisingly apprehensive, she pushed it open. As she stepped into the hallway, the air smelled heavily of burnt wood peppered with a hint of dampness. Inside, the house was dark and cavernous as if the fire had hollowed it. She heard the slow drip of water falling from high above on to the flagstone paving of the hallway. Glancing upwards, she could see patches of charring on the handrail on the second floor where the flames had flickered as she had been carried to safety. That must be where the fire had come from, she thought. Somewhere up there and only yesterday. It seemed out of time now. Less than twenty-four hours before she had lived here but today this was an abandoned place.

Mirabelle gripped Panther's lead and took the stairs upwards. The door to her flat was open too – the fireman had had to break it in in order to save her and now the lock hung useless from the splintered frame.

'Hello,' she called gently.

Picking up on Mirabelle's nervousness, Panther let out a gruff bark. There was a squeal from inside and Vesta appeared in the hallway with a clipboard in her hand. Her nails were painted a bright cerise that shone in the gloom and she was wearing all black with a fashionable pink feather hat perched on her head. Mirabelle judged this outfit must have been laid out the night before in readiness for church.

'Mirabelle!' Vesta sounded concerned. 'Are you sure you want to come in? The place is a bit of a mess.'

That was an understatement. As Mirabelle walked into the drawing room, the extent of the damage became apparent. Sodden newspapers had swollen into thick bricks over the floor and the walls were smeared with grit. In places, the soot obscured the window so thoroughly it was almost black and instead of the pure, bright light off the ocean that usually made the flat sparkle, strange, dim shadows cast over the furniture. Mirabelle peered into the bedroom. It had not fared any better than the drawing room. An eerie atmosphere leeched from the soot-damaged walls. It was as if the house had died, and yet she felt she belonged here. It was as if the old place wanted to claim her from beyond its grave. She ventured into her bedroom and opened the creaky wardrobe door. Her clothes were thick with the smell of burning. Everything felt soiled.

'Don't worry,' Vesta fussed protectively. 'The Prudential will have the whole place cleaned and redecorated inside and out. I'll get on to them first thing tomorrow. It looks bad but it's only smoke damage and clearing up the mess the firemen made. I don't think the fire got into the roof.'

Utterly shocked, Mirabelle sank on to the end of the bed. Her lip quivered and she found she couldn't control the tears that rolled down her cheeks. Her hands were shaking and Panther's lead dropped to the floor.

'Now, now.' Vesta put an arm around her. The girl smelled of amber, fragrant in contrast to the musty smell of burning that pervaded everything else. 'You'll see. It'll be a new start.'

Mirabelle nodded but she didn't stop crying. She felt terribly ashamed. These were only bits and pieces, after all. Foolish things – kitchen cupboards and old clothes. Upstairs, a man had died: that was far more important. Still, this was her life – the dresses she had bought in London before the war, the shoes and stockings she'd picked up after it, eking out her rations. The copies of the *Argus* that she'd never managed to fling out were destroyed, among them the one she'd read the day Jack died. She remembered sinking down then, just like this, and crying – realising that no one must ever know about the decade of their affair. She didn't want a flat that was better than new. She wanted the old one, with all its memories.

'I'm sorry,' she managed to gasp. 'It's silly I know.'

Vesta hugged her. 'It's just the shock, I expect. Shall I make a cup of tea?' She glanced doubtfully in the direction of the kitchen, where a filthy packet of Vim that had survived the fire was sitting ironically on the worktop.

'Tea?' Mirabelle laughed at the ridiculousness of the suggestion. This would be her third cup this morning and she hadn't so much as taken a sip. 'I'm not sure tea will really help.' She sniffed. 'I tell you what...'

Beside the sofa there was a decanter of whisky and she wasn't shaking so much that she couldn't pour herself a glass. She held up the musty cut crystal to offer Vesta a dram. Vesta shook her head. 'It's the only thing in the house that's meant to taste smoky.' Mirabelle knocked back the shot and felt the complex flavour expand over her palette in a comforting wave. 'A new start,' she said, as if she was trying out the idea.

Vesta nodded hopefully. 'Yes. I thought the walls might suit a pale blue patterned paper. And we can probably have the chairs and the sofa re-covered. Hannington's has some wonderful fabrics these days. It'll clean up all right – you'll see. And for the kitchen I wondered about daffodil yellow – it's very fashionable. I'll pop into the newsagent and pick up a copy of *House Beautiful*. Maybe we'll get some ideas.'

Mirabelle squinted, trying to imagine the flat being clean again, never mind redecorated. Above the fireplace there was the snow scene Jack had bought in a gallery on Bond Street as a Christmas present for her in 1949. He'd loved snow scenes. Now the pristine landscape looked as if the thaw had set in and a sea of mud was reasserting itself. You couldn't clean snow. Mirabelle shrugged sadly.

'I don't care if it smells of smoke, I just have to have my hat,' she said, setting off for the hallway where she had left her navy pillbox the night before.

Vesta regarded the list she'd started. 'I wondered about that headscarf,' the girl said absent-mindedly as Panther woofed at Mirabelle's back.

'Shush,' Mirabelle soothed the dog. But Panther would not be quietened and woofed again. He took a step towards the hall and stared plaintively at Mirabelle who was pinning the hat into place and gingerly sniffing her clutch handbag before deciding that it would have to do. Panther gave another gruff bark.

'What is it?' Mirabelle's tone was offhand.

'It must smell very odd to him,' Vesta called out.

Mirabelle pushed the door of the flat open further. They often joked in the office that Panther should have been named Parker – Nosey Parker. When he was a tiny puppy the name had been suggested but Bill had said it was cruel. Still, it would have suited him. Mirabelle picked up the dog's trailing lead and Panther brightened as he began to climb the stairs. Mirabelle lingered on the landing and he looked down at her as if to say, *Can't you see I'm trying to tell you something?* With a shrug, she followed him upwards. The runner squelched beneath her feet. The fireman had drenched everything to douse the flames. Up-stairs, the door to the flat lay open just as hers had. Mirabelle hesitated. She hadn't even known Mr Beaumont had moved into the building and it seemed disrespectful now to simply wander into the poor man's home where he'd died, after all, only a few hours before. The dog strained on the lead.

'No,' said Mirabelle, pulling him back. Panther let out another airy bark and kept straining. 'Well really.'

She was just about to turn and drag Panther

41

back downstairs when she heard a movement inside. The dog looked up and kept pulling. Mirabelle relented. Curious, she knocked on the door but no one answered. The flat fell still again as if it was waiting for something. The places where people died often felt that way. Mirabelle had noticed it before.

'Hello,' she called.

Anyone could be in there. The doors had lain wide open all night. She advanced inside. Dougie Beaumont's flat was laid out in the same way as her own but the ceilings were lower on this upper floor and the place had been decorated quite differently. Now, more burnt-out black than anything else, Mirabelle could just make out that the walls had been painted dark green in the hallway, opening on to a burgundy drawing room with what was left of two dark, leather sofas and a forest-green smoking chair upholstered in velvet. A couple of mahogany side tables had been toppled where the firemen had done their job and a silver cigarette box had fallen, scattering its contents across the floor where two dozen sodden Dunhills lay ruined by the water. Up here, the fabric of the place was more damaged. The fire had burned into the walls. One chair had been entirely charred and part of one sofa had been eaten away, as if the fire had torn it in a lopsided, ragged rage. The floorboards in the middle of the room were black and uneven where the flames had burned longest. This was where it had started, she realised. She walked in, recreating the scene. Dougie Beaumont stringing himself up, here in this room. Looking up, she shuddered to see a scrap of rope still fixed to the

42

chandelier. That was where he must have done it. He'd kicked away a stool beneath him and it had fallen into the fire, embers spilling over the grate, setting the place alight.

Jerked out of this grisly realisation, Mirabelle jumped, hearing a footfall in the bedroom, and stepped back as a tall man emerged. She reckoned he was thirty perhaps, and well dressed in a grey coat and a homburg that he had not taken the trouble to remove. There was nothing immediately remarkable about the fellow – he looked like a hundred other men of his age, except his skin was pale and his eyes were ringed by heavy bags as if he hadn't slept. Where they protruded from his coat cuffs, his hands looked very white and now and then his fingers twitched. He hovered on the threshold and wouldn't meet her gaze.

'I'm sorry,' she started. 'I heard movement. The dog.'

'What are you doing here?' the man snapped.

'I'm Mirabelle Bevan. I live downstairs.'

'Were you here last night?'

Mirabelle nodded.

'Did you see anything?'

She shook her head. 'Only outside. Afterwards. I saw him then. I'm sorry. Are you ... an investigator?' She held out her hand. A moment passed as the man decided whether to introduce himself. 'Are you a relation?' she encouraged him.

'George Highton.' His grip was firmer than she expected as he shook her hand. 'Dougie and I weren't family. Not really.'

'But you knew Mr Beaumont?' Mirabelle checked.

'Didn't you?' Highton batted back.

'No. I didn't even know he had moved in,' she said sheepishly. 'I saw him win a race once. That's all.'

Highton seemed to relent. 'I came down as soon as I heard what happened. I've known Dougie since we were kids. I cover racing events for the *Daily Telegraph,* you see. I just wanted to see where it had happened. I can't quite believe it – him gone like this and the place is nothing but a wreck.'

Mirabelle pulled back. 'Mr Highton, I'm not sure you should be here.'

George Highton's expression didn't waver. 'He was a wonderful driver. Lots of them are reckless – some to the point where it's a death wish. There are plenty of ex-fighter pilots who can't live without the adrenalin rush. But Dougie had just enough wildness coupled with control. He had a talent for driving in wet weather – I've never seen anyone able to hug the bends in the rain like he could. Racing cars is fun, Miss Bevan. We had a good time. I always thought if he went early it would be a crash... An accident.'

'How old was he?'

'Twenty-seven.'

'I'm sorry. When did you see him last?'

'Ten days ago.' Highton shifted on his feet as if he was suddenly uncomfortable. 'I'll miss him. He wasn't the type. You know. To kill himself.'

'I'm not sure there is a type.'

He met her eyes properly for the first time. 'I best get on,' he said and pushed past.

Mirabelle listened as his footsteps retreated down the stairs. She went to the window and squinted past the shards of smashed glass, watching as George Highton emerged, turned left along the front and disappeared round the corner. Perhaps he had parked on one of the streets that led up to the main road. It was strange he'd come, she thought – all the way from London too, and so soon after Beaumont had died. But then Mirabelle knew that pull. During the war, acquaintances and friends had been killed on a daily basis. The dead had a kind of glamour. You wanted to remind yourself of them. You wanted to make a connection to prove that their lives meant something and that, by association, your life meant something too. She'd visited the site of a bomb on more than one occasion – just to feel close to a friend who'd died there. She decided George Highton wasn't just rubbernecking or, for that matter, on the prowl for a story, although the suicide would probably make the papers. Still, there was a gravity about the man that bespoke a real connection. If Highton seemed uncomfortable it was no wonder – the poor fellow was in shock.

Mirabelle turned back into the flat, thinking how lucky she had been. How lucky she was. Downstairs, Vesta was busy reassembling her life. Bill had come in especially and McGregor had been immensely kind. On the floor above, it seemed Dougie Beaumont had only a colleague to mourn him. Where was his mother – the woman in the pink dress? Several silver picture frames had toppled off the wrought-iron mantelpiece and Mirabelle leaned down to pick them up. Damaged by the flames, the glass smeared with soot, she could still make out three: two that contained the long dark motor car with the number twenty-six on its side – the one Beaumont had driven at Goodwood – and in the other frame, behind smashed glass, was what must be a family portrait, taken some years ago judging by the clothes, perhaps in the early days of the war. Mirabelle squinted. Dougie Beaumont looked incredibly young – a schoolboy in fact – and behind him there was the same woman – his mother – smiling, and, beside her, a man in naval uniform whose face seemed oddly familiar, but, for the life of her, Mirabelle couldn't quite place him.

'Beaumont...' she murmured. And then it came to her. 'Oh my goodness,' she whispered. 'Of course.' The man was none other than the Member of Parliament: Elrick Beaumont. She'd heard him speak at the hustings during the general election earlier that year. He'd been impressive – singing the praises of Eden's leadership – a fresh start for the country under the Conservative party. In the photograph, Elrick Beaumont looked far younger than he had at the debate. His hair was slicked back and he wore a thin moustache that no longer graced his upper lip. But he was recognisable. He squared up to the camera just like he had squared up to the crowd. She felt a sudden wave of sympathy. Losing a son must be terrible under any circumstances, but losing a son like this was especially dreadful. They must be beside themselves. She laid the photograph carefully on the mantelpiece and made a sound, which she imagined might bring Panther to heel. 'Come on, boy,' she said as she led him back into the hallway.

In the first-floor flat, Vesta was pulling on her

coat amid the chaos. Mirabelle smiled. Since she had married Charlie the previous year, Mirabelle had noticed small changes in her friend. Little by little, Vesta was growing up. She had acquired a bicycle to take her in and out from the new house and as a result she had slimmed down. At the same time, though she had always had an air of efficiency, Vesta's style had changed. Today she sported patent leather heels that set off her well-formed calves and her skirt was well fitted. Mirabelle thought that would be troublesome on the bike but there was no denying that it looked marvellous. In the past the girl's outfits had often seemed flung together but marriage had brought with it a measure of sartorial maturity. These days Vesta closed her coat properly and checked her hat was in place. Mirabelle eyed the clipboard – the paper attached to it was covered in Vesta's untidy scribbles – a long list that wavered this way and that like a shaky tower that might tumble. She hadn't become tidier in all things. 'I hope Bill found a locksmith,' Vesta said. 'That's the first thing.'

Mirabelle glanced around the gritty, grey walls as Vesta took her by the arm and guided her downstairs.

'I just don't understand why.' The girl's eyes followed Mirabelle's up to the second floor in a kind of salute as they left the building. 'Why would somebody do that? Someone with so much going for them?'

Mirabelle didn't reply. Outside, a blustery autumn breeze seemed to breathe life into the wide blue sky. Brighton felt alive, the white stucco buildings reaching upwards as if they were fitness fanatics. It was difficult to believe that this burnt-out shell would ever rejoin them. Panther fell into step as Vesta wheeled her bike along the pavement and they made their way back towards town.

Chapter 4

It's not what you look at that matters, it's what you see

That evening the boarding house was almost full. Before dinner, the guests took sherry in a sitting room overlooking the small back garden. The room was decorated in a mass of shady greens as if it might be part of the planting outside. With the autumn chill setting in, Miss Brownlee had laid a fire in the grate. The dancing flames were reflected in the glass of the French doors. Outside Mirabelle could make out a sturdy wooden table and chairs where drinks were no doubt served before dinner during the summer months.

The guest house was proving well run. Tonight there were half a dozen people staying despite the fact the season was spent. The fire crackled encouragingly as Mirabelle introduced herself and managed not to explain why she was lodged here or, for that matter, the reason she was wearing a navy woollen day dress in the evening. Most people seemed to be in Brighton for a few days on holiday. In the main they chatted about the sights. When the gong sounded, everyone moved through to the dining room and took their places at separate tables. Miss Brownlee had placed Mirabelle in the bay, overlooking the street, and she felt suddenly uncomfortable as she sat alone. The feeling dissolved into relief just as service commenced, when McGregor arrived, removing his coat and hat as he came through the door. Mirabelle grinned gratefully as he slipped on to the seat opposite her. There was a ripple of interest as the other guests wondered or perhaps assumed that Mirabelle was married to this competent-looking man. Certainly Mirabelle thought she could sense a change in the way they were regarding her – a woman on her own, after all, was a vulnerable creature and much to be pitied.

She suddenly became aware that she and McGregor could be overheard, although, luckily, the closest table was occupied by a mother and her daughter who were talking in high spirits about a walk they had taken along the seafront, which had culminated in a trip to the aquarium. 'Tomorrow,' the girl enthused, 'we must get over to Hastings and see the site of the battle.' She pulled a guidebook from her bag and read out the entry for Battle Abbey.

'It fits. Looks nice,' McGregor commented with a nod at Mirabelle's outfit.

'Thank you. I don't quite know what I would have done...' Her voice trailed. 'It's very kind of you.'

'You'd have organised yourself, I imagine.'

'Vesta's doing a good job of that.'

'How are you feeling?'

49

Mirabelle did not reply immediately, as Miss Brownlee appeared at her elbow holding two plates of soup, which she set down carefully. Surprisingly, it smelled delicious.

'Mushroom,' Miss Brownlee announced and turned to serve the other tables.

'I feel better than I did,' Mirabelle confided as she leaned in. 'Though it's awful about Mr Beaumont. I keep coming back to it. Poor man.'

McGregor nodded. 'I broke the news to his father this morning. I thought, as he's a Member of Parliament and I'm the senior officer, I ought to be the one to do it. I attended, after all. The boy was an only son – there's a daughter but, well, that'll be the end of the family name. He took it quite well all things considered. We'll release the body later this week.'

McGregor paused and the conversation halted at this impasse. Many churches refused to bury someone who had killed themselves. Mirabelle felt a rush of sympathy. It must seem like insult on top of injury for Dougie Beaumont's family and then there was the shame – everyone would know what he had done. Everyone would wonder why.

'Was there a note?' she enquired.

McGregor shook his head. 'Not that we can find. Of course the fire may have done for it. The scene is a mess.'

'Yes. I was there today.' Mirabelle lifted her spoon and took a sip. Miss Brownlee had evidently used a good deal of butter and the soup was delicious. A serene look passed across her face.

'It's a crime scene, Mirabelle. What were you doing there?'

Mirabelle felt herself prickle at McGregor's tone. This was quickly followed by a stab of guilt. The superintendent, after all, was her saviour. She ticked herself off for feeling inappropriately independent not to mention ungrateful for his help, and told herself that the least she could do was answer his question.

'I went to have a look at my flat. Vesta was making an inventory of the damage. I know it's ghoulish but I went upstairs.'

'When?'

'It was late morning. Perhaps eleven or so.'

'Did you move anything?'

'I picked up a couple of photographs from the floor and put them back on the mantelpiece,' she said slowly, deciding not to tell the superintendent about Mr Highton. He was exercised enough as it was. 'I wasn't aware, that is to say I didn't think...'

'I don't mean in the drawing room – I mean in the bedroom. Did you move anything in the bedroom?'

'The bedroom?'

'Yes. Did you touch anything? Take anything away?'

Mirabelle shook her head. 'Of course not. I didn't even go into the bedroom,' she said. 'Why?'

'It's nothing.'

'You can't get away with that, Alan McGregor!'

McGregor picked at his bread roll before he relented. 'There was a drawer. An empty drawer. It was left open.'

'Mr Beaumont was a bachelor, I believe.'

'I know. Bachelors are hardly tidy. And the flat is

in chaos anyway with the fire and then the brigade picking it through. But it makes no sense. It's the top drawer beside the man's bed, you see. The drawers below it are filled with bits and pieces – it just seems odd that the top one is empty and left open too. It's the only thing that isn't quite right. At first I thought Beaumont must have taken out whatever was in there before he, you know, did it. Perhaps he'd been planning to kill himself for a while. Perhaps that's where he kept the rope. But then, checking against the other drawers – the amount of grit and dust and so forth. The water from the hose. Well, I don't think it was open during the fire. It was dry inside and if it had been open when the fire brigade went in, it's unlikely it would have stayed that way when everything else was soaked. I think someone took whatever was in the drawer, and left it open. After the fire. After it was all over, I mean.'

Mirabelle bit her lip.

'The firemen – well, now and then, you get a bad one,' McGregor reasoned. 'Sometimes it's too much temptation. He could have kept anything in there. I'm making discreet inquiries...'

Mirabelle recalled George Highton's inability to meet her eye when he first emerged from his friend's bedroom. Perhaps his shifty expression wasn't the result of grief. Perhaps Highton was guilty of removing something from the scene?

'Will there be a funeral? I mean, does anyone know yet where the poor man might be buried?' she asked.

McGregor shook his head. 'The body will be released after the post-mortem. It's up to the family to make the arrangements.'

'That day we saw him – well, he was a talented driver, wasn't he? You don't get to that level without having a good amount of nerve, I imagine. It doesn't make sense.'

McGregor dipped a piece of bread into his soup. 'You mean, if he was so brave what was he doing killing himself?'

'No. I mean if he was so brave what was it that drove him to do it? That's a different question. A more pragmatic one. Poor fellow.'

McGregor grinned. 'Oh no,' he said. 'I know that look. You leave this to me, Mirabelle Bevan. You have more than enough on your plate.'

Mirabelle directed her attention back to the soup. The superintendent had a point, but still, poor Mr Beaumont had been a neighbour. And then there was the look on his face as he swung his mother around the day he'd won the race. Once more she considered telling him about George Highton and once more she dismissed the notion and instead decided to change the subject.

'Miss Brownlee tells me you bought this place.'

McGregor smacked his lips as he scooped the last mushroomy smear into his mouth.

'Yes. Alfie Brownlee won't be coming out. I'm sure Betty told you that as well. I was renting a room further up in Kemptown. It was fish and chips most nights. I've never been good at doing for myself and I always meant to buy somewhere and settle down. I had some savings and a bit of money I inherited. It seemed like a good arrangement. She's a nice lady.'

'It's a nice house.'

'I took the best room, on the first floor. It was the old drawing room – like in your flat, but not so grand. There's plenty of space so I can read beside the fire if I happen to be in. And Betty's a good cook, don't you think?'

Mirabelle nodded. She had never thought of the superintendent as much of a reader or for that matter much of a gourmet. To say nothing of him being a proprietor. Her surprise must have shown.

'It's mostly case files that I read,' he admitted. 'And the newspaper. But the library is just down the road. I like George Orwell, believe it or not.'

'That's revolutionary.' Mirabelle smiled.

'We Scots are revolutionary.'

'I thought that was the Irish.'

'James Joyce...' McGregor paused as Miss Brownlee removed his plate. 'I don't understand a word. It just goes on and on.'

'And you don't mind the guests being here?' Mirabelle kept her voice low. 'I mean, they seem perfectly nice.'

'I don't mind it at all – there's company if I want it. I don't have to join in. And the place turns a tidy profit.' McGregor's eyes danced. 'I'm not so revolutionary that I object to that.'

After a creditable chicken stew and a warm slice of treacle tart with a dollop of thick cream, they decided to take a walk along the promenade rather than retire to the residents' lounge for coffee. The evenings were drawing in now the summer was spent. Mirabelle slipped her arm through the superintendent's and they fell into step along the front.

'Vesta arranged insurance,' she said. 'The flat is

covered – she's going to organise the whole renovation. It needs to be completely cleaned and refitted.'

'She's a wonder.'

'I don't know how long it will take.'

'You're welcome at the guest house for as long as you like. I owe you my life, remember?'

Mirabelle shrugged off the comment. She'd rescued McGregor and Vesta when they'd been kidnapped a couple of years ago not half a mile from here. But then McGregor had risked his life for her in Paris the year before. She didn't want to think about that now.

'It's a lovely evening,' she said.

Beyond the pier the front stretched for miles. As the sky darkened, the sea became enticingly blank. Tonight there was a breeze rolling off it that was bracing but not unpleasant. She could hear the tide breaking on the pebbles, the soothing swish as they shifted. The deep cold of winter had yet to descend, the chill evening air only a warning of what was to come. A scratch of dead leaves skittered along the pavement and caught against a gatepost.

'We could pop into the Cricketers,' McGregor suggested.

When Mirabelle didn't reply he stopped, took her in his arms and kissed her. He tasted of treacle tart still – sweet and insistent. She kissed him back.

'I don't want to push you,' he said. 'We're living under the same roof. It seems as if I have the advantage. You've had a terrible shock.'

Mirabelle's expression was quizzical. 'The advantage? We know each other too well for that.'

Some people might have found it risque to share lodgings, but, Mirabelle thought, Vesta and Charlie had shared digs on a far more intimate basis than she planned to with McGregor. And now Vesta and Charlie were happily married – very happily indeed. It was difficult to think of McGregor in those terms, and yet there was no question that as time passed Mirabelle found the superintendent increasingly attractive. He hadn't pulled away, his strong hands holding her firmly. She leaned backwards, hinging his grasp on the curve of her back and letting him support her. But somehow she couldn't settle to the idea. Not entirely.

'Perhaps a gin and tonic would be nice,' she said, standing upright and smoothing the collar of her coat.

McGregor put his arm around her shoulder as they turned away from the sea and she moved fractionally closer. She told herself it was for warmth, but that wasn't entirely true. Away from the swish of the waves on the pebbles, their steps sounded different today. Usually the percussive beat of her stride on the paving stones sounded a staccato tattoo against McGregor's steady rhythm but in flat heels Mirabelle moved almost silently as if she wasn't even there.

'Charlie is playing this evening,' McGregor said absent-mindedly. 'There'll be jazz.'

Jazz or no jazz, Mirabelle thought, the Cricketers was bound to prove a distraction. But then thinking of it that way was odd in itself, as if she didn't want to recognise her relationship with McGregor or consider poor dead Dougie Beaumont. She kept seeing the image of the poor boy's body on the stretcher in the dark, or worse, imagining him hanging from the brass chandelier beside the wrought-iron fireplace. It was disconcerting. Somehow he hadn't gone. It was as if his ghost was needling her from the fringes.

'Do you know how the fire started?' she asked.

'I'll speak to the pathologist tomorrow but it looks as if when Beaumont did it, he kicked off from a stool that toppled into the grate. The fire set it alight and that ignited the whole room. He wouldn't have known a thing.'

'Yes, I thought that,' she said.

Mirabelle wondered if Dougie Beaumont had newspapers or books around his favourite chair. If he had they would have fed the blaze. It would have been easy enough for the fire to spread.

'It's not that I'm responsible,' she tried to explain as McGregor held open the pub door and she swept inside to the warmth and the music, 'but I still feel awful. I mean, at least I ought to have known the poor chap was there.'

Chapter 5

The first and simplest emotion is curiosity

Mirabelle paused with a pencil in her hand as she perused the London telephone directory the following morning in the office. She and McGregor had stayed in the Cricketers for more than an hour. Charlie had played the drums like George Wettling at McGregor's special request and now she beat the rhythm on to the page with the end of her pencil as the image of her and McGregor dancing flickered across her memory. The beat just wouldn't go away. Really, she scolded herself, she ought to get on. Bill had already left the office for the day and Vesta was detailing her proposed renovations on Mirabelle's flat. The assessor was due to arrive shortly and the girl was determined to be prepared. She had typed her lists in triplicate and now she was marking the margins with potential workmen to undertake each task, each trade allotted a differently coloured pencil.

With only a glance to ensure the girl was fully occupied, Mirabelle abandoned the beat and instead slid her finger down the page until she came to the entry for Elrick Beaumont MP. It seemed Mr Beaumont lived just off Sloane Square. Mirabelle paused. Elrick Beaumont represented a Brighton constituency but this address would be handy for Westminster, she supposed.

The sky was grey this morning and it threatened rain. Mirabelle stared out of the window and wondered what a bachelor might keep in his top drawer.

'What does Charlie keep in his bedside cabinet?' she asked Vesta. 'Top drawer.'

Vesta looked up. 'What?'

'Charlie? What does he keep in his top drawer?'

Vesta perused the office while she thought about it. Generally when Mirabelle asked a strange question it was because she had read something mysterious in the newspaper or come across an unexpected piece of correspondence. Today, however, the newspaper was folded tidily on Bill's desk and Mirabelle appeared to be looking at an entry in the London telephone directory.

'The top drawer of his bedside cabinet is socks,' she said, her head to one side as she tried to decide if Mirabelle looked satisfied with this answer. She did not. Mirabelle found herself wondering what McGregor kept in his drawers. When they got back to the Arundel from the Cricketers she had kissed the superintendent as they stood on the first-floor landing, the doors to their rooms opposite each other, both resolutely closed. She had felt drawn in two directions at once and evidently so had McGregor. They hovered as if held in mid-air by some kind of magnetic force and in the end it was he who had backed away as if he was forcing himself, his hands held palms upwards in an informal surrender. When his bedroom door clicked shut, Mirabelle had found herself wondering if going to bed with Alan McGregor might be like it had been with Jack. But how could it be? That the question had occurred was most disconcerting.

'This is the dead fella, isn't it?' Vesta said. 'It's his drawers.'

Mirabelle nodded. 'Someone appears to have removed the contents of his top drawer. After the fire.'

'Maybe a diary?' Vesta tried. 'Or some cash?'

'Maybe.'

'But not the telephone directory...'

'He wasn't in the telephone directory.' Mirabelle bounced her pencil off the page. 'He only moved in a few weeks ago. This entry is for his family up in town. I can't imagine how they must be feeling today.'

Vesta stood up and stretched. She wandered over to the hooks by the door and removed Mirabelle's green tweed coat. 'Go on,' she said, her tone businesslike. 'They're listed so you know where they live.'

Mirabelle got to her feet and Vesta held out the coat. It was only good manners to offer her condolences, she thought as she slid her arms into the sleeves.

'Charlie had heard of him, you know,' Vesta said.

'The father?'

'No. The dead bloke. The driver. Boys and their toys. Charlie learned to drive during the war. The Yanks had food-supply trucks so he got a licence on one of those – a great big lumbering thing. He likes an engine. Not that we'll ever have a car, I expect. Certainly not a racing car. I always fancied myself in a Ford convertible with the roof down – if we ever get a sunny day. Racing down a country road in a Deluxe or maybe a Ferrari 166. That's glamour.'

'Thanks,' Mirabelle said, laying a hand on Vesta's arm gratefully. 'If I rush I'll catch the next train.'

Vesta stepped back. She knew from experience that Mirabelle sometimes just needed to get away. She'd had a shock, after all. She might have died. 'Leave all this to me,' she said and opened the door so that Mirabelle could sweep through.

After boarding a first-class carriage at Brighton Station, Mirabelle took a seat opposite an old man puffing a pipe. It was a curious fact that on cold autumn days the smoke in a train made it feel more welcoming, somehow, and warmer. The smell of tobacco usually reminded Mirabelle of being a child – coming downstairs in the morning when the dinner party her parents had hosted the night before was cleared away, but the scent of cigars still lingered. Today the smoke on the air didn't invoke such rosy memories. She shuddered, imagining what it would feel like to be sitting on the train in a fog, surrounded by smoke yet again. There had been something awful about not being able to see – worse even than the flames, she realised. It was the smoke that had really terrified her. It had pressed on her lungs. She kept coming back to the thought that she might have died that way, the world masked by a thick, grey shroud and she choked by it. As the train pulled out, she swapped to an empty carriage and made a conscious effort to keep her eyes on the view and try not to think about what had happened. It wouldn't be long before the leaves were off the trees and the smell of bonfires started to pervade the weekends. I wonder how I'll feel about bonfires, she thought.

At Victoria she took a cab, which dropped her at a very grand street only a couple of minutes from the station. She stopped to gather her thoughts. The houses here were wide and solid – the terrace chequered now and again by one that was greying. The buildings were the same era as the town-houses along the front in Brighton but they were bigger and somehow more self-important. Mirabelle noticed the peeling paint and the chipped windowsills. It was difficult to keep things up during the war and after it nobody had had much money. The Beaumonts' house, however, looked pristine.

She hovered on the pavement until the clouds let rip and large raindrops began to bounce off the paving stones. Scrambling, she moved more decisively than she felt towards the old-fashioned wrought-iron bell-pull, tugged it and waited. A moment later a woman opened the door with a snap. Mirabelle felt immediately off balance. She had expected a butler or a maid at the least. It took a moment before Mirabelle recognised the woman framed before her as the lady in pink at the race-track. Today she was wearing a dark grey dress with a smear of what looked like egg down the front. Her thick rope of pearls seemed out of place. Her hair was tousled and, clearly, she had been crying.

'I'm so sorry to trouble you,' Mirabelle said.

The woman sniffed and pawed at the watery trail of mascara marking each of her cheeks. She had the air of someone who had been caught in the middle of a sentence, suspended in a spotlight.

'I shouldn't have answered,' she said.

Mirabelle was unsure what to say. 'I came to see Mr Beaumont,' she tried.

The woman stiffened. 'He had to see to everything. I can take a message.'

'You are Mrs Beaumont?'

The woman nodded.

'My name is Mirabelle Bevan,' she introduced herself. 'I live in Brighton. In the flat below your son's. I'm so sorry – I came to offer my condolences. I was there, you see. I was in the building the night he died.'

Mrs Beaumont couldn't contain her grief. Her lip quivered and she brought her hand to her mouth to try to cover it but it was useless. Her face twisted and she began not so much to cry as to howl. A raw, desperate sound emanated from her lips. She laid her hand on the wide doorframe as if this alone would keep her upright.

'I'm so sorry. I shouldn't have come.' Mirabelle backed into the rain but Mrs Beaumont reached out and grasped her arm.

'Come in,' she sobbed. 'Please.'

Bundled inside, Mirabelle looked around. It was obvious that Mrs Beaumont should not have been left alone. A house like this must have staff but perhaps the family emergency had scattered them. The hallway was furnished with dark, carved oak that looked practically medieval but nobody had lit the lamps on the side tables and the light from the long windows was limited by the unrelenting banks of grey cloud outside. Mrs

Beaumont led Mirabelle into a rather grand sitting room decorated in the latest style but with a display of stuffed heads over the fireplace – a zebra, a lion and two dyk dyk. The poor woman sank on to a pale blue sofa – a bright oasis amid the gloomy surroundings.

'My husband went into town,' she said, pulling a crumpled linen handkerchief from her sleeve. 'There has been a good deal to do. And he needed help, so they all went one by one. And today is cook's day off.'

Mirabelle hovered uncomfortably. Her eye was drawn to the photographs that were propped haphazardly on the mantelpiece next to a bank of printed invitations. The first picture was of a wedding that had taken place quite recently if the cut of the dress was anything to go by. Then there was one of Dougie Beaumont that appeared to have been taken some years before. He was wearing a uniform and standing beside a light aircraft in the sunshine.

Mrs Beaumont followed Mirabelle's eyes and dissolved once more into tears. 'That was taken when Dougie was in Nairobi. When he got called up,' she sobbed.

'After the war?'

Mrs Beaumont nodded. 'He missed the fighting by a few months. I can't tell you how relieved I was. Dougie had a simply marvellous time out there though of course I missed him terribly. You always worry, don't you? I mean they come out of school and they get sent goodness knows where. I worried that Africa might be dangerous. But it's not a lion that got him or a poison dart.' She sank deeper into the sofa, her hands trembling. 'For Dougie to do it himself. Oh God.'

Mirabelle looked around. Mrs Beaumont seemed to suddenly notice that she was hovering. 'Please.' She shifted along the padded cushion and motioned Mirabelle to join her. 'Would you like a cup of...'

'No. Thank you. I only came to pass on my condolences. He seems to have been such a strapping young man. It is a dreadful tragedy. I can't imagine how you must feel. I'm a neighbour, of course, but I never met him. I saw him race at Easter at Goodwood. He won.'

'Dougie spent the summer racing. He'd only just got back from Europe.' Mrs Beaumont sounded eager. The recently bereaved often mired themselves in small details as if the last meals and travel arrangements of the people they'd lost took on a strange and symbolic importance. 'He spent the last few months on the Riviera, between Grand Prix, of course. He simply loved France.'

Mirabelle thought of the previous year when she had been drawn back to her own past, in Paris.

'He spoke French terribly well,' Mrs Beaumont continued. 'You'd think he'd been brought up there. Our name – Beaumont – in hotels abroad, they often assume we're French. Dougie could bring that off. He felt at home there. And he always said that the French circuit was the best in the world. He hadn't won it yet but he would have. He'd set his sights on Le Mans.'

'It sounds as if he liked speed.'

'Yes. Since he was a little boy. It was horses at

first. Well, ponies, really, but as soon as he discovered what a motor could do...'

'And he flew. I didn't know that.' Mirabelle nodded towards the photograph.

'He learned in Africa. Boys are like that, aren't they? So good at picking things up. He was such a lovely little boy.' She started to cry again, softly. 'I'm sorry. This is why Elrick left me here. He's quite right, of course. I mean I can't go about just howling like this. I'd only get in the way and there's so much to attend to. I keep thinking of Dougie. I can't help it. I wonder where he is now. And then I remember that he's in Brighton. In the mortuary.' She heaved a sob.

'It sounds as if he was a wonderful son.'

Mrs Beaumont grasped Mirabelle's hand. 'He was. Such a tremendous help. I don't know how we'd have managed without Dougie. Did you see him, Miss Bevan? I mean afterwards? Did you see him?'

Mirabelle took a breath before she admitted it. 'Yes. They brought his body outside. After they had carried him out of the fire. I recognised him almost straight away.'

Mrs Beaumont's hand flew to her throat, her fingers darting behind the thick rope of pearls. 'I just don't understand why he did it. Everything was going so well. He loved driving. He said it was what he had been born to do. My poor, poor boy.'

'You had no inkling?'

Mrs Beaumont shook her head. 'He had even made plans for next summer – an alteration to his car. My son was an innovator, Miss Bevan. A whizz kid, my husband called him. Elrick was quite right, of course. And Dougie was dreadfully good with money. They were altering his engine as an investment, you see. He'd come up with something that was going to add speed. I don't understand that kind of thing but Dougie was excited. They all were. Dougie's career has become something of a family obsession, you see. We're all right behind our boy.'

Mirabelle found her head moving to one side. She had never thought of a motorcar as an investment. On the contrary, she was sure they cost a great deal. 'It was his life's work, then?' she said encouragingly.

'Oh yes. And now no one will be able to drive the thing as well as he could. He fixed things, you see. He was always fixing things. His friend had a place – a garage, I mean. He spent hours there just playing with engines. I think it's where he was probably happiest. He'll be buried quite close to it, now. When we get his body back.'

'Oh, I wondered where he might be buried?'

Mrs Beaumont dabbed her nose with the handkerchief. Her stare was fixed. 'Not here. At home. The canon came at once – I was hardly up and dressed,' she said, waving her hand dismissively towards the street beyond the window.

'Your local church, you mean?'

Mrs Beaumont nodded. She seemed to be struggling, trying not to speak, but her eyes flashed with temper and she lost the battle. 'The nerve of the man,' she spat furiously. 'He wouldn't have it – Dougie's funeral, I mean. My family has lived here for generations. I'm a Roedean girl, you know. My father paid for the stained glass in the apse and I've a mind to take a hammer to it now. And that man, calls himself a Christian. An Anglican, no less. He expects to sit in my home and preach to me, having refused the only thing we have ever asked. And I'm supposed to feel ashamed of my son. Well I won't. Dougie was worth a hundred of those heartless...'

'Please.' Mirabelle tried to calm the poor woman. 'You said that you've found a place for him. Near his friend's garage.'

'Yes. Chichester. The bishop is a friend of my husband's and he has agreed to do it ... to allow... It doesn't seem real. I mean Chichester is so far away. But Elrick says it's for the best. I suppose Dougie loved Goodwood and it's close to that.'

A tear trickled down Mrs Beaumont's cheek and Mirabelle remembered the horror she'd felt at the idea of Jack's body going into the ground. She hadn't attended his funeral. As Jack's mistress it would have been entirely inappropriate, but that wasn't the only reason she'd stayed away. There was something unbearable about the damp, dark earth closing over a coffin and the still, empty flesh that was inside. She had attended a hundred funerals, but when you really loved someone there was something too final about a burial. Something brutal.

'I'm glad you have arranged somewhere. Somewhere he would have liked. That's a comfort,' Mirabelle said, and immediately bit her lip. She knew perfectly well that in such an abyss of grief, nothing was really a comfort. It was only something that people said to each other.

'Elrick intends to name a race after him. A silver

cup. He mustn't be forgotten you see,' Mrs Beaumont continued wistfully. 'I don't know how we are going to stand it. I keep thinking that it is such a waste. I said to my husband, "We can't go back to Nairobi." Usually, we go as a family every Christmas. It has become a tradition. The boys love it – some kind of adventure – and it's wonderful to get away from the cold weather. But I'm not sure I could stand it this year.' Mrs Beaumont stopped to dab her nose. 'Dougie was the most engaging young man, Miss Bevan,' she continued. 'And so popular. I mean girls followed him about, like puppies. They flung themselves at him. He was terribly charming.'

Mirabelle wanted to hug the poor woman. 'I'm not sure you ought to be here on your own, you know. Not today.'

'Oh, Enid is coming,' Mrs Beaumont said, as if it was an afterthought. 'My daughter and her husband,' she explained.

Mirabelle's eyes raised to the other photograph on the mantelpiece – a blond bridegroom, who looked rather stern, she thought, and his starry-eyed bride, who must be Enid, her face half covered by a veil that had been caught in the breeze. 'That's good. I shouldn't like to think of you being alone.'

'People...' Mrs Beaumont sounded mystified and Mirabelle understood.

What good would people do? The only person who mattered wasn't there.

'This is a very historic building.' Mirabelle cast her eyes around. Apart from the heavy carved wood the place seemed so empty. The frantic maelstrom of Mrs Beaumont's grief was the house's only content. When it was built, Mirabelle couldn't help thinking, the women who lived here would have worn hooped skirts. What tragedies had they had to face?

'We did it up quite recently. None of our forbears had bothered and the old pile was in a dreadful state.'

Mirabelle watched as Mrs Beaumont pulled herself together. In less than a minute, she changed from a heartsore, devastated mother into an MP's wife – the sort of lady who might open a summer fete or visit a hospital. It was as if the sense of discretion that had deserted her suddenly reinstated itself. She could swear even the egg stain looked less obvious.

'I hope I haven't embarrassed you, Miss Bevan,' she said, her fingers alighting on the rings that adorned her wedding finger. 'Elrick would be cross if he could hear me rattling on.'

'Not at all. I only wanted to pay my respects,' Mirabelle assured her. 'And to offer – if there is anything I can do. Especially in the matter of your son's flat. I live in Brighton and we'll have workmen in the building anyway. I'm happy to help.'

Mrs Beaumont stood up. 'Thank you.'

Mirabelle followed suit. 'He'd only just moved in above me, you see. I imagine he'd hardly unpacked.'

Mrs Beaumont shrugged. 'Dougie travelled light in life,' she said. 'He knew it was people who were important.' She managed a smile as she saw Mirabelle to the door.

Back in the street, the rain had relented. It

would soon be the weather for boots. As Mirabelle picked her way down to the main road, she couldn't help wondering what Mrs Beaumont had meant when she said her son was a help. That was, in Mirabelle's experience, a word a mother might use more usually about her daughter. The poor woman was engulfed in grief but still. People gave away everything if you only let them speak. She was a woman who had defined herself by her husband, her son and her old school. Nothing else.

She looked back before crossing the road and, standing at the bus stop, she couldn't help wondering if she'd met Dougie Beaumont on the stairs as she came home, what side of himself he might have shown – the risk taker, the man who could hug the bends and not turn over the car, the family stalwart or, if she was lucky, perhaps the part of him that had seemed so engaging – the part of him that had smiled at his mother so warmly when she had congratulated him that day he won the race. If she had met him might she have understood why he had killed himself? His death seemed such a waste, a tragedy, even. But then, there was another word for it – mystery.

'Perhaps I'll just look into it a little more…' The thought trailed through Mirabelle's mind as the bus pulled up. The route would take her eastwards – and that was most convenient.

Chapter 6

Question everything. Learn something.
Answer nothing.

Vesta stood silently in the middle of Mirabelle's drawing room, while Mr Timpson, the Prudential's assessor, surveyed her list.

'Very thorough,' he intoned, looking up with a half-smile.

'I used to work in insurance.'

'Good. That will make matters easier. Terrible business this. It just seems strange this catastrophic incident came so soon, Mrs Lewis. After the policy was taken out, I mean. Mr Evans, downstairs, has been with the Prudential for eight years but Miss Bevan...'

Vesta folded her arms across her ample chest and a worried expression flitted across Mr Timpson's face. Formidable at the best of times, Vesta looked as if she was squaring up for a fight. She knew the man was only doing his job, but she was going to do what she saw as hers. 'If you are suggesting that my colleague, Miss Bevan, arranged for her upstairs neighbour to kill himself and set fire to the premises in such a manner as she might die in the blaze, and only with great good fortune escape with her life, then much as I respect my colleague's abilities, you have endowed her with a good deal of foresight and, indeed, luck.'

'I am not suggesting any such thing, Mrs Lewis. No indeed, I am not.'

Vesta's shoulders appeared to broaden. 'Good. I understand that you have to ask, Mr Timpson. So for your information, I organised this insurance among other policies, towards the end of last year because we had made a substantial profit in the business.'

'I see.' Mr Timpson took a note. 'Do you know if there is any other insurer with an interest in the property?'

'You mean upstairs?'

'Yes.' Mr Timpson nodded. 'Because that isn't one of ours.'

'I don't think it would be right to call the family so soon after poor Mr Beaumont died. You may, however, wish to do so. The telephone number is in the directory – they live in London, I believe.'

'Thank you.' Mr Timpson sucked his teeth so that momentarily the sound of a deflating balloon echoed around the room. Then he relented. 'It will all have to be cleaned to start with and you're quite right, the kitchen cannot be entirely re-covered. There will have to be substantial replacements. We will draw up a schedule of works based on what you have started. I fear for the wiring with all this water. We'll have to have it checked. The fire brigade do not consider such matters.'

'Too busy saving lives.'

'This kind of damage can kill people too.' Mr Timpson stuck to his guns. 'It is going to take some weeks. Just to be clear.'

'I know.'

Mr Timpson nodded curtly. He put away the

sheaf of papers in his well-worn leather satchel and sighed. 'Well, thanks to your efficiency, I'm finished far earlier than I expected.'

'And if I understand you correctly, you are happy to underwrite the cost of cleaning, refurbishment and replacement as required?'

Mr Timpson looked over the top of his spectacles. Really, this woman was a marvel. Often when he turned up at the site of a large claim there was only confusion. Most times if there was a woman there, she'd burst into tears. Mrs Lewis's professionalism was inspiring. 'You understand correctly,' he confirmed with what could only be described as a toothy smirk. 'And if I might just ask, will you be dealing with the claim on Miss Bevan's behalf?'

Vesta nodded.

'Well, she is, I think, extremely fortunate to have you. Now, as I'm finished here, I wonder if I might tempt you to join me for a drink? It is almost that time.' Mr Timpson gave another smile and checked his watch. It was a quarter past midday, easily time for lunch, liquid or otherwise. 'I'm running rather early, you see. I expected this business to take well into the afternoon and I confess I'm curious to find out how you ended up here, Mrs Lewis?'

'Working for McGuigan & McGuigan?'

'No. Here in Brighton, I mean. One doesn't expect such an exotic person...'

Vesta stiffened. He wasn't trying to be rude. 'I'm a London girl really,' she cut in. 'From Bermondsey. And I'm afraid I need to get back to the office.'

Mr Timpson's eyes strayed only momentarily across her figure. 'That's a shame.'

Vesta made a move for the door. A couple of years ago she'd have taken up Mr Timpson's offer. She'd have smiled and laughed and won him round so that he wouldn't think of the colour of her skin before he thought of anything else. These days, since she and Charlie had got hitched and the trouble they'd had with the neighbours when they moved out of town, the truth was that Vesta felt a good deal less inclined to bring people round, one way or another.

'And where is Miss Bevan?' Mr Timpson made to follow Vesta downstairs.

'She's gone up to London. She needed some essentials.'

'You seem very protective of her.'

'She's more than just my boss. Over the years we've become friends.'

'And I can't tempt you to just one little drink?'

'I must get back to work. Thanks, though.' Vesta closed the front door with a sense of finality. She locked it and held out her hand. Mr Timpson shook it and watched her as she wheeled her bike into place so she could mount.

'It's an easy cycle along the front,' she said.

Mr Timpson raised his hat as Vesta's figure receded along the promenade, wishing he could have been more persuasive. He'd expected the girl to be keener but there was no accounting for taste. Still, he thought, there was plenty of time – the renovation would take a couple of months and he'd have every opportunity to take Mrs Lewis for lunch on another occasion. Turning towards

Hove, where he had parked his car, he wondered if Miss Bevan was as much of a honey as her clerk. Perhaps he'd have the opportunity to take her for lunch at some point, too.

Mirabelle hopped on to a Routemaster and headed eastwards. As the bus drove through town, she stared out of the window. The pavement was dappled in autumn light and the air felt warmer than it had on the coast. She had not set out for town with the sole reason of a visit to the Beaumont residence in mind. Before she left Brighton she'd had the foresight to make another appointment but Madame Vergisson had not been able to see her till three o'clock so there was plenty of time to undertake more investigation. The bus filled and emptied by turns. At Fleet Street, she alighted only a few yards from the *Daily Telegraph's* office, an imposing Victorian building fronted by a line of stone columns.

When she enquired after George Highton at the reception desk, the girl who was stationed there didn't even check. 'He's out to lunch,' she said.

Mirabelle looked at her watch. Often she simply forgot that most people punctuated their days with food and drink. 'Do you know when he might be back?' she enquired.

The receptionist looked confused as if Mirabelle had asked when Mr Highton might be landing on the moon. There was a pause, then she said decisively, 'I couldn't possibly say.'

'Does he have a secretary?' Mirabelle pushed.

The receptionist shook her head in alarm. The

ritual of lunch on Fleet Street was generally accorded a quasi-religious respect and it would seem callers who ascertained that Mr Highton was so engaged seldom asked any further. Mirabelle folded her hands as if she was set to wait. There was a small bench to one side and she eyed it.

'I suppose you could speak to Mr Vinestock, if you like,' the girl said. 'He writes about the Grand Prix and that sort of thing. He's upstairs. Second floor.'

'That's very helpful. Thank you.' Mirabelle smiled as she turned to take the stairs.

In the second-floor hallway there was a glass screen through which she could see the news-room. It wasn't busy at this time of day – the morning editions were long gone and the pressure was off until tomorrow. Over half the desks were abandoned and of the journalists who remained in the office, several were smoking laconically as they spoke on the telephone or read newspapers other than the one they were employed to produce. As she walked through the glass door, their voices joined in concert with the clacking of typewriters. She paused in front of the bank of desks, taking in the layout to see who she might ask for help. In the event there was no need. A stocky, blue-eyed young man caught her eye and raised his hand in greeting. He strode towards her and held out his hand.

'Mr Vinestock?' Mirabelle checked.

'That's right.' He grinned, revealing a wide, white smile. 'How can I help?'

'I understand you work with George Highton. I wondered if you might know where I could catch up with him?'

'And you are...?'

'Mirabelle Bevan.'

'From?'

'Brighton. I was up in town on other business and I wanted to drop in. I bumped into Mr Highton yesterday when he was down on the coast.'

Vinestock paused. He ran his hand through his hair, releasing the scent of pomade on to the air, then he hooked his thumb into his waistcoat pocket. 'He'll be out on the town, Miss Bevan. He's been out on the town ever since, you see.'

'Since yesterday, you mean?'

The man nodded.

'Since the fire?'

'You know about it, then?'

'I was in it, Mr Vinestock. Dougie Beaumont lived directly above me.'

Reuben Vinestock seemed to relax a little. The explanation of a tragedy was always difficult because you never knew how people might react or how much it was politic to tell them. Mirabelle, after all, might have been anyone. In this case the matter was now sufficiently illuminated. Mirabelle had an interest.

'You can call me Reuben,' he said, drawing a bashed silver cigarette case from his trouser pocket and offering it in her direction. She shook her head, and he lit a smoke for himself, regarding her carefully. Mirabelle knew that look – he had realised she had a story. Journalists and policemen always wore the same slow-eyed expression when their interest was aroused. He glanced momentarily back towards his desk.

'Do you think you might be able to point me in the direction of Mr Highton's drinking spree? I'd very much like to catch up with him.'

Reuben shrugged his shoulders and drew deeply on his cigarette. 'Why?'

'I have a couple of questions. Things to clear up.'

'Such as?'

Mirabelle paused. There was no point in being coy. 'I have reason to believe he removed something from the scene of the fire.' Vinestock took another draw and waited for her to continue. 'The police don't know Mr Highton was in Brighton on Sunday and I didn't tell them he had visited Mr Beaumont's flat. He has been bereaved, after all, and sometimes people do odd things. But I think he took something that belonged to Mr Beaumont and I'd like to know what it was.'

Mirabelle let her words settle.

'That doesn't sound like George,' Reuben said, doubtfully. 'He's not a sneak thief. Perhaps he had lent Dougie something. Perhaps it was a photograph or a keepsake. He was pretty cut up about what happened. They spent a lot of time together. They'd known each other since they were children.'

'Yes, perhaps it was something like that. There's no need to get the authorities involved but I'd very much appreciate your help. Do you think you could help me track him down?'

It took a moment or two as Reuben weighed up Mirabelle's resolve alongside his own curiosity. There was no doubt that given the state George Highton was in, he was far better speaking to this woman than the police.

'Let me get my hat,' he said. 'There's a couple of places we could try.'

Outside it had started to rain again. A mist of fine drizzle descended like a blanket over Fleet Street but this time it did not obscure the bright autumn light. Reuben had brought a long-handled black umbrella and he opened it, motioning for Mirabelle to shelter underneath.

'Well, this is cosy,' he said.

'I understand you cover events on the racing circuit. The Grand Prix and so on?'

Reuben shook his head. 'Only if George can't get his copy in for one reason or another. Mostly I write about foreign policy. I just fill in sometimes when people are off.'

'You've got languages then?'

He nodded. 'You can say it, if you like. I mean it's obvious, but you can ask if you want to.'

'Ask what?'

He cast a glance sideways at her. 'I'm Jewish, Miss Bevan. I'm one of those clever, hard-working Jews. You know: the lucky ones. I speak just about everything – French, Russian and, for that matter, Arabic. And yes, I speak German too. That's what everyone always asks. "Do you speak German?" As if the whole war was our fault because we stupidly settled in Germany and picked up the mother tongue. So, yes, I have languages. It's less awkward just to get the thing out.'

Mirabelle faltered. 'Well, that's none of my business,' she said and cursed herself for sounding prissy.

Reuben laughed. He took her arm and guided her around the corner on to Red Lion Close, skilfully manoeuvring the umbrella to miss the low-hanging shop signs and wall-mounted lights. This part of town had character but that came with disadvantages in wet weather.

'No. I mean it,' Mirabelle insisted, recovering from the frankness of his admission. 'There's really no need. You sound so very het up. I wouldn't tell you anything like that about me.'

Reuben eyed her. 'Church of England?' he snorted. 'Nothing to tell. Look, it's very nice of you, but I know what everyone thinks. I mean, the English at least try to be polite. I just wish I was half as good with money as you lot assume.'

'We didn't fight the war...' Mirabelle's voice trailed as he met her eyes with a glance that could freeze water. He lifted the umbrella higher to let her enter a pub beside the advocates' chambers. Inside, the atmosphere was subdued. If anything it was darker than outside, despite the downpour. The place smelled of stale cigarette smoke and vinegar. Two men dressed in legal gowns huddled over glasses of oily-looking brandy. Reuben Vinestock made for the bar where a tall, thin fellow in a crumpled plaid shirt was cleaning a beer pump.

'What can I get you?'

'I'm looking for George Highton.'

The tall man shrugged. 'I ain't seen him, mate. Not since yesterday.'

'Who was he with?'

The barman eyed Mirabelle, considering perhaps if he ought to say.

'With a woman, then?' Vinestock guessed.

The man nodded.

'Just the two of them?'

He nodded again. Vinestock checked his watch. 'Right,' he said, ushering Mirabelle back out on to the lane. The door banged behind them and he motioned her towards Fleet Street.

'He'll be somewhere in Soho,' Reuben said. 'He'll have taken the girl drinking and dancing, whoever it was. He'll stop off somewhere, get some sleep. He'll be up by now more or less and, well that's my guess, he's probably back in Soho, drinking. Everyone knows him round here. Yesterday the whole world was commiserating with the poor guy – regrets and regards, all that. All the fellows in the office dropping by one by one to pay their respects. I think that's the worst thing – everyone feeling sorry for you when someone has died. Everyone trying to help when the truth is that nobody can. About now, if I were George, I'd want to be alone. Look, I'm sure he didn't take anything valuable from Dougie's flat, Miss Bevan. He wouldn't remove anything he didn't have a right to. He isn't like that. But if he's over in Soho, I don't want to intrude. He's probably blind drunk and he's gone there to avoid people.'

'And the girl he was with when he was here...?' she asked. Reuben's eyes shifted slightly. 'He doesn't have a regular girlfriend, then?' Mirabelle pushed.

Reuben skipped only a beat. 'It'll just be someone from the typing pool.' He looked over his shoulder and Mirabelle just knew. Sometimes people gave themselves away without even realising. Reuben Vinestock had the air of being frank, but it was what he hadn't said that was important. That and a remark Mrs Beaumont had let drop about her son – girls followed him around like puppies – she had emphasised that, almost as if she had been convincing herself. Now, understanding dropped into place like a penny in a slot.

'It was always Dougie Beaumont for George Highton, wasn't it?' Mirabelle pressed her suspicion home. 'And his feelings were reciprocated. That's why Highton came down to Brighton after the fire. That's why everyone was commiserating with him. And that's why he's so cut up. It was more than just a friendship. They were lovers, weren't they, Mr Vinestock?'

Reuben stared blankly. If there was any suggestion that what Mirabelle had said was untrue, most people would take tremendous offence. Reuben Vinestock did not. 'What do you want me to say?'

'Well, it seems to me you're a young man who says what he thinks. Only a few minutes ago, you were extremely frank.'

Mirabelle was surprised at the flush that bloomed across Reuben's cheek.

'What George and Dougie got up to is their business, not mine. They're decent blokes, both of them. Look, I need to get back.'

He stepped away. A fine mist of rain dusted Mirabelle's skin, or at least what little of it was protruding from her outfit. Reuben held out the umbrella. 'You can take it, if you like.'

'Mr Vinestock, I have to ask. Is this why Dougie Beaumont killed himself? I mean, it can't have been easy for him. His father is a member of parliament–'

'I don't know,' Reuben cut in, but he shook his

head as he said the words. Homosexuality was illegal, but worse than that was the shame. Reuben shifted on his feet.

'I'm not accusing you, Mr Vinestock. To be honest, I feel a lot of empathy. The more I find out about this young man – he had such tremendous talent but that meant a lot was expected of him. And it can't be easy... I mean, Dougie Beaumont might well have felt tremendously guilty.'

'Well if he did, none of us knew,' Reuben relented. 'I mean why should he? People think that they're perverts or ingrates or whatever but whose business is it? People are just different from each other. Dougie seemed absolutely fine the last time I saw him.'

'When did you last see him?'

'Last month. In Deauville. He was excited because he'd had an idea about how to modify the steering column. He was planning to have a prototype to try out in time for Goodwood next year. You can't tell what's going on inside people.'

'Did Beaumont keep a diary? A notebook of some kind?'

'I don't know. Why?'

'I'd still like to know what George Highton removed from Beaumont's flat.'

'It's not your business. Look, the chances are it was probably something private – I mean, between them. A revelation would be the last thing the family would need now and the last thing Dougie would have wanted. Don't break his mother's heart by making a point of this. All it would take is a nosey copper to decide it was his duty to hunt out the sodomite. I don't like witch-hunts. Or fag-hunts. Or Jew-hunts. You must know what the police are like. Please. I think you should drop it. George is devastated. That much I can definitely tell you. I really ought to get back now.'

Mirabelle followed Reuben on to Fleet Street. As the drizzle dried up, a rainbow appeared between the clouds. From this angle it looked as if it ended at the Old Bailey. Vinestock picked up his pace and she fell into step with him as he strode back towards the office.

'I'm not like that,' she insisted, 'I believe in live and let live.'

'Well, you should leave it be, then. I don't want to know anything more about it,' Vinestock mumbled. 'I can't get involved.'

Mirabelle felt suddenly wise – a woman of the world. Her friend, Eddie Brandon, was brazen in his love affairs, but then Eddie knew a lot of secrets. If the police were to arrest him they would risk an unholy security breach. Once it had been suggested that his sexual behaviour was risky for the department.

'Why?' he'd asked, his tone characteristically cool.

'Well, you know.' The man Eddie had been speaking to was his superior. He'd dealt with war crimes, corruption and espionage, but somehow he couldn't find the words for this. 'There's a fear you might compromise us, Brandon.'

'The thing is–' Eddie retained a twinkle in his eye '–we all know about me. I never deny it. So what is someone going to threaten to do? Unmask me for the unholy sybarite I am? Report me to the police for sodomy? What I don't know

85

about the Commissioner isn't worth knowing.'

Eddie hadn't said it, but the implication was that he also knew a good deal about his boss too. Somehow he managed to straddle two worlds – one respectable and the other one very far from it. He truly didn't care what people thought. Few were that lucky.

Mirabelle struggled. 'This isn't a witch-hunt and it doesn't have to become one. I'm only trying to understand what happened.' She stuck to her guns. 'I was rescued from my flat in the middle of the night. The place is a wreck because of the fire and I didn't even know Dougie Beaumont had moved in. If I'm going to go back and live there, I want to know why he did it. And that involves George Highton and whatever he took from the scene.'

Reuben stared at her. 'There are no ghosts, Miss Bevan,' he said. 'That's something I know from personal experience. You can search for them as much as you like, you can try to reason things through for weeks and months and years, but there are no ghosts. There's only the here and the now. That's what we have to get on with. If you truly believe in live and let live you'll go back to Brighton and leave George to deal with his grief.'

Reuben didn't pause for more than a second before he swept inside the office. 'Goodbye,' he said over his shoulder and the door clicked closed.

Mirabelle looked around as if he might have dropped a clue on the damp paving stones. At least she felt closer to understanding. Dougie Beaumont, shining star of the racing circuit, had a secret and one that would not be welcome in his family home or his father's London club or the back rooms at the palace of Westminster where political careers were made and broken. Things were often more complicated than they first appeared and this was no exception. She doubted if Beaumont's mother was even aware that homosexual acts were commonplace, let alone that her son had indulged in them. If the boy had always tried to please his family, he would have kept his predilections secret, but might Elrick Beaumont be more worldly wise than his wife, Mirabelle wondered. Did he know? A homosexual son was a heavy burden for a man in his position.

On the other hand, Reuben said everyone in the office had commiserated with George Highton so maybe among the staff, the men's shameful secret was simply accepted. And if the staff at the *Daily Telegraph* knew, who else was in on it? Was the affair between Beaumont and Highton accepted in the laissez-faire world of the French Riviera? There was a pleasing camaraderie in that. Perhaps the men had constructed a life where they could be honest and then, somehow, the real world had intruded and Beaumont hadn't been able to take the shame.

At least in the light of what she had uncovered, the tragedy in the flat upstairs made more sense. And Reuben had a point – George Highton might have removed photographs or a notebook or private letters, something day-to-day that was incriminating. Over the years Mirabelle had known several men who had been put in prison for the crime of gross indecency. Dougie Beaumont might be dead but George Highton at least had the foresight to protect his lover's memory, the Beaumont family and, for that matter, his own reputation. It might be a good thing he had removed whatever Dougie Beaumont kept in his top drawer.

Mirabelle set off westwards. The revelation had left her feeling quite cheery. Madame Vergisson's salon was in Fitzrovia and, checking her watch, she calculated that she had time to walk there. It had been years since she'd had lingerie made to order, but when she had telephoned, Madame Vergisson remembered her immediately. In fact, she had sounded delighted. In her heyday, Mirabelle had regularly bought silk undergarments – brassieres, slips and smooth French knickers that buttoned at the waist. When clothes rationing ended that summer it had crossed her mind to come up to the salon but the trip had seemed too frivolous somehow. Well, she was here now and today she would buy a set in peach silk from the ready-to-wear rail, just to tide her over. Then she'd order some replacements for her ruined wardrobe and perhaps pick up something nice for Vesta, as a thank you.

Before Mirabelle turned off Fleet Street she cast a glance back at the *Daily Telegraph*. All in all, she thought, this was tidier than the mysteries she generally got caught up in. The revelation about Dougie Beaumont's sexuality tied things up nicely. She decided that she'd tell McGregor about the boy's proclivities when she got back to Brighton. She wouldn't divulge any names but she was sure the superintendent would be pleased that she could so easily explain the open drawer in Beaumont's bedroom and, for that matter, provide a potential reason for the suicide.

Two minutes from Fleet Street she passed a bombsite, now overgrown with weeds. She paused, struggling to recall what it used to be. The old London was fading from her memory. She no longer expected to see the shops that had been bombed when she passed familiar streets. In many places the sites were being redeveloped. That's what seemed real now – the new buildings and the flats above them. As she hit her stride, Mirabelle smiled. It felt good to be in the big city again and on her way.

Chapter 7

There are no secrets that time does not reveal

Bill Turpin was about to grab his jacket and head home at half past five when he heard footsteps on the stairs. Seconds later there was a businesslike rap and Superintendent McGregor appeared in the doorway.

'How do?' Bill smiled. He hadn't known McGregor when he was on the force. Bill's job had been to look after the sniffer dogs and McGregor had only just arrived in Brighton around the time he was being dismissed. Besides, the superintendent had gone straight into criminal investigation at Bartholomew Square whereas Bill had always

89

been based at the station on Wellington Road. Still there was always a bond between coppers past and present, and the men rubbed along.

'She's not in then?' McGregor put out his hand and Bill shook it.

'No, sir. Vesta said she'd gone up to London. Shopping.' Bill raised his eyes to the ceiling. 'There'll be a lot of shopping to be done, I expect.'

'The building is in a hell of a state. I was down there today.'

'It's a crying shame. Dougie Beaumont was a great driver.'

'I didn't know you were a man for the racing circuit, Bill. Did you see him drive?'

Bill nodded. 'Yeah, once or twice, just at club meetings. I heard Jaguar wanted him on the team. He had a hell of a season in France this summer, drove for them a couple of times and then he turned them down flat for next year's club meetings. He had an idea of his own, I heard. But how could you do that – cool as a cucumber? Turn down the chance of driving for Jaguar, eh? The D-type is a proper masterpiece. He'd have ended up taking it – he'd have had to.'

McGregor removed his hat, withdrew a flask from his pocket and waved it in Bill's direction.

'Don't mind if I do,' Bill said, holding out a teacup.

McGregor poured a generous measure. 'Busy?' He nodded towards the papers on the other side of the desk.

'It's always busy in here.'

'Do you miss the force?'

'You've got to go forwards, don't you? And I've

90

landed on my feet. It's a smashing place to work, this. Isn't it, boy?' Bill leaned over to pat Panther who was snoozing at his feet.

'Well I'm glad. I like to think there's someone with proper experience in here. I mean, I worry sometimes – two women on their own. Debt collection isn't a natural business for the fairer sex...'

'Well, I gotta say, Miss Bevan and Mrs Lewis aren't your regular wallflowers. I've seen them both on the doorstep and they're the match of any fella.'

'But knowing there is an officer here, I mean, an ex-officer, it gives me confidence.'

'Cheers.' Bill lifted his cup and the men took a meditative sip in tandem. 'The nights are closing in.' He nodded in the direction of the window.

'We've got a few weeks yet. I don't mind it so much down here. At home it gets dark so early in the winter. I always feel the south coast's got it easy.'

'It's Edinburgh you're from, isn't it?'

McGregor nodded. 'I probably won't go back.'

'Northern Lights. Well, I'm sure Miss Bevan will be pleased to hear that.' Bill had a twinkle in his eye. 'Especially now. She'd never say, but she had a helluva shock. I mean, she needs you, doesn't she?'

McGregor wasn't so sure. It had shaken him to find Mirabelle in such a fragile state when he turned up at the scene of the fire. Over the years, he'd seen her in a myriad of difficult situations and her nerve had always held. When he'd realised the address of the emergency he'd been surprised at the effect it had had on him. His heart had raced.

When he saw her lying on the pavement he felt overwhelming relief that the firemen had got her out of the building. As he put his hand on hers, her fingers had fluttered, trembling beneath his own. Then, afterwards, when he bundled her into the car to take her home she'd clearly been suffering from shock and he had found himself feeling surprisingly protective. At the Arundel, he'd helped her up the stairs and into bed and she'd fallen asleep immediately, like a child. 'Sleep's the best cure,' Miss Brownlee had said when he'd told her that Mirabelle would be staying. Still, the idea that Mirabelle might need him remained an alien one.

'We'll see,' he managed.

There was an awkward hiatus during which Bill finished his whisky. 'Well,' he said, 'I'm sad to see Dougie Beaumont go. It must be tough on the family.'

'The mother was in hysterics,' McGregor admitted. 'It's hardly surprising. Sometimes I think it's like watching someone slipping over the edge of a cliff. They're just hanging on by their fingernails when they get news like that. And we haven't even told them the worst yet.'

'Told them what?'

McGregor stood up and laid the cup back on the desktop. 'Sorry,' he said. 'I shouldn't have said. There have been developments and with you being an officer... It was a slip of the tongue.'

'It's all right, mate. You don't have to tell me.'

McGregor was about to reply, but then the office door opened and Mirabelle swept in. Fresh-faced after a brisk walk down Queen's Road from the railway station, she was carrying a couple of boxes wrapped in brown paper, which she laid on her desk.

'You don't have to tell Bill what?' She smiled.

McGregor shifted. 'Oh, nothing,' he said. 'How was London? Did you get everything you needed?'

'The rest will be sent on.' Mirabelle removed her gloves and glanced at the mail on her desk. It appeared no one had had time to open the afternoon delivery. 'Were you looking for me?'

'Yes. I thought I'd walk you home. That is, if you're finished for the day.'

Bill reached for his hat and coat. 'Well, I'll be off,' he said, shaking McGregor's hand.

'I'll lock up,' Mirabelle offered and Bill disappeared out of the door, with Panther padding behind him. 'What were you two talking about?' Mirabelle turned back to McGregor. Men always made her curious. Even in the days when Big Ben McGuigan had run the firm, she knew the conversations that went on when she left the room were different from the ones that went on when she was in it.

'I think Bill would like to know.'

'Know what?'

'About us.'

Mirabelle fumbled in her handbag. 'That's none of his business.'

McGregor stared at her frankly. 'I'll admit, I'm curious myself. Belle, last night I hardly slept. I mean with you in the house ... the thought...'

'I don't want to make things awkward.'

'No. That's not what I mean. I don't want to end up ... behaving badly.'

Mirabelle's glance did not waver. 'Behaving

93

badly doesn't sound like you and it certainly doesn't sound like me, Alan. I'm perfectly comfortable with the things we do. I wouldn't do them otherwise.'

McGregor shifted on his feet. Mirabelle's candour had disarmed him. Business as usual, he thought. As she met his gaze, he felt his heart quicken. He'd thought about her most of the night and all day. When he was working, he kept coming back to the danger she'd been in. He couldn't help thinking that if the fire brigade had arrived only a few minutes later or if she hadn't opened that window, Mirabelle might have died. The sum of it all was that he had decided that he wanted to propose. The truth was, he'd wanted to for a long time, but the moment never seemed right and Mirabelle was impossible to read. He had no idea what she might say. Somehow, given the way his day had turned, a proposal hardly seemed appropriate. But here he was, the steady gaze of her hazel eyes unequivocal.

'The thing is, if this wasn't a murder inquiry...' he started.

'When did it become a murder inquiry?'

McGregor's expression froze. 'Damn it,' he cursed, and then immediately apologised for his ungentlemanly language. 'Mirabelle. I'm sorry.'

'Do you mean Dougie Beaumont was murdered?'

McGregor nodded. He noticed that by contrast it was easier to talk to Mirabelle about Dougie Beaumont's death than it was to declare his feelings for her. Her gaze didn't falter as she waited for him to explain. 'The post-mortem turned it up,' he said, giving in. 'Actually I should have noticed at the scene, but I was so worried about you that I didn't pay proper attention to the body. It was the mark around the neck.'

'The welt?'

'Yes.'

'It was quite wide, wasn't it?' Mirabelle had been trying not to think about Dougie Beaumont's body, his head to one side, eyes too still, as the medic stood over him, but now she pictured it again, it was obvious that the wide red mark on him was wrong somehow.

McGregor nodded. 'The thing is, he'd been strangled first. Before he was strung up. He probably wasn't quite dead when he was hung. The marks, well, when you're hung the rope cuts into the skin high up and at an angle.' McGregor demonstrated, pulling his finger across his throat and then upwards behind his ear. 'But in this case, the earlier strangling left a straighter mark lower down. He was hung after that so the two marks joined together at the front of the body and diverged towards the back.'

Mirabelle sighed.

'It was probably quick after he was on the rope. There was no smoke in his lungs. He was gone by the time the fire got going.'

'But that turns up another question,' Mirabelle reasoned. 'If there was somebody else in the room when Beaumont was hung, he didn't just kick over a stool that caught fire. Someone must have set the blaze deliberately. It was arson.'

McGregor cursed inwardly. She came to conclusions so quickly. He wished his officers were half as bright. 'Mirabelle, I shouldn't have said anything to you. Or to Bill – I seem to have my foot in my mouth this evening. We haven't told the family yet. I'm going to speak to them tomorrow.'

'So who do you think would have wanted to kill Dougie Beaumont?'

'I don't know. So far, he seems to have been a golden boy. He was rich and talented – his driving appears to have been in demand. We're working on who he had beaten at the track over the summer. If there had been any bad feeling. There was a big pile-up at Le Mans – a lot of deaths – you must have read about it. But he wasn't involved in that, apart from simply driving on the same track. We're looking into a number of possibilities. I wondered if there may have been a vendetta of some kind. Car racing is highly competitive. Ruling things out, he doesn't seem to have owed anyone money, in fact he was pretty flush by all accounts. The racing world is more upmarket than the gees, that's for sure,' McGregor said with a smile. In the past, both he and Mirabelle had undertaken investigations at Brighton's racetrack where the seamy underside of the city found its stride. 'Beaumont rubbed shoulders with the rich and famous – aristocracy and film stars. More than that, they seemed to have admired him. He was a talented young man with the world at his feet. Maybe someone took exception to that. Anyway, it's a proper investigation now. His flat is a murder scene and, obviously, I'm keen to find out the contents of that drawer. It's possible that whatever was in there may be the reason Beaumont was killed.'

Mirabelle paused, considering whether to be generous with her information. McGregor, after all, had only told her what he knew by mistake. She decided to relent. 'Actually, I might be able to help you with that. I'm afraid Dougie Beaumont was...' she picked her words carefully '...a homosexual.'

'What do you mean?'

Mirabelle shrugged awkwardly. 'What do you think I mean?' She'd felt worldly wise in London talking to Reuben Vinestock about his friends' sexual preferences, but things felt a lot more difficult with McGregor. This made no sense. Over the years McGregor had seen her in more than a few tricky situations. They'd risked a great deal for each other, and still it was tough to get this out. 'You know. He was unusual. Sexually.' She felt herself blush at the word, as if even saying it was going too far.

'Of course. I'm sorry.' McGregor recovered himself. 'Well, that puts a completely different complexion on the matter.' His eyes were still as he thought it through.

'I only found out about his ... predilection today but I think that the material in Beaumont's bedside cabinet was removed by one of his friends. A lover, I mean. A man. To protect Beaumont's reputation, or his own reputation, or even the family. I don't know what it was, but my guess is that the contents of the drawer were incriminating. Letters. Photos. Something of that nature. I don't imagine that whatever it was was necessarily connected to the murder. It was removed the day afterwards.'

'You can't know that.'

'Actually, I do. I know who it was. I saw him there. In the flat. After the fire, on Sunday morning. He was grieving and he'd come to see where it had happened. At the time I thought he was just a friend, but it's turned out to be more than that.'

McGregor eyed her. 'Why didn't you tell me last night?'

'There didn't seem any point. I mean, it was suicide.'

McGregor's voice was flat. 'You should have said something, Mirabelle. Withholding evidence is a misdemeanour. Not that I'm entirely surprised.'

'What do you mean?'

The superintendent removed his flask from Bill's desk and slipped it into his pocket. 'You always withhold evidence. You're just not very ... open.'

'You're angry.'

'Of course I'm angry. If you'd told me this earlier, then I'd be further on. And instead I'm lumbering behind you like a fool and I've spent all day trying to figure out something that I ought to have known since yesterday. Dougie Beaumont was murdered. Do you understand? If you met a fellow trespassing in his flat it's important. And if what you're trying to tell me is that the victim was queer but that doesn't have anything to do with it, well that simply holds no water. You know it's the perfect motive, one way or the other.'

'You've already decided it's the motive and I don't necessarily agree.'

'What's this man's name – Beaumont's lover?'

Mirabelle froze. If she gave McGregor what he

was looking for, he could arrest George Highton – not only for taking the material from Beaumont's flat, but for soliciting or sodomy or gross indecency, or whatever the superintendent made up his mind to put on the charge sheet. It was clear he had already as good as decided Highton was guilty and, even if his workmates at the *Daily Telegraph* were understanding, McGregor blundering into an investigation would mark, if not the end of the poor man's career, at least a large dent in it. It didn't seem fair when poor Highton had just lost his lover and still retained the presence of mind to try to save both their reputations. 'Can't you take it on trust?' she said.

'Of course I can't take it on trust,' McGregor snapped. 'This man returned to the scene. He might be the murderer. If there was incriminating material in the flat then he's the only person so far who has anything even approaching a motive. Even if he isn't guilty he's the person most likely to know what actually happened. You know, you're lucky he didn't assault you. He could be a killer for heaven's sake, and you disturbed him at the scene. I'll have to bring him in for interview.'

'I wasn't in any danger. You've got this all wrong, Alan. Look, if Beaumont's lover was the murderer why didn't he take the material with him when he perpetuated the killing?'

'That's for me to investigate. I'm the policeman and this is a promising lead. You have to tell me who it is.'

Mirabelle took in a breath. McGregor might be right – George Highton might have had something to do with the murder, but the superintendent wasn't the least bit open-minded and for Highton the stakes were high. 'I don't have to tell you anything when you're this angry. In fact, I won't tell you – you're trying to bully me.'

She waited to see what McGregor would do. It crossed her mind that he was within his rights to arrest her for withholding evidence. The superintendent's eyes narrowed.

'Why don't you ever make it easy?' He spat the words. 'This is just like you. You won't give a thing. Not information. Not anything. It's as if there's part of you that closed down during the bloody war. Sometimes I think there's part of you that's missing. What happened, Mirabelle? What is it that's made you so cold?'

Mirabelle heard herself breathe out. A soft 'Oh,' escaped her lips. Her heart shifted in her chest at the same time as her brain stopped thinking in words. She couldn't be sure if the pause lasted only a moment or longer but however long it went on, McGregor glared as she stood stock-still, her fingertips tingling. When she finally managed to form a thought, it chilled her. Was this what Mc-Gregor had thought of her all this time? Her resolve hardened. Well so what if she wasn't a pushover? So what if she had some mettle and didn't wear her heart on her sleeve? She had done everything she had done for the best. For king and country.

'I'm not going to give you the man's name,' she said slowly. 'You're not thinking straight.'

The superintendent seemed to suck his fury into his chest. 'Right,' he said as he swept out of the office.

Mirabelle waited. She wouldn't have been surprised if she had blacked out as she leaned against her desk. She stood motionless, listening as the superintendent slammed the door on to the street. The sound felt somehow final. All at once, the office felt too empty. She stood there, trying to get over the feeling that she was reeling, falling from a great height with no one to catch her. Then, slowly taking possession of herself, she picked up her bag, snapped off the light and slipped into the hallway to lock up. It was shady outside, the shadows criss-crossing as they fell on the stairs. She hesitated at the bottom before she stepped on to the pavement, turning in the opposite direction to the Arundel. There was an unassuming little boarding house just off the front in the direction of the Lawns. She passed it almost every day. She'd book herself in there.

Chapter 8

Every day is a journey

The next morning when Mirabelle arrived, McGuigan & McGuigan was a hive of industry. After a mostly sleepless night, she slipped behind her desk and got on with opening the mail alongside Vesta. Between them the two women brought the ledgers up to date and filed the paperwork. The electrician called to pick up the new keys to Mirabelle's flat so that he could check the wiring.

Bill embarked on his rounds at ten o'clock and after that, bent over their desks, the women barely spoke until it was time to switch on the kettle at eleven.

As the hands of the clock clicked into place, Vesta pulled three home and housekeeping magazines from her shopping basket and laid them on Mirabelle's desk. 'These are for you to have a look at. If you see anything you like let me know and I'll include it in the renovation. I'm really not sure what to do with the kitchen. How do you feel about yellow?'

Mirabelle eyed the little tower of printed paper. 'I don't know,' she said, 'I don't spend much time in the kitchen.'

The sound that emanated from Vesta's lips strongly resembled a stifled snort. Mirabelle ignored it. Instead she passed over one of the brown boxes she'd picked up the day before in London.

'What's this?'

'It's a present to say thank you. I really don't know how I would have managed without you, Vesta.'

Vesta's grin lit up. She scrambled to rip the paper aside and gasped when inside, wrapped in tissue, she found one of Madame Vergisson's creations – a beautifully cut wisp of black satin fashioned into a slip with intricately embroidered lace straps. 'Oh,' she said, 'it's gorgeous.' She ran her palm over the material and held it against her clothes, looking down to inspect her figure. 'It's so delicate. I love it.'

'I hoped you would.'

'Thanks, Mirabelle.' Vesta turned back to

making the tea. 'Well,' she said, 'I don't want to pry but Charlie said you and the superintendent were dancing the other night in the Cricketers. He said you were smoking.'

'I don't smoke. Neither does Superintendent McGregor.'

Vesta giggled. 'No. It's jazz slang. You know.' She put on an American accent. 'Smoking.'

'Oh.' It surprised Mirabelle how far her heart sank. She had spent several hours the night before, sitting in the dark telling herself that at least she had seen the real stuff the superintendent was made of. She had managed not to cry. 'Well, Mr McGregor enjoys his jazz.'

Vesta stirred the tea in the pot. She tapped the spoon decisively on the side before pouring. 'What happened?'

'Nothing,' said Mirabelle.

'No, really, Mirabelle. What happened?'

'It's a murder. Dougie Beaumont was murdered.' This, she decided, was easier than answering the question and it was, at least, part of what had happened.

Vesta placed the cups carefully – one on each desk. 'Gosh,' she said, considering this development. 'So did someone set the house alight deliberately?'

'It seems that way. Superintendent McGregor will let the family know today.'

'I had best keep Mr Timpson informed.' Vesta sipped her tea. 'It doesn't change what we have to do but I'm sure he'll want to know. That makes it arson, doesn't it?'

Mirabelle nodded. 'I wonder how the Beaumonts are taking it,' she mused. 'The poor boy's mother was devastated as it was. I'm not sure if it makes things better or worse, to be honest – whether he did it himself or someone killed him. He's dead either way.'

'Does McGregor have any idea who did it?'

Mirabelle shook her head. 'Not yet.'

'Do you?'

'Certainly not.'

Vesta flipped through one of the magazines. 'I suppose you'll probably prefer something more old-fashioned for the kitchen.'

'Yes. I should think so.'

Vesta nodded. 'All right,' she said.

Mirabelle shuffled the papers on her desk. She cast her eyes over the pile Vesta had been working on. 'If it keeps up like this we'll need to take on someone else, won't we?' She picked up the paper on top of the pile next to her.

'Another collector? Or someone on the office side?'

Mirabelle shrugged. She leafed through the papers Vesta had been processing. 'It's going to be difficult for Bill to get around everything. It's not only Brighton and Hove any more, is it? Look, this job's in Bognor Regis.'

'Well, I wouldn't have taken that one normally, but it's a tidy sum. It'll make it worthwhile Bill rattling up and down the coast. Bognor is only an hour away.'

Mirabelle read the letter. It concerned a hotel that hadn't paid for a large order of beer and spirits. The sum had been outstanding for months. The correspondent said McGuigan &

McGuigan had been recommended by a brewery outside Brighton that they had helped with a similar problem the year before. 'Bognor Regis? I might take this one myself.' She removed the paper from the sheaf.

'Mirabelle, what *is* going on?' Vesta demanded.

'I'm finding it difficult to settle down,' Mirabelle admitted. 'The other night was such a shake-up and I can't quite find my feet. Maybe a run along the coast would be good for me.'

Vesta eyed her friend dubiously. 'I could ring the doctor, you know.'

'What on earth can the doctor do? No, I'm sure some fresh air will work wonders. It just might take a little time,' Mirabelle said as she reached for her hat.

She chose to sit on the south side of the train in order to get the best view. The coastal route stopped at Shoreham, Worthing and Littlehampton before it pulled into Bognor Regis. However, when the train ground to a halt, Mirabelle did not disembark and remained seated in her first-class carriage. What she could see of the town looked down-at-heel. On the way in she had spotted several boarding houses that were shuttered, their gardens overgrown. The glimpses afforded of the sea between the buildings appeared similarly unpromising. Brighton could manage outside the summer season because it was big enough and places like Shoreham were scenic, with its little harbour dotted with pastel sailing boats at anchor. By contrast, Bognor was shabby. Mirabelle sat back in her seat and fiddled with the edge of her glove. She didn't like lying to Vesta. The ticket inspector opened the carriage door.

'Chichester next stop, madam,' he said cheerfully.

It was only twenty miles, not many minutes, before she stepped on to the platform and asked for directions. Outside the station, the streets were busy. Chichester wasn't only a cathedral town but a market town too. Mirabelle set off smartly past the humdrum shops on South Street, wondering what exactly it was she wanted to find as she slipped past the housewives with baskets over their arms. A man in an ecclesiastical dog collar dotted into a shop to pick up a wrap of tobacco. A little girl waited for her mother outside the butcher, loitering in the doorway with a terrier at her heel, the dog sniffing hopefully. A van stopped to make a delivery to a shoe shop but Mirabelle found herself disinterested in the wares on display. Quite apart from the cathedral, which she had already ascertained lay further on, there were church buildings here and there – a deanery and a little chapel. She peered down Canon Lane where three men in black were engaged in conversation as they walked slowly along the wide paving stones. A chicken that had escaped from its coop perched on a rough stone wall and clucked contentedly as they passed.

Mirabelle continued past the City Cross and the cathedral appeared on the left opposite the Dolphin Hotel. The scale of the building was impressive, but then cathedrals were constructed to make an impression. A peal of bells emanated from the half-ruined bell tower, on cue, as Mirabelle took her bearings. You always entered through the door on the west side of a large church – that was the public way in. As she crossed a stretch of grass, there was a whisper of music on the air – snatches of an organ and a choir singing from the hymnal – children's voices. Stepping over the threshold the music grew louder, echoing round the impossibly high ceiling. Taking her bearings, Mirabelle inspected the body of the cathedral. It stretched so far that you couldn't see to the end of it and it struck her that Mrs Beaumont could be justifiably proud that her son would end up somewhere so grand. No one would need know Chichester had been the family's second choice and now, of course, no one need think that the bishop was doing the Beaumonts a particular favour. Dougie had been murdered, which was both a tragedy and a crime, but not one that reflected on either the poor boy's state of mind or the state of his soul.

She slipped into a pew. The choir was singing 'When I Survey the Wondrous Cross'. To one side, next to a pale, carved medieval tomb, she made out a plump deacon, who was conducting the singers mustered in one of the chapels. The deacon drew circles in the air as if he was nipping the music into place. As he turned to the right she could see his round face contort, not singing, but mouthing the words to the children. He seemed utterly taken up by what he was doing. At the end, he held his first finger and thumb high overhead and, as he brought them together, there was perfect, high-ceilinged silence. One of the children coughed. The deacon paused, waiting for the echo to fade. Then he stepped backwards.

'Almost.' He kept them hanging. 'We are getting there. Yes.'

To say that the choir relaxed at this pronouncement would be an overstatement, but Mirabelle felt their relief. The group seemed to widen a little as shoulders came down and the children breathed out. The group was made up of youngsters of many ages but – she squinted – the youngest surely couldn't be older than seven or eight years. The deacon shuffled his papers. 'Well, that'll do until Friday, Prebendalians,' he said. 'Practise the staccato in the first hymn, that's the main thing.' He let out a trill to demonstrate. 'Love of God. Don't forget.'

The choir shifted as they moved off in an orderly fashion and, murmuring, disappeared through a mahogany door into the cloisters. From above, the organist emerged, his steps echoing on the stone floor. Mirabelle reckoned the boy was perhaps seventeen years old. With a folder of music under his arm, he moved to join the others.

'Peter,' the deacon pounced. 'A minute, if you will.'

Peter approached.

'You know what I'm going to say. The legato, Peter.'

'Yes. I see.'

'Let it breathe, boy. Let it linger.'

'Yes, sir. I'll mark the music.' He scurried away.

Mirabelle wondered why churches always smelled the same – the musty scent of hymnals and wooden panelling. They were perpetually dim – even here where the windows were the length of

108

several storeys. She got to her feet, her steps echoing as she walked down the aisle.

'Excuse me.'

The deacon turned. 'Yes?'

'I wonder if you might be able to help me. I want to find out the details of an upcoming funeral.'

The deacon's face settled into a solemn expression. 'What is the name of the deceased?'

'Dougie Beaumont.'

The man hesitated. It was only a fraction but it was enough to convey his discomfort. 'That service will be family only, I understand, miss.'

'Mirabelle Bevan.' She held out her hand. 'I was Mr Beaumont's neighbour.'

'Ah, I thought you might be... We have had a few enquiries about where to send flowers. Mr Beaumont appears to have had a number of ardent fans in the area. Not only females,' he added awkwardly. 'Nothing like that.'

Mirabelle did not explain Dougie Beaumont's proclivities. 'I expect that I'm rather too old for that kind of thing,' she said dismissively. 'No. I live downstairs from poor Mr Beaumont. The fire brigade rescued me on the night he died. I'm the lucky one, I suppose. I keep thinking about it. I didn't know him, you see. He moved in only a short time before he died. I paid my condolences to his mother and–'

'I don't really deal with this kind of thing,' the deacon cut in as he shifted from foot to foot. 'A couple of the other fellows are far more adept ... really they have me here for the music. The bishop is very keen on music in the cathedral, and art too, of course. I can find you a verger if you'd like to talk to someone. You know – emotionally.'

'Ah.' Mirabelle was surprised she had said so much – maybe it was to the good that this man wasn't someone who was terribly interested. 'Well. Anyway. It's a lovely church,' she said. 'The choir sang beautifully.'

'The cathedral has a school. A music school. Why don't you come to the vestry? I'll see if I can find someone to show you round.'

'No. I'm all right. Really.'

It seemed strange now that she had come all this way. The funeral would probably be delayed, after all. McGregor wouldn't release the body as quickly now it was clear Beaumont had been murdered. She wondered if the bishop even knew yet that the death certificate would state murder, not suicide.

'Mr Beaumont's favourite racetrack was nearby, I understand.' It was something to say.

'Goodwood? Yes. It's the only racetrack.' The deacon fumbled, bundling a sheaf of musical notation under his arm. 'We don't have any of the Gordon-Lennox family buried in the cathedral. Most of them rest at Boxgrove, but we do have a few noble departed – medieval in the main. You know, over the last few years there have been several deaths at the track and we also have some of those poor souls. They drive at speed, you see. Quite reckless. The bishop had to have words with the duke. There is something so very tragic about unnecessary loss of life – well, I hardly need to tell you. We interred one chap last year as a result of a collision.' The deacon gesticulated in the direction of the apse. The walls were peppered with stone carvings, ancient tombs and brass plates and it was unclear to which he was referring.

'Mr Beaumont didn't crash, though.'

'No. Such a waste.'

Mirabelle didn't correct him. After all, a murder was as much a waste of life as a suicide, or a car crash.

'It seems before he died, Mr Beaumont was planning renovations to his motor. He had a friend with a garage somewhere nearby.'

'There are a lot of garages around Chichester. On account of Goodwood, you see. People round here are quite potty about motor cars.'

'Yes, I visited once. It was fun. I live in Brighton and the main point of sporting interest is horse racing. There were thousands of people though, the day I came to Goodwood.'

'It gets busy. Sometimes I think the chaps round here will race just about anything. People get terribly excited. All that rushing about. It puts me in mind of the William Tell Overture.'

Mirabelle laughed. 'It was very nice to meet you,' she said.

Outside, she loitered a moment, near the gate to the school. This would be a pleasant place to be laid to rest. She didn't mind thinking of Dougie Beaumont being buried here. She strolled back across the grass trying not to wonder what Superintendent McGregor was getting up to today. He'd probably informed the Beaumonts of the news by now and would be setting himself to the task of investigating the murder. Turning out of the laneway, she noticed a group of older boys, the organist, Peter, and one of the singers from the choir among them, ducking across the road and into a pub. She decided to follow, though it seemed a rough kind of place – the windows needed cleaning and the paintwork was badly chipped. As she walked through the door there was a strong smell of stale beer.

'You looking for someone, love?' the man behind the bar grunted.

'I thought I might have a gin and tonic.'

'I ain't got no tonic and we don't serve ladies if they're unaccompanied,' he said without looking up.

As Mirabelle turned, she noticed that she was the only woman in the place. 'I'll accompany you all right, dearie,' a man growled from the corner. There was a cackle of laughter and she spun on her heel. Back outside, she stared in the direction of the station and cursed herself. What was she thinking of walking into a place like that on her own? She really ought to know better. She decided that she'd get off at Bognor Regis on the way back and see what she could do about the outstanding debt. There had been no point in her coming. She was about to get going when the organist emerged on to the pavement.

'Excuse me, miss,' he said. Peter was fresh-faced, now she saw him in daylight. 'I'm sorry–' he jerked his head towards the interior '–that was rude. If you like I'll walk you down to the Ship. They'll serve a lady.'

'It's early to be looking for a drink anyway,' Mirabelle said. 'Your playing sounded lovely. I was sitting at the back.'

The boy blushed. 'I always need one after rehearsals. Deacon Bartholomew has us all on tenterhooks. He's an odd fish but he gets the best out of you.'

'Are you allowed...?' Mirabelle cast her eyes back towards the pub.

The boy shrugged. 'Not really,' he said. 'But in the final year it's one of the perks. As long as no one gets too mashed up they turn a blind eye. It's a hole in there, really. Please, let me take you down to the Ship. It's the least I can do.' He held out his arm and Mirabelle took it. They set off in the direction of South Street. 'There's a restaurant in the pub – it's quite fancy,' Peter said. 'I've only been in when my parents visit.'

'I was just hoping for a gin – a stiffener, I suppose. I came to Chichester looking for a friend but I haven't found him.'

'Really? Who?'

'A man called Dougie Beaumont.'

'The racing driver?' The boy's face coloured. 'Haven't you heard what happened?'

'I heard. I was looking for sight or sound of him, I suppose. Some kind of trace. He's to be buried at the cathedral and I know that he liked it here. I'm not sure what I hoped to find, really. It's silly.'

'I met Beaumont once in the pub in Tangmere. I got him to sign my autograph book. It was a couple of years ago. I was younger then. I had to sit outside.'

Mirabelle stifled a smile. The boy seemed hopelessly young and if anything his good manners made him seem even more childlike. They came

113

to a halt outside the brick façade of the Ship. 'Was that at RAF Tangmere?' she asked.

The boy considered for a moment. 'Yes. There's an aerodrome all right. I was with my father. He came down to visit and we'd been to watch the racing. Afterwards he had a beer and I got a lemonade. I was supposed to sit outside on the bench.' He rolled his eyes. 'Anyway, most of the drivers went back to the big house. We were just lucky to bump into Mr Beaumont and his mate. They'd sneaked off for a chat, I think.'

'The Bader Arms is the pub in Tangmere, isn't it?' Mirabelle recalled the name being changed in honour of Douglas Bader who'd flown missions from the base during the war. She'd read about it in *The Times*. Jack had said something about naked commercialism and that Bader probably wouldn't have appreciated the gesture. 'It's not much of a war memorial, is it?' he'd snapped and Mirabelle had pointed out that there were plenty of pubs named after Nelson.

'The Bader Arms? I wouldn't mind seeing that,' she said.

'I'd guess it at three miles.' The boy's eyes followed the line of the road. 'There's a bus but it's hardly regular.'

'Thanks,' said Mirabelle. 'It's a lovely day. I might as well walk. You've been very kind.'

Chapter 9

There are only two forces that unite – fear and interest

She always thought Sussex was God's own county – a glorious mixture of seaside and landscape that was the best of England. The hedgerows were losing their leaves and there were berries, bright against the muddy track, and now and then a tree with a blaze of orange fluttering on its branches almost ready to fall. On the road out of Chichester short rows of cottages were set back here and there. The harvest was over and the fields were tidy, mostly finished for the year and now set for the long, fallow winter. She met a boy walking three cows along the winding back road. He stepped aside to let her pass, like a medieval peasant, as if the road was not wide enough for both of them. 'Thank you,' Mirabelle said briskly as he doffed his cap. A couple of times the old-fashioned atmosphere was broken by the sound of an airplane passing overhead but Mirabelle wasn't overtaken by a single car and only saw a tractor in the distance, moving silently across the naked fields.

Coming into Tangmere there was a rash of houses, a small village green and a telephone box. An old stone church punctuated the main street, a tiny cemetery spread around it. Some of the trees here had already lost their leaves and skirted the graveyard like black sentries. The pub was in a two-storey building, half brick and half white pebble-dash. Across the road there was a village shop from which a woman's face peered at Mirabelle as she pushed open the door of the pub. Inside, the Bader Arms was like a hundred country drinking holes. The bar was carved mahogany with a short rack of spirits behind and two beer pumps. Chairs and tables were spread around the room, which was mostly empty. At the wide fireplace, a woman with hair so blonde that it could not possibly be natural was on her knees, setting the fire, a cigarette suspended between pursed, painted lips. She had just set a tower of kindling alight and was now balancing two logs on top.

'Hello,' said Mirabelle, glad after her experience in Chichester that there was a woman in charge.

The girl nodded and got to her feet, removing the cigarette and brushing the sawdust off her palms. Mirabelle couldn't help noticing she was wearing white patent leather stilettos that did not belong in a rural setting. 'What can I get you?'

'I'd like a gin, please.' Mirabelle removed her gloves.

The blonde slowly headed for the bar, where a tin ashtray by the till was full to overflowing. She picked up a glass. 'Anything with that, love?'

'Tonic, if you have it.'

'Sure.' The girl smiled and reached for a measure.

'It's quiet in here.' Mirabelle looked around.

'We hardly see a soul till they come off shift at the airfield at four.' The girl laid down the glass

116

and poured a small bottle of tonic into the gin. 'Are you meeting someone?'

'No. I came because an old friend used to drink here.'

'A pilot, was he? You aren't a widow?'

'No.'

'We used to get a lot of that after the war. Less now. Can't get anything right today, can I?' The girl stubbed out her cigarette. 'And none of my business anyway.'

'I don't mind. My friend was a driver, not a pilot. I know he liked it here. Dougie Beaumont.'

'The racing driver? Mr Harrison's chum?'

'Mr Harrison?'

'Yes. He's a retired gentleman. He lives outside the village. Calls himself the tinkerer.'

'The tinkerer?'

'Yeah, cars and that.'

Mirabelle sipped the gin. It was refreshing after the long walk – lighter than whisky. 'You mean he's an engineer or something?'

'Not that he comes in here all covered in grease. Nor in overalls neither. He's a proper gent. It's just a hobby – no money involved or nothing like that.'

Mirabelle leaned in. 'I wonder if he might be the chap who was helping Dougie? I know he was planning to do something to his car.'

'Nah. I doubt it.' The girl pulled a grubby-looking cloth from beneath the sink and held a glass up to the light to check if it was clean.

'Why not?'

'They had an argument right after the Easter races. A proper bust-up. Mr Beaumont and Mr

117

Harrison. I ain't seen them together since. I ain't seen Mr Beaumont at all, come to that. Shame. He always dressed nicely – one of them hounds-tooth jackets and his hair all slick. Suntanned too. Just like he looked in the papers. Handsome devil.'

'Do you know what it was about?'

'What?'

'The argument?'

The girl shrugged. 'I dunno. But there wasn't a stand-up or nothing. They was gentlemen. You've heard, haven't you? About Mr Beaumont?'

'Yes.' Mirabelle was about to push the girl further when the door of the pub swung open and she was surprised to see a black man enter carrying a small box filled with wine glasses.

The girl sniffed. 'Put it down there,' she said cursorily, indicating the end of the bar.

'Yes, lady.' The man had an accent that Mirabelle couldn't place but she held back from asking. It drove Vesta quite potty when people asked where she came from. One thing was sure this fellow did not hail from Bermondsey. He was wearing military overalls. 'You're from the airfield?' she asked.

The man's eyes fell to his shoes. 'No, lady. I'm not RAF.' He grinned as if the suggestion was ridiculous and then gave a vigorous salute that left Mirabelle in no doubt he had never had any military training. 'Mister just got me these for today,' he said, indicating his outfit.

'You're helping out?'

'That's the ticket. I'm helping out. Yes. When the plane comes in.' The words were alien in his

118

mouth, the vowels long and low, like music.

Mirabelle smiled and raised her glass. 'Well, you're very welcome.'

The girl picked one of the glasses out of the box. She sniffed once again.

'I washed them all, missy,' the man said, still grinning. It struck Mirabelle that smiling was this man's defence mechanism – a filter he put between himself and the world.

'Still. I better do them myself. Properly,' the girl said and lifted the box over to the sink.

The man seemed unfazed by the implication. 'Mr Crowe said to thank you very much for lending them.' He grinned again and the girl barely nodded.

From behind, Mirabelle could hear the fire crackling in the grate as the blaze the girl had set spread to the logs. By the time the men came off shift at the airfield there would be a bed of glowing embers and the room would have warmed up. She could feel the heat already, as it advanced across the room. It felt uncomfortably as if the fire was sneaking up on her from behind. She shifted at the bar so she could keep an eye on it.

'Was there a party?' she asked.

The black man rubbed his hands together, clearly enthusiastic about making conversation. 'Yes indeed. Mr and Mrs Crowe are party people.'

'It must be pleasant to work for them. Do they live in the village?'

'We are up from London,' the man said. 'It is a sad day. But there is business that has to be done when somebody dies.'

'Oh I am sorry,' Mirabelle replied. She was

119

about to ask another question when the fire suddenly crackled and spat a flash of hot sparks on to the brick floor. Mirabelle faltered, almost losing her footing.

'Don't worry, missy.' The man rushed forward to stamp out the bright embers.

Mirabelle felt the colour drain from her face. 'Oh dear,' she said, ashamed of having jumped. She tried to recover herself but found that she couldn't control her breathing. 'I hadn't quite realised...' she said. Her heart was beating strangely and she felt woozy as the gin glass tumbled out of her hand on to the floor. It didn't even feel that she was in same room any more. When the man offered his arm, she grasped it. He was small, no taller than Mirabelle, but he was steady. She felt grateful as he guided her to a wooden chair.

'Are you all right?' the barmaid turned. 'Hey, you, nig-nog, leave her alone.'

But Mirabelle wasn't all right. A wave of nausea started in the pit of her stomach moving upwards and she realised that she was shaking. She bent over, head between her legs, but it didn't help and she kept watch on the fire out of the corner of her eye. She knew her blood pressure must have dropped because she found it impossible to clench her fingers. Then there was a clicking sound, which she realised was the barmaid coming to help. The girl pushed the black man out of the way and he stepped back, holding his hands in the air as if in surrender. 'Are you all right?' the girl repeated.

Mirabelle kept her attention focused on her breathing. That was what you were supposed to do and it seemed patently obvious that she wasn't all right. More than anything she felt foolish having such a silly reaction. Then, as if in the distance, she heard the girl snap, 'Fetch Doc Coughlan. Over the road. Go on. Hurry.' The black man's shoes moved away and the pub door creaked.

'I'm sorry,' Mirabelle managed. It took a good deal of effort to get out the words but once she'd done it, she found herself repeating them. 'I'm sorry,' she said again. But there was nothing she could do. This appeared to have overtaken her. How ridiculous, she thought, that I should feel like this, after everything I know, everything I've seen. Her skin flushed and then a sheet of fog engulfed her slowly as if it was rolling all the way from the long-dead blaze at the Lawns. The last thing she managed to say before everything went dark was 'Be careful of the fire.'

When Mirabelle woke, she was in a sitting room, laid on a sofa that was upholstered in grey glazed cotton. Turning, she made out the corner of the Bader Arms through a small sash and case window to the right, and, as she did so, she remembered what had happened. Outside, a motorbike zoomed too quickly along the village street. The room was pleasant, with a few watercolour landscapes on the walls and a small brick fireplace on the other side of a loosely woven green rug. The clock on the mantel sat at just after one o'clock and next to it was a leather case containing binoculars, which was decorated on one side with a clutch of enamel badges on cord – passes from racing days. She could just make out a white one, the latest addition, which read 'B. A. C. Goodwood 1955'. She felt glad the fire was not lit and cursed herself for being so foolish. She began to wonder whose house this was, when from behind the closed door she heard movement. Then the knob turned and a man in a RAF uniform came in. He was an officer.

'Ah, you're awake,' he said, his Irish accent apparent immediately. 'Good show. How are you feeling?'

'Sheepish,' Mirabelle admitted. 'I'm so sorry.'

'Not at all. The gin over at the Bader Arms often has that effect.' The man grinned, which set his blue eyes alight. 'I'm Desmond Coughlan – the doctor at the base.' He crossed towards her and Mirabelle noticed that behind him there was a well-dressed woman with her hair styled in a smart Italian cut. 'This is Enid Crowe, who heard you had been unwell and came to see if you were all right.'

Mirabelle, still slightly woozy, struggled to place the name.

'How do you do?' the woman said. 'I think one of my husband's men, Kamari, fetched Dr Coughlan when you got into difficulty.'

'Ah. He's Kenyan?' Mirabelle was not so woozy that she didn't recognise an unusual name. 'I wondered about his accent.'

'Yes. My husband's family live in Kenya. How clever of you.'

'Now,' Dr Coughlan cut in, checking Mirabelle's pulse, 'I'd like to see you eat something, young lady – you're my patient, you know, so it's doctor's orders. I've asked my housekeeper to fetch you some sandwiches and a cup of tea.

Let's start with that.'

'Thank you, but...'

'But nothing. I'll bet you haven't eaten anything today, have you?' Mirabelle gave a tiny shake of her head. 'Well, we need to look after you, Miss...'

'Bevan. No. You're quite right.'

'Are you undergoing ... treatment for anything? Based here, I have very few female patients. Tell me, is there anything I ought to know?'

'If what you are tiptoeing around, Doctor, is whether or not I'm pregnant, then most emphatically I am not. I suspect I am suffering from shock though. It's silly, really.'

Mrs Crowe laughed and sat down eagerly on a chair to the side. She had the air of a schoolgirl, despite her smart outfit. 'There, Desmond, Miss Bevan will have none of your Dublin pitter-patter, the long way around.' Behind them the door opened once more and an older lady carrying a tray of tea things came in and deposited them on a side table. Her shirtsleeves were rolled up to reveal forearms as sturdy as prize hams and Mirabelle caught a faint whiff of bleach as she leaned over. 'Let me,' Mrs Crowe insisted. 'Please.' She poured the tea as the housekeeper turned out of the room.

'You said you had a shock, Miss Bevan?' Dr Coughlan pressed.

Mirabelle felt foolish. After all, on an RAF base the doctor had no doubt seen terrible accidents and, if he had been stationed here for very long, he'd have tended men who'd flown wartime missions and not returned. 'I don't want to make a fuss. Really, it's nothing. You're very kind.'

'I can't help you if you don't tell me.'

Mirabelle paused before she relented, telling herself that he was a doctor, after all. 'I was in a fire in the early hours of Sunday morning. The brigade rescued me and I'm fine, really, but for some reason it keeps coming back into my mind. I've noticed a few times and just ignored it – chaps smoking on the train and so forth – but then in the Bader Arms the fire in the grate suddenly spat and I felt awful. I couldn't think of anything else. It brought the whole thing back and I expect I passed out. The next thing I knew I was here. It's silly, really.'

Mrs Crowe delivered a strong cup of tea into Mirabelle's hand and Mirabelle sipped it. Perhaps everyone had been right all along – the tea certainly made her feel better almost instantly. Mrs Crowe on the other hand appeared suddenly all nerves. She perched on the corner of her seat, a cup in her hand.

'Where was the fire?' she asked.

'It was upstairs from my flat. In Brighton.'

'The Lawns?'

'Yes.'

'Oh no.' The girl's hands began to shake and she deposited the cup and saucer on to the floor.

'Enid?' Dr Coughlan crossed the room and slipped his fingers on to Mrs Crowe's wrist to check her pulse. 'It's clearly a day for it,' he said cheerfully.

'Are you a journalist?' Enid snapped in Mirabelle's direction.

'No,' Mirabelle replied. 'Certainly not.'

'Because that just isn't on. It isn't on, you

know.' Mrs Crowe extracted her wrist from Dr Coughlan's grasp and instead took hold of his hand. 'That's *where* Nug died, Desmond. That's *when* Nug died. On Saturday night, or Sunday morning, in his flat in Brighton.'

Dr Coughlan's blue eyes fell unblinking on Mirabelle, demanding an explanation. 'Well, Miss Bevan?'

'I didn't mean to alarm you. You are Mr Beaumont's sister, aren't you? Enid. I recall the name now. I'm sorry if I gave you a fright.'

Enid's stare was unforgiving. 'What are you doing here?' she asked.

'Don't worry. I'm not a journalist. Nothing like that. Your brother bought the flat upstairs from mine. I had no idea he was even there that night. I feel guilty about it. The thing is that since the fire I have found myself compelled ... well, I just want to know a bit more about him. I almost died and it seemed odd that I had no knowledge of Mr Beaumont, what with him being a neighbour. I had seen him race once, you see. At first when it looked as if he had killed himself, well, one can't help but have tremendous sympathy for someone so very unhappy. Later, when I heard he had been murdered–'

'How do you know that?' Enid cut in. 'The police only told us this morning.'

'Oh. Yes. I've been helping with their inquiries,' Mirabelle stumbled. 'I found out yesterday. I'm so sorry. I'm really not explaining terribly well. It's only that it happened just upstairs, you see. I was there that evening. I must have slept right through it – his death I mean. It's been dreadfully

125

unsettling and rather on my mind. I knew your brother was to be interred at Chichester so I came to have a look and then I heard he drank sometimes at the Bader Arms, so I came here to get a sense of him. And then the wretched fire scared the wits out of me. You see, I'm far too hopeless to be a journalist, Mrs Crowe. I'm sorry – you've had enough on your plate this week, I'm sure, without me blundering in.'

Enid nodded, accepting this haphazard explanation. Dr Coughlan squeezed her shoulder. 'Now then,' he comforted her. 'I think what we have here is a coincidence. After all, Miss Bevan couldn't possibly know Dougie's car was coming in today.'

Mirabelle paused. 'Mr Beaumont's car?'

Enid appeared to deflate. Mirabelle had a sudden vision of her as a schoolgirl with her hair in plaited pigtails. She seemed too young. Nonetheless, she shooed off the doctor and picked up her teacup. Dr Coughlan peered towards the tray and passed round the plate of sandwiches. Enid waved away the food but Mirabelle took one gratefully – most people complained about Shipham's paste, but she liked it.

'Thank you,' she said.

Enid shifted in her seat. 'You don't blame Nug, do you, Miss Bevan?'

'Whatever do you mean?'

'Well, I think I might blame him. You know, if I had almost died in a fire that he had somehow caused. I'm sorry that I accused you. My father warned us that there might be press interest. He is in the public eye so he is aware of that kind of thing and Dougie, after all, was quite well known.'

126

'It must have been a terribly trying couple of days for you, Mrs Crowe. Were you close to your brother?'

'Yes. Of course I was. I looked up to him. It is terribly strange being here without poor Nuggie.'

'Here?'

'Oh, I don't mean "here" in any existential sense.' She smiled sadly. 'It's just I only ever came to Goodwood to see him race. It's a relief in a way that it turned out he didn't kill himself. Suicide – really. When the news first came through, it was just so awful, and even my husband looked at me strangely, as if he was waiting for me to top myself too. People think it's a weakness and they worry it might run in the genes.'

'When did you come up?'

'Last night.'

'Ah – the glasses that Kamari returned to the bar.'

'Yes. We put on drinks for the base commander and a few of Nug's friends from the village. Everyone has been tremendously kind.' Here she was interrupted by the sound of an airplane engine flying low overhead and she paused and sat up. 'That'll be the car.'

Mirabelle cast her eyes to the ceiling. 'You mean it's being flown in?'

'Yes. From France. That was why Nug came home this week,' Enid replied. 'They use old transport planes to deliver racing vehicles internationally. When Goodwood's on, sometimes it feels as if it's raining Bugattis. One of us had to deal with it – the bally thing was always going to come back – so here we are. Daddy is tied up in

London. Mummy wouldn't be able, you see.'

'Yes. I delivered my condolences to your mother.'

Enid's eyes narrowed. Oblivious, Dr Coughlan took another sandwich from the plate and ate it in one. 'Well,' he said, 'I pronounce you a lot better, Miss Bevan. I can prescribe sleeping tablets, if you'd like. Or something for your nerves? A little morphine works wonders.'

'Thank you, but I think I just have to get on with things,' Mirabelle replied. Jack had always said 'worse happens at sea'. He wouldn't have taken pills if he'd fainted though the truth is he probably wouldn't have fainted in the first place. She put down the teacup and slowly got to her feet with the sinking feeling that somehow she had let down the side.

'All right?' Dr Coughlan checked and she nodded. Then the three of them collected themselves before passing through the cottage's dark hallway and into the street. Outside, the sky had clouded over and looked as if it threatened rain. The gates of the base were only a couple of hundred yards away and Mirabelle fell into step with the doctor and Enid Crowe – it was the right direction for Chichester. The guard on duty scrambled to attention as they approached the barrier.

'I hope you have a safe drive back to Brighton,' the doctor said.

'I haven't driven in years,' Mirabelle admitted. 'No. I shall walk back into Chichester and catch the train.'

'Oh no,' Coughlan turned, suddenly insistent,

understanding dawning. 'I can't have that. I assumed you must be in a car.'

'I'm fine, really.'

'No,' he took Mirabelle firmly by the arm. 'It's miles, for heaven's sake, and you only just came round. Tag along with us. I'll see if I can get a driver from the base to take you. I insist, Miss Bevan.'

Enid said nothing. She doesn't like me, Mirabelle thought. Still, she could understand that. To Enid it must seem strange that Mirabelle had come here, on some kind of quest, looking for traces of a man she'd never met.

'A lift into town would be most welcome.' She smiled.

The guard saluted as they passed through the gate. The base was large – a mixture of brick and prefabricated huts. From the direction of the runways the hum of engines surged towards them and the air was scented with an odd mixture of airplane fuel and the aroma of over-boiled soup that was being served in the canteen. Tangmere had been a key airfield in the final months of the war. D-Day wouldn't have gone as smoothly without the men who had worked here. Two airmen in a jeep passed on the road and the throaty sound of men laughing emanated from the mess.

'What will happen to Mr Beaumont's car?' Mirabelle asked.

Enid continued to look straight ahead. 'I don't know exactly. My husband is interested in cars, though not to the degree Nug was. Poor Nuggie – he was obsessed.'

'I heard he was planning some renovations.'

'Perhaps we'll implement his design for the car,' she sighed. 'I mean, that's what he would have wanted. Michael said he thought that might be for the best and Daddy seemed quite keen. I don't care, to be honest. I'd just like all this to be over. I suppose the main thing now is that we find out who murdered my brother. And that we bury him.'

'I'm sorry,' Mirabelle said. 'Of course.'

Ahead of them, Kamari appeared from one of the prefabricated huts. He must have spotted the group's arrival.

'Oh hello.' Mirabelle sounded cheery. Kamari grinned. Neither Dr Coughlan nor Enid acknowledged the man's presence. It struck Mirabelle as extraordinary how perfectly pleasant people behaved entirely differently according to the colour of another person's skin. After four years working alongside Vesta, she had ceased to be shocked by such behaviour but she still felt outraged by it. Mirabelle found bad manners rankled her – probably too much. Kamari fell in faithfully behind Enid Crowe. The party halted at a brick building that must be the officers' mess.

'See to it that Miss Bevan is given a lift back to Chichester, will you? To the railway station,' Dr Coughlan ordered him.

Kamari's eyes slid towards his mistress, who nodded in confirmation, before she held out her hand towards Mirabelle to say goodbye.

'Well, I hope you're feeling a good deal less groggy, Miss Bevan,' she said.

'Oh much better,' Mirabelle said, as she shook her hand. 'Thank you so much for your help. If Kamari hadn't been there I hate to think what might have happened. It was very kind of you to take an interest when you must have so much else on your mind.'

Kamari gestured to show Mirabelle the way, just as the sound of screeching tyres suddenly ripped through the social niceties. Dr Coughlan stepped back as a Land Rover swerved on to the side of the road in front of him and pulled up sharply. Mirabelle did not immediately recognise the driver, who was wearing sunglasses and had his shirtsleeves rolled up – which was notable as the autumn weather was fine but not exactly warm.

'I'm in time, am I? I didn't want to miss it. Is the car here?'

Enid stepped forward. 'George,' she said. 'We hardly expected you.'

George Highton removed his sunglasses and pecked her on the cheek. 'Why not? I have to protect my share, don't I?'

A man appeared at the door to the mess and Mirabelle recognised Enid's husband from the photograph on Mrs Beaumont's mantelpiece. He reached out to shake George Highton's hand and simultaneously clapped his arm around the other man's shoulder. These were people who knew each other well.

'You might have let us know, old man,' Michael Crowe said.

Highton's eyes were bloodshot. The smell of raw alcohol was palpable, not only on his breath but seeping out of his pores. He seemed lankier than the last time Mirabelle had seen him – taller and slimmer, as if his grief had stretched him. Still, she thought, I hate to think what I looked

131

like two days after Jack died.

'I better fetch my jacket,' Highton said, looking back at the car.

Enid walked across and laid it over her arm. 'Don't worry, Dingo, I'll get it for you,' she said, as the men entered the mess.

Mirabelle felt momentarily glad that George Highton hadn't recognised her. It would be another awkward thing to explain to Enid Crowe, who was collecting herself once more on the doorstep.

'Goodbye, Miss Bevan,' Enid said, her tone marking her, if not an MP's wife, then an MP's daughter.

Mirabelle could not for the life of her think of a way to engineer staying on. 'I'm so very sorry for your loss, Mrs Crowe.'

She turned away with Kamari, who appeared to know exactly where he was going.

'Mr Beaumont's car has arrived then?' she said cheerily.

Kamari's grin was immediate. 'It is a beautiful car, missy. Beautiful.'

'Where will it be kept?'

'Mr Crowe has seen to that. It's going to a friend's garage.'

'I'm sure that's what Mr Beaumont would have wanted.'

'Yes, miss.'

'Did you meet him?'

'Mr Beaumont? Sure. I've worked for Mr Crowe a long time. When I was a boy, and Mr Beaumont was first stationed in Nairobi, he used to spend the weekend at Old Mrs Crowe's place.'

'Gosh. In Kenya?'

'Oh yes. He liked the monkeys. He used to play with the monkeys and Old Mrs Crowe would go crazy. "You can't play with those monkeys. You'll encourage them into the house." But Mr Beaumont still played with the monkeys. He used to feed them and once he got an old monkey drunk.'

'Was this when he was in the RAF?'

'Yes, miss. Mr Beaumont was a flight lieutenant.'

'A pilot?'

'Like Mr Crowe. The master keeps a plane at Nairobi airport and the two of them liked to fly it. One day Mombasa for dinner. Another day round Kilimanjaro. They went all over the place.'

'And you look after Mrs Crowe too, do you?'

'Yes, miss,' his grin, impossibly, seemed to widen even more, though his eyes were grave, as if this was a particular responsibility.

'It must have been very nice for them, as friends, I mean – Mr Crowe and Mr Beaumont – when Mr Crowe married Mr Beaumont's sister.'

'When the master met Mrs Enid it was true love. Dinner at the Muthaiga Club and then on safari.'

'And when they got married they brought you to live in London. How do you like it?'

The sides of Kamari's mouth slid into an unaccustomed straight line. 'In my country now, it's no place. The Mau Mau have ruined everything,' he said, passionately.

'The Mau Mau?' Mirabelle recalled the uprising in the papers but she was curious as to what Kamari might say about it. It was odd, she thought, she'd expected him to make a joke about the weather and instead he had become angry.

'What would the country be without the white men? We owe them everything and the Mau Mau are killing people, Miss Bevan. They are bad, bad men. We have to bring back order. We must do whatever it takes.' The poor man looked so tearful Mirabelle wondered if he might actually cry.

'I'm sorry to hear that,' she said.

Kamari appeared about to say something more, but then he pointed towards a line of three jeeps that were parked down the side of an office block. 'Here,' he said. 'I'll make sure you get a good driver. Some of the chaps are crazy. They think they are in an airplane, when really they have got their tyres on the ground.'

Mirabelle laughed. 'That's the last thing I need today,' she said. 'Really I don't know what I would have done without you.'

Kamari disappeared inside the building and Mirabelle waited. She wondered what was being discussed inside the officers' mess. Still a little shaky, she didn't feel she could go back over and ask George Highton what he'd removed from Dougie Beaumont's bedroom the morning after the fire. Perhaps this was enough for today. It was odd, though, she thought, that Enid Crowe had said that the main thing was they caught the person who had killed Dougie Beaumont. The girl had clearly been fond of her brother and of course her desire for justice was bound to be marked. That was the way Superintendent McGregor thought of the case too – he was focused on finding the person who had done this horrible thing. That was the traditional approach. The police way. Who not why. When not how. But it occurred to

Mirabelle that the issue wasn't catching the culprit – that was only part of it. The main thing, without question, was finding out why Dougie Beaumont had been killed. That would uncover everything.

Chapter 10

True friends are a sure refuge

Mirabelle was surprised to see the office lights were still on when she walked down East Street. She hadn't intended to drop in to work on her way back to the guest house, but somehow it was as if she was on automatic pilot when it came to choosing a route home. She lingered on the pavement and checked her watch. It was just after six o'clock. Perhaps there had been a problem.

A tang of vinegar hung in the air as she mounted the stairs so it was no surprise when she opened the office door to find Vesta at her desk, a packet of chips wrapped in newspaper in front of her. Sitting at Bill's desk, Vesta's husband, Charlie, was similarly supplied. He grinned as he licked his fingers and got to his feet.

'Mirabelle!'

'See, Vesta, she's fine.'

Mirabelle turned to Vesta. 'What does he mean? Is anything the matter? I thought you would have gone home by now.'

'I was worried about you,' Vesta retorted.

Charlie moved to leave. 'I'll be in the pub,' he

said, gathering his packet of chips into a manageable bundle with one hand and reaching for his hat with the other. Mirabelle watched him go as Vesta pushed the packet in front of her to one side.

'You didn't turn up,' she said. 'I thought something awful must have happened.'

'Didn't turn up?'

'At the hotel in Bognor. Superintendent McGregor rang and left a message. I thought you would want it, so I rang ahead. Where on earth have you been, Mirabelle?'

It occurred to Mirabelle that of late she seemed to be making many of the people around her angry or suspicious. Upsetting Vesta, however, was worse than upsetting anybody else. 'I'm sorry,' Mirabelle said. 'It's Dougie Beaumont.'

Vesta bit her lip and crossed her arms. 'I figured,' she replied. 'I know you and an unsolved murder. I just don't understand why you're being so secretive.'

'I don't think...'

Vesta cast her eyes to the ceiling at the very murmur of denial. 'Mirabelle, you can't just disappear like that. You gave me the fright of my life.'

Mirabelle sank into the seat opposite her friend. 'I think I am in shock. I know I do this all the time. McGregor said the same. But I'm not quite recovered from the fire. I keep thinking about it. At night I can't sleep until I've figured out an escape route. In case it happens again.'

Vesta relented. She squeezed Mirabelle's hand and then offered her chips. They smelled delicious. Mirabelle removed a glove, picked a plump

136

one from the packet and popped it into her mouth. 'Wow,' said Vesta. 'You don't normally eat anything on the hoof.'

'I moved out of McGregor's place into a B&B just off the front,' Mirabelle admitted. 'I don't expect the landlady there cooks much. Breakfast was dreadful.'

'Ah.' Vesta's eyes twinkled. 'Well that makes sense of the message.'

'Message?'

'From McGregor.' She scrambled for her notepad. 'He says he would like to meet you for dinner. He said Miss Brownlee makes the best kidney pie he's ever tasted and he invites you to join his table if you wouldn't mind coming home. Home,' the girl repeated with an expectant look.

Mirabelle gazed at the chips. They seemed far less complicated than kidney pie at the Arundel. Her gaze shifted to a sheaf of coloured papers beside her in-tray. Vesta was easily distracted.

'Oh. White for the kitchen with new tiles in pale turquoise.' The enthusiasm was evident in her voice. 'Dove grey for your bedroom and I thought light blue for the drawing room. And something like this pale stone colour in the hallway. Oh, and the bathroom – peach, I thought. We still need to pick fabrics, but it's a start.'

'Thank you. This is just what I'd like, Vesta.'

Vesta grinned and returned to attacking her chips with gusto. Mirabelle joined in less enthusiastically, picking another one from the newspaper and sitting back to savour it. Vesta knew her well, from her likely choices of what to eat to her preference for pared-down simplicity at home. In

137

the house that Vesta and Charlie had bought, the girl had chosen pillar-box red wallpaper and a primrose bedroom in which Mirabelle could not imagine settling down to sleep. At the house-warming, the young couple's friends had filled the place with music and Vesta's parents had come down from London. The family had managed an uneasy rapprochement after almost falling out over Vesta's insistence on an unconventional wedding but the house-warming party had set matters right. Immediately afterwards, Vesta had adopted two cats – a ginger kitten called Frisky and a tabby that Charlie had christened Mr Cool. Everything about Vesta was lavish, generous and welcoming. By contrast Mirabelle knew her flat would feel austere.

'At least you're in time for dinner,' Vesta pointed out, checking the office clock above Mirabelle's head. 'Kidney pie, eh?'

Mirabelle thought of Miss Brownlee's mushroom soup. She certainly had an appetite – the only thing she'd eaten today was the paste sandwich at Dr Coughlan's. 'We'll see,' she said.

'I wouldn't be surprised if McGregor didn't intend, you know...'

'Intend what?'

Vesta gestured towards her ring finger. 'You know. He's been smitten with you since you first met him. He's always sniffing about. I see how he looks at you. You must have noticed.'

Mirabelle felt her lips purse. 'I don't think so. The last time I spoke to Superintendent McGregor he was anything but smitten, believe me.'

'Lovers' tiff,' Vesta pronounced like the old

married lady she now considered herself to be. 'Charlie and I used to have tiffs all the time. Promise me you won't go off like that again.'

Mirabelle nodded.

'And you have to fess up. Where did you get to?'

'Chichester. Dougie Beaumont is going to be buried there. At the cathedral. It's lovely, actually.'

'Did you track down the murderer?'

'No. I met Beaumont's sister though. His car was being flown in from France and she went down to pick it up.'

'Flown in? How glamorous!'

'I expect, quite apart from anything else, they want to settle the estate.'

'What do you mean?'

'Well, death duties. People like to get those things over and done with – burial, probate... I wonder if he left a will.'

'I can find that out tomorrow. And that reminds me.' Vesta held out her hand as if she was waiting for something.

'What?'

'Bognor, of course,' she said. 'I'll need the paperwork if Bill's going to try to get the money out of that hotel.'

Mirabelle took the sheet from her bag and handed it over. Vesta was a marvel – she never forgot anything.

Loitering on the pavement outside the Arundel, Mirabelle could see that the guests hadn't gone in to dinner yet. They would be having sherry in the sitting room. She checked her wristwatch. It was two or three minutes before seven and it was nice

139

to feel that somewhere things were running to a regular rhythm. Perhaps that was what having a home felt like. It had been some day. Slowly, Mirabelle let herself in. A low hum of conversation floated into the hallway, punctuated by a woman's high-pitched laughter. Suddenly, she felt quite exhausted and considered turning tail but then Miss Brownlee appeared from the kitchen with the stick she used to beat the dinner gong.

'Oh hello, Miss Bevan,' she said. 'May I take your coat?'

Mirabelle allowed herself to be fussed over. She slipped her arms out of the sleeves and handed it over. Miss Brownlee did not mention her absence from the Arundel the night before, but then, Mirabelle thought, she must be accustomed to people coming and going. Betty sounded the gong smartly and retreated before the door of the sitting room opened and the guests began to file through. The mother and daughter were still in residence, Mirabelle noted. Today the girl was talking enthusiastically about the South Downs. They nodded their hellos and Mirabelle fell into step and took her seat in the dining room at the table by the window. She felt her temper rise as the last of the guests took their seats. If Superintendent McGregor couldn't turn up on time when he had invited her to dinner, then she might as well go back to the other place. This line of thought ceased abruptly as Miss Brownlee served the first course – a rough pâté with a dollop of onion marmalade and a hot bread roll. It smelled divine and, giving in to her hunger, Mirabelle picked up her cutlery just as Alan McGregor dived into place.

'I'm sorry,' he apologised. 'I got held up. It's delicious, that, isn't it?'

Mirabelle nodded as she let the first piece melt in her mouth. McGregor tore a patch of bread from his roll and slathered it in pâté. The silence was awkward. It was the superintendent who finally broke it. 'It's difficult to pick a favourite day of the week to have dinner at the Arundel, but this is definitely a contender,' he said cheerfully. 'Betty does a wonderful job.'

'Is the menu always the same week in, week out?'

'More or less. Now and then there's a substitution.'

'Miss Brownlee said she was a lady's maid.'

'Yes. Somewhere quite fancy – a country house in Derbyshire, I think. But Alfie got her involved in one of his schemes and she was fired. She became a kitchen maid after that, somewhere more downmarket in Brighton. It must have been quite a comedown but it has left her with a certain set of skills. Occasionally, she makes scones. Only now and then. High days and holidays, but they are delicious.'

'I expect that now rationing is over she'll be able to get any ingredients she wants.'

McGregor grinned. 'She's always got whatever she wanted and I just turn a blind eye to where it comes from. Many of the women in my life appear to require the same. Mirabelle, I'm sorry. You were right. I tried to bully you. I was wrong.'

Mirabelle pushed her plate to one side. 'Thanks. I don't think it's you, to be honest. I haven't been myself the last couple of days.'

141

'What do you mean?'

'The fire was a terrible shock. I was unwell today. I fainted, actually.'

'Are you all right?'

'Yes. I mean, I got myself home.'

'Where did you stay last night?'

'I booked into a bed and breakfast place not far from the Lawns.'

McGregor looked over his shoulder. 'Don't let Miss Brownlee hear you say that!'

Mirabelle couldn't help but smile.

'I was up half the night worrying,' he admitted. 'I was going to try to find you but I decided against it. I thought it might seem even more high-handed. I hoped you would come home. Here, I mean.'

'Did you get any further with the Beaumont case?'

McGregor wagged his finger across the table. 'Oh no,' he said. 'We're not going to talk about that. I've learned my lesson.'

Miss Brownlee cleared the plates silently and the kidney pie was served. It was just as delicious as McGregor had promised. After, she produced baked apples stuffed with moist plump raisins and served with a generous dollop of thick vanilla custard.

'It's like being a kid again, isn't it?' McGregor enthused.

Mirabelle recalled the food of her childhood. The cook her parents employed in their London house would never have served baked apples or meat pie for dinner. She recalled a variety of pâtés and terrines, thin soup and a good deal of

142

roasted fowl with over-boiled vegetables. Perhaps she might be keener on food in general if Betty Brownlee had been employed by the Bevans.

'You can't beat home cooking.' McGregor sat back in his seat. 'Do you fancy a stroll? It's a nice evening.'

'I'm tired, I'm afraid. I expect a proper night's sleep would do me no end of good.'

McGregor nodded. 'Of course.'

Mirabelle got up from the table and he followed her through to the hallway. She loitered at the foot of the stairs.

'Well, good night,' he said.

'Good night.'

Mirabelle caught Betty Brownlee's attention. 'My coat, please. That was an absolutely delicious meal, Miss Brownlee.'

McGregor looked taken aback as Betty helped Mirabelle slip into the green tweed. 'But...' he managed to get out. Mirabelle pulled on a glove and he caught her by the arm. 'What are you doing?'

'I'm going back to the other place. I'm booked in.'

McGregor's expression darkened. 'You're trying to teach me a lesson. That's it, isn't it? I've apologised, Mirabelle. Can't we go back to normal? Please.'

Out of the corner of her eye, Mirabelle noticed the girl who had been excited about the scenery of the South Downs hovering in the doorway to the sitting room, pretending not to notice the unfolding drama. McGregor saw her too. He pulled Mirabelle towards the threshold of the dining room where they couldn't be seen.

'It was a delicious dinner,' Mirabelle said, keeping her voice low, 'and I'm grateful for your help. But I can't stay here, Alan. It's far better than the place I've chosen in every way. It's nothing to do with that. It's only...'

'It's only me. Is that what you're trying to say?'

Mirabelle suddenly realised that she couldn't breathe very deeply. 'I don't want to lead you on. I know we've spent a lot of time together. I enjoy your company but...'

McGregor's eyes were limpid and trusting. She didn't want to hurt him. After all, there were times she had relied on him for her life. There were times when she'd kissed him and the rest of the world had disappeared. But he just wasn't Jack. He never would be. And, unlike Vesta, Mirabelle couldn't see herself living with McGregor. Not in a bed and breakfast or anywhere else.

'It's just not appropriate,' she managed to get out, trying not to sound snobbish. 'I'm sorry.'

'Would you like me to walk you back? See you home, I mean?'

'No. I'll be fine. You go up and read George Orwell.'

He stared blankly.

'Go on,' she insisted. 'I'll see you soon, I promise. You need to get this Beaumont case out of the way.'

Chapter 11

Truth is the torch that gleams through the fog

The renovations at the Lawns were well underway and Mirabelle walked along the front the next morning to inspect them. The cleaning company Mr Timpson commissioned had arrived promptly the day after his visit. Three operatives – all grey-haired men wearing overalls the colour of brown paper – worked silently, so accustomed to scenes of personal disaster that they seemed to simply know what to do without any instruction. At first, Vesta had fussed over them like a tiny, frantic bird tapping repeatedly at a window, but as it became apparent that slow and steady they could not be either diverted or aided, she finally relented and let them get on.

Over the two days the men had been in Mirabelle's flat, the cupboards had been emptied, the furniture sent for specialist attention and the contents of the wardrobe dispatched to a laundry in London that was renowned for its ability to remove the smell of smoke from almost any fabric. It was yet to be established whether some items of clothing could be renovated at all. As to the rest, Vesta had made a list of the pieces it was impossible to clean. These included three shelves of Penguin paperbacks that lined the hallway and the thin silk lampshades that Mirabelle had chosen for the side lamps when she first moved in. It had been agreed that most of the soft furnishings would need to be re-covered. Some of the damaged plasterwork had been chipped away and between the water from the fire engine and the grit that was now trodden into them, the carpets were declared ruined.

Outside, a team of workmen was constructing scaffolding across the façade so that the smoke damage to the stucco could be cleaned and re-painted. The electrician had submitted his report about the state of the wiring, some of which would need to be replaced. All in all, the house no longer felt abandoned though, if anything, it probably looked worse than it had directly after the fire. The rooms were stripped, wires hung from the walls and tea chests and cardboard boxes were piled haphazardly, waiting to be loaded into the van.

Mirabelle knew it would be weeks before the flat could be inhabited again but, despite Vesta's efficiency, she still felt drawn to see for herself. She tried to visualise how the old place would look when it was cleaned up. Even if it was pristine, would the memory of the fire make it impossible for her to settle down? If she'd learned anything the day before it was that it wasn't only the house that needed to recover. Now she loitered in the main hallway unsure if there was anything useful that she could do. It would appear that the Beaumont family hadn't thought to start work on Dougie's flat. The lock upstairs had not even been repaired, and while the two lower floors were at least started on the process of recovery, the upper one remained blackened and deserted, pressing down heavily on the rest of the building like a thick, filthy London fog. The sound of scaffolding being bolted together outside punctuated the morning air as Mirabelle stared upwards, hesitating only a second or two before deciding to have another look at the scene of the crime.

The door creaked as she pushed it open and she worried that someone might notice, but there was no change in the rhythm of the house below. In the rest of the building the burning smell was starting to air, but here it still hung heavily. Now the flat had been designated a murder scene, there were some chalk marks in the drawing room where the fire brigade and police had tried to reconstruct what had happened. The overturned side tables had been moved and the chandelier had been lowered from the ceiling so it could be examined. Passing by, Mirabelle shuddered and crossed the hallway again into the kitchen. There was almost nothing in the cupboards. Two bottles of champagne and a jar of mustard stood forlornly on the shelf like awkward guests at a cocktail party. Evidently Dougie Beaumont didn't cook at home. Bachelors generally ate out, she supposed, and in that he had made a good choice in Brighton – there were plenty of hotels and restaurants close by. Mirabelle carefully closed the cupboard door so as not to make a noise that would attract attention downstairs. Then, keeping the most intriguing for last, she crossed the living room once more to enter the bedroom.

The wardrobe was open but it only revealed a few clothes. Even for a man who travelled light in life, as Mrs Beaumont had described her son, it seemed too little to leave behind. Wooden coat hangers with balls of cedar hanging from them looked as if they had been abandoned. There was only one suit of clothes and two starched cotton shirts, which must have been white originally though now, of course, the material had been daubed in grey smoke. Mirabelle opened the drawers on both sides of the bed, discovering two pairs of socks and two sets of underwear, a packet of Du Maurier cigarettes and another of Dunhill, a box of Swan matches, a pair of braces and a leather travelling wallet which contained Beaumont's passport and some ticket stubs. She stared at the small black and white photo on the main page of the passport. Then, flicking through, Mirabelle realised that Beaumont was not only good-looking but also well travelled. She'd known he'd got around, but the pages were crammed with exotic stamps that read like some kind of biography. Nairobi appeared near the front and it reappeared often, long after Beaumont had demobbed, always around Christmas as Mrs Beaumont had said, and then again, occasionally, over the summer. This year Beaumont had visited Italy, France and Holland. Late in August, he had gone to Kenya for a trip that barely lasted a week. The final stamp testified that Beaumont had left France only three days before he died. It must have been an extraordinarily busy summer and not all easy. McGregor had confirmed Dougie Beaumont was on the track the day of the big crash at Le Mans. The bust-up had made all the papers. Over eighty people had died when a car ploughed into the viewing stand and horrifyingly the race had not been stopped to let the ambulances through. Driving, it seemed, was an obsession for those who were involved – more important than life or the saving of it. In such a world, Dougie Beaumont must have been completely focused on success. The passport was testament to that as he trailed around Europe from one track to another. With so much to live for, who had he fallen foul of? she wondered. It made his murder seem all the more senseless.

Raising her eyes, Mirabelle peered across the bed at the empty top drawer, which, after all, was the reason she had come. She wondered if whatever it had contained were the only truly personal effects in this, Dougie Beaumont's immediate estate. The handle had been dusted with powder – presumably McGregor hoped his men might be able to isolate any fingermarks despite the scattering of grit and soot on the exterior. Carefully, she pulled the drawer clear of its runners. Now she'd started, this was simply habit more than anything else. Mirabelle knew how to search a room. She'd helped to write a manual about it when the first internment camps had been set up.

First she checked whether Dougie Beaumont had concealed anything to the rear of the drawers – this was by far the most common hiding place in a bedroom. He had not. With a sigh, she stood up and continued the routine, running her palm underneath the mattress. The cover smudged grit on to her coat but, unperturbed, she felt as far as she could, then walked to the other side of the bed and did the same. When her fingers alighted on something hard, sewn into the mattress, she lifted it up and snapped the thin thread that held the lining in place. Slipping her fingers between the springs, she retrieved a small leather packet. Mirabelle looked round, almost afraid of what she'd found. How had McGregor missed this? Fingers quivering, she opened the tan leather flap and stared at a sheaf of large white five pound notes which were unsullied by the fire. Counting quickly, she calculated that there were two hundred pounds or so – a small fortune. Below the money there was a strange-looking key. She turned it over in her hand. It was a peculiar shape – an oval at the centre with two shafts running in opposite directions. Perhaps it was something to do with a car, she thought – it looked as if it might be designed to loosen screws. Below the key, there were two black and white photographs. The first showed Dougie Beaumont and his sister, sitting on matching wicker chairs outside, somewhere sunny. They were laughing. Enid had flung her hands in the air in delight, clearly demonstrating by her naked fingers that she wasn't yet married or even engaged. And, in the background, Mirabelle squinted, Kamari was serving drinks on a tray. On the back of the photograph someone had written in pencil 'Christmas at Diyane Beach', but there was no date. The second photograph showed a racing car, not pictured from the front, but the rear, with Beaumont peering out from under the engine with a spanner in his hand. Under the last photograph was a slim silver snuffbox. Mirabelle flipped open the lid and sighed. It contained white powder, finely milled. Businesslike, she licked her pinkie finger and picked up a tiny smear. 'Cocaine,' she whispered as she felt her gum numb where the powder touched it. That put a different complexion on things. Perhaps Dougie Beaumont hadn't been such a golden boy, after all. She wondered what on earth had been in the bedside drawer if these were the things he'd hidden under the mattress? You couldn't get more personal than this little collection. Had there been more money? Something incriminating that he had decided to keep to hand? That was odd in itself. The mattress was a safer hiding place, more out of the way. Did George Highton find what he had been looking for?

Mirabelle was recalled by the sound of steps approaching. She scrambled to conceal the packet, shoving it into her handbag.

'Are you up here?' It was Vesta's voice.

Mirabelle dusted down her coat but the grit from the edges of the mattress had embedded itself in the fibre of the tweed. She was just about to make her way out of the bedroom when the girl appeared in the doorway.

'There you are. What are you doing?'

'He died up here,' Mirabelle said simply, it coming to her rather suddenly that if she left with the tan case in her bag she was effectively stealing two hundred pounds and a tin of drugs from a crime scene.

'My, you are maudlin.' Vesta reached out and took her by the arm. 'Come downstairs and we can talk about what the decorator will have to do.'

It took several hours before Mirabelle managed

151

to get away from the office. Vesta had insisted they have lunch at a café and after that there had been the mail to see to. At about four o'clock two separate debtors had arrived, both keen to pay a portion of what they owed. Mirabelle frequently found in-office payments disconcerting – people were never at ease and appeared either cowed by the formality of the process or bitter because they felt hard done by. At least it was generally quick – they never lingered – and with everything seen to, she worked at her desk until Vesta was ready to pack up for the night. The women hovered as Vesta locked the door and, once downstairs, the girl wheeled her bike alongside Mirabelle as far as the top of East Street and then set off home-wards, pedalling up the hill. Mirabelle waited until her figure had disappeared and then turned left past Bartholomew Square police station. The lights were on in McGregor's office but she couldn't make out any movement. She wondered how his investigation was coming along and if he had managed to uncover George Highton as Dougie Beaumont's lover. The men had moved in secretive circles, after all, and a woman asking questions was undoubtedly in a better position to find out more than a policeman.

The hoardings on Prince Albert Street were peppered with tattered posters for the last of the summer shows. Vera Lynn had headlined in the variety at the Palladium. McGregor and she had meant to get tickets but the summer had slipped past. Now the loose edges fluttered in the breeze that whipped around the streets off the sea. Cutting down a tiny lane that only the observant would notice that ran along the side of the pub, Mirabelle disappeared from view. The alleyway looked abandoned, weeds tumbling out of fissures in the high wall that skirted one side and here and there an empty bottle of blue billy, abandoned by some desperate drunk. Halfway along she rapped on the door of a tatty cottage. A minute later, her friend Fred opened it.

'Ah, Mirabelle.' He always sounded delighted, as if she was a particularly welcome dinner guest. 'Come in. What can I get you?'

When Fred had first moved to Brighton a couple of years ago, the front room of the little house had been stocked with black-market goods – anything that was still being rationed or was in short supply. On one occasion he had sold Mirabelle a gun that later saved her life. These days, however, he specialised in the rare and unusual and was expert at finding objects of desire – French lace and silk, Italian perfume, gourmet chocolate and, she was sure, risqué films for a certain clientele. Mirabelle knew Fred's customers came from all over the country. Whatever you wanted in the way of luxury, he was your man. By contrast, the little cottage was almost falling apart. The ceiling was full of holes, the planking beneath the plaster exposed. A pipe that ran up the back wall slowly dripped dirty water into a strategically placed bucket. Mirabelle noted that the room was emptier than it used to be in the days when Fred traded boxes of eggs and bags of sugar. At one time every surface had been stacked high and she had been afraid to touch anything in case the towers tumbled. Now there were a mere half a dozen tea chests and a few cardboard boxes. Two paintings were stacked under the window, half-obscured by a grubby sheet, through which glimpses of their rococo frames protruded.

'Gosh, I think this place gets more down-at-heel every time I visit.'

'We don't want anyone knowing what's going on.' Fred winked. 'Or we'll be knocked out cold with the tax bill. Whisky is it?' he asked, leaning against the table that doubled as a shop counter.

'These days I'm keener on gin,' Mirabelle admitted. Whisky reminded her of Jack but in the old days her usual had always been a gin and tonic. Perhaps as time passed, she didn't need to be reminded any more – perhaps she had become less nostalgic.

'I've got London gin. Burleigh,' Fred offered. 'I can do you a deal.'

'That's not what I came for.' Mirabelle cocked her head as she felt inside her bag. She opened the little leather pouch without bringing it out and withdrew the key. 'I thought you might know something about this.'

Fred felt inside his pocket and pulled out a small magnifying lens in a black loop. He inserted this over his right eye, picked up the key and peered at it. 'Foreign,' he said, turning it over slowly in his hand.

'Foreign?'

Fred had the demeanour of an expert. During the war he'd applied his photographic memory to matters of national security. He'd been one of Jack's best men in the field. Now he had turned his skills to items of commercial rather than

154

national value, and he had learned quickly how to date silverware and take the measure of gemstones to identify what was worth his trouble and what wasn't. 'If you push me I'd say it's probably French and it's an old one. It's the key to a clock, see.'

'Are you sure?'

'You can fit a lock anywhere, of course, but once you've seen one of these, you'd know it again. What you've got there is the key to a carriage clock. From 1810, 1820. Later than that and they made the keys out of brass but this one's steel. They're not particularly hard to come by. Still, if you've got the clock to go with it, I'll make you an offer, Miss Bevan.'

Mirabelle thought back to Dougie Beaumont's flat. She hadn't seen a clock anywhere. She cast her mind over the Beaumonts' house in London but there definitely hadn't been a clock on the mantel, she was sure of it. There had been a huge grandfather clock in the hallway but a key of this size wouldn't touch that.

Fred removed the loop from his eye. 'How are you?' he asked cheerily. 'Got yourself a boyfriend, yet?'

Mirabelle felt her cheeks redden. 'I'm afraid my love life hasn't been going terribly well.'

Fred inhaled, sucking air through his teeth as much to say that Mirabelle was somehow not trying hard enough. 'I hope you're juggling one or two fellas, Miss Bevan. That's the way to do it. Keeps them on their toes. Who have you got on the go?'

'Right now? A racing driver. He's the one I'm

mainly interested in.'

Fred made exactly the same noise with his teeth, which this time clearly indicated his disapproval. 'Fast crowd,' he pronounced. 'Not that I think you can't handle whatever comes your way.'

Mirabelle smiled. 'What do you mean?'

Fred reached across the table to a small shelf, which Mirabelle noticed housed a few packets of cigarettes, a brandy flask and a crumpled newspaper. He must have been in London earlier that day because he'd picked up an *Evening Standard*. Oblivious, Fred opened the paper, turned over the front page and pointed. 'See. A body at Goodwood,' he said. 'There's a racetrack there, isn't there? They built it after the war.'

Mirabelle nodded and cast her eyes across the text. The article included a photograph of the exterior of Goodwood House which, she realised, must have come from a photo library because the trees were in leaf, setting off the green copper domes at the four corners of the flint building.

'Is that today's?' she checked.

'Picked it up myself at Victoria just after lunch.'

Mirabelle snatched the paper from his hand and shook it to open the page properly. Beneath the photograph of the house there was a smaller black and white shot of a man next to a motor car with the number '26' painted on the side. Time slowed as Mirabelle recognised the car from the grit-marked photograph on Dougie Beaumont's mantelpiece and then her gaze flickered as she also recognised the man's face. It was George Highton. The caption underneath the picture said, 'Racing journalist, Highton, mingled with the smart set.'

156

She scrambled to read the story, gulping in the details so quickly she had to slow herself to make sure that she was taking them in. 'But I saw him only yesterday,' she said, her voice low as she read that Highton had played a round of golf the afternoon after she'd left, and booked into the coaching inn on the Goodwood estate. He was invited to dinner at the main house and stayed on to play backgammon until the early hours of the morning. Then, the report said, he left late – perhaps after two – to take the short walk back to the inn. At first light his body had been discovered a few hundred yards down the driveway. 'Drink had been taken,' the *Standard* pronounced.

'Oh no.' The words slipped from Mirabelle's lips as in her mind's eye she saw him, jumping out of the Land Rover the day before. Still grieving. Poor George Highton. Her stomach turned as it dawned on her that if she'd given his name to McGregor, the fellow might have been taken into custody. That at least would have kept him alive. She had made a terrible mistake.

'That isn't your man, is it?' Fred checked.

Mirabelle handed back the paper and picked up the key. 'I have to go,' she managed to get out as she made for the door.

Fred was nimble and cut in ahead of her. 'Are you all right?' he checked. 'I don't like to think of you having a fright. Do you know that fellow?'

'Yes,' she said. 'Sort of.'

'Don't you go getting involved, Miss Bevan. I don't want to have to supply you with arms again. Not after what happened the last time. Couldn't you find yourself a doctor or a lawyer? A respectable kind of bloke?'

Mirabelle barely nodded as she opened the door. As far as she was concerned she was involved already and plenty of the professional men she'd bumped into over the years had turned out to be less than respectable. 'You know me and a murder,' she said.

'It doesn't say it's a murder, Miss Bevan. It doesn't say that. Poor chap might have had a dickie ticker.'

Mirabelle looked dubious. 'He might have,' she said.

Chapter 12

Investigation: a formal inquiry or systematic study

It was dark by the time Mirabelle arrived at the coaching inn where George Highton had booked in the night before. All the way down on the train, and then on the journey to the inn, having secured a car and a driver, she couldn't shake the guilty feeling that somehow she might have prevented his death. There had been no streetlights since they left Chichester but the driver clearly knew the road and took it at some pace, the harsh light of the headlamps throwing up sharp bends skirted by thick hedgerows. Mirabelle couldn't help think of the deacon at the cathedral saying people round here would race anything as she was flung one way and another in the back seat. The cold nipped at her ankles as she got out of the car and hovered on the fringes of the tarmac to pay the driver. Then she watched as the vehicle disappeared into the thick, black countryside. The small windows of the coaching inn glowed golden but the light hardly reached as far as the other side of the road. Clutching her handbag, Mirabelle made for the door. Inside, the bar was pleasant, an open fire burned in the grate and the low hum of conversation was punctuated by dominoes toppling at a table where a game was in play. When Mirabelle asked for a room the barman chose a key from the rack over the till without really looking. His hands were huge and rough and the key, which was attached to a lozenge of rounded wood, looked tiny as he handed it over.

'Do you work on the estate?' she asked.

'Yeah. In the sawmill. I'm just helping out tonight. They wanted to have a fella around. Your room's upstairs, miss.' He gesticulated towards a door that led to a set of wooden stairs.

Following his vague directions, Mirabelle left the bar and climbed upwards to a dim corridor with a runner of thin carpet tacked along it. She turned the key in the lock and switched on the light. The room was hardly luxurious but it would do – a bed, a lamp and a side table with a sign saying there was a bathroom at the end of the hallway. It struck her she was becoming accustomed to sleeping in a strange bed. In London during the war she sometimes didn't make it home for days on end. In the air-raid shelter at work there had been lumpy, makeshift mattresses on the floor. When she first moved to Brighton, the flat on the Lawns had felt luxurious and it had seemed as if she was settling down, sleeping in the same bed every night, in the same place, the darkness uninterrupted by any hint of emergency. It had felt as if all her difficulties were over.

Mirabelle clicked off the bedroom light and peered out of the window. Outside, the night sky was so completely unsullied by artificial light that she could almost believe the blackout was still in force. In Brighton it was difficult to make out the stars but here the sky was peppered with them. The vista stretched cloudless – the cold moon only a sliver. The glass felt icy to her touch and clouded around her fingertips. She wondered momentarily if this room was the one George Highton had hired the night before. What exactly had he meant when he arrived at Tangmere saying he had to protect his interest in Beaumont's car? And given what she'd found today under Dougie Beaumont's mattress, were Highton's red eyes and jumpy demeanour only down to his grief? She wouldn't blame him for trying to block out his lover's death with spirits or powder or both. She'd hit the bottle hard after Jack died. If only I'd given McGregor Highton's name, she chided herself. If he'd been arrested he would have been safe. As the guilt turned in her gut, she tried not to dwell on her regrets. Telling the superintendent about Highton wouldn't necessarily have saved his life. As it stood there was no point in crying over spilled milk. She might as well get on.

She slipped downstairs and, without attracting attention, went outside again into the cold. The winding B road that led back to Chichester lay silent until a fox darted out of one hedgerow and disappeared through another. As if this called her to action, Mirabelle walked a few yards to the west where she was surprised to find that the inn was almost next door to the gate of Goodwood House. Not much after nine, the stone gatehouse that guarded the entrance was in darkness, the place closed for the night. With a shrug, Mirabelle slipped over a small stone wall to one side and began to walk up the drive. The inn quickly disappeared from view, the thick night shrouding it like a blanket. Fallen leaves crinkled underfoot as Mirabelle followed the driveway, unable to see what lay ahead. To the side, skeletal branches stretched above, visible only because the thin moon's low light contrasted them against the sky. The chill autumn air nipped her skin and, as her eyes became more accustomed to the darkness, the outline of Goodwood House appeared like a looming black shadow ahead. Somewhere on this path, the night before, George Highton had died walking in the opposite direction, returning to the inn a mere twelve hours after she'd seen him in Tangmere. How far had he got down this road?

As the driveway curved, Mirabelle glanced behind and noticed a moving light a few hundred yards off, approaching unsteadily in her wake. She stepped off the tarmac, secreted herself behind a tree and waited for it to pass, picking out the shape of a policeman who had propped a lamp on his bicycle as he made his way towards the house's grand front entrance. The portico was dimly illuminated by the lamp and it suddenly seemed as

161

if the whole place was built of insubstantial shadows. Mirabelle picked up her pace as the bobby dismounted. Then two pinpricks of orange – cigarettes in the darkness – betrayed one officer relieving another of his duty. Now well within hearing distance, she stuck close to the façade of the building, keeping one hand on the cold stone to remind her this was real.

'Sorry I'm late,' the policeman said.

'It's perishing.'

'Anything doing?'

'The staff went home after five and not a peep since.'

'You been inside, then?'

'Yeah. Before.'

'My Trisha would love to see it. A bit of the high life and that.'

'Mostly it's just estate offices – there's a nice old ballroom, though they've carved it up and there's rows of desks instead of the grand and the good. Shame really. We cordoned off the room where they were gaming.'

'I won't be relieved until six. It's a long night.'

'I don't envy you, mate. It's bitter.'

The off-duty policeman walked past Mirabelle, who loitered in the shadows as he headed back down the drive, his cape drawn around him against the chill. She wondered how long it would take the man to get home. Meanwhile the other fellow smoked his cigarette, inhaling deeply as his friend retreated. Careful to make no noise, Mirabelle turned away from the front door and slipped down the side of the house to check the windows one by one. None had been left open – not at this time of year. Then, continuing towards the rear, she crept around some bins and discovered a service door that was locked too. There was something indomitable about Goodwood House. It seemed impenetrable. The goings-on in large houses were always unpredictable but, in her experience, they were usually busy places. This building appeared to have swallowed any sign of life. It was a citadel. There must be people in there, but the old place was so huge and so dark it was impossible to tell.

At the rear she hit an impasse – a courtyard with high wooden gates that were bolted. She backed up and at last made out a small row of lights, which were visible on the first floor. On tiptoes, in the flat shoes McGregor had sent from Hannington's, she strained to see the room, which was furnished as a private drawing room. Perhaps only members of the family were at home tonight, recovering from the tragedy. Unable to continue further, Mirabelle made her way back to where she started. The policeman on duty had moved off and, luckily for her, was easy to spot, still smoking a cigarette as he walked along the darkened exterior of the wing that stretched in the other direction. If Mirabelle scrunched her eyes she could just make out the orange dot, a couple of hundred yards away, where the officer was peering through a set of French windows. She dodged out of sight between the pillars.

Then, just to be sure, she turned the front doorknob. She hadn't expected it to open, but, to her surprise, the door did just that. Glancing over her shoulder and hardly able to believe her luck, she slipped inside. She couldn't help smiling. It was so like the English upper classes to make sure the house was locked and shuttered, but not to expect a thief in the night to have the temerity to use the front entrance. This was where George Highton must have been received when he came for dinner.

Tentatively, Mirabelle moved into the hallway and was glad of her unaccustomed low heels – the entrance was floored in what sounded like marble but in these she could cross it almost silently. The house was as grand inside as it had looked from the exterior. She could just make out the curve of a Georgian cornice and the sweep of the staircase – evidence of the high life the policemen had mentioned. Still, Mirabelle knew that while the darkness might mask the house's beauty, it would also shield its dilapidation. Places like this had been taken over during the war and had become hospitals and staging posts, development centres and extra billets. In 1945, England's country houses had been handed back bruised, chipped and worn, and most had not been returned to their former glory. If the family here had had to make their ballroom into offices, that told its own story.

Mirabelle peered through the window beside the front door and made out the policeman who was now returning to his post. Then, by the dim light the windows afforded, she took her bearings. The officer going off duty had talked about a room that was cordoned off. If policemen were posted at the front door it was probably close to that. And that made sense. A house like this would have its ballroom and dining room on the ground floor, and if there was a room used for post-dinner drinks or gaming it was probably within easy reach of those. Squinting, she scanned the hallway and could just make out a white cordon across a doorway to the right. She made for the tape, dodging underneath it. Inside, the smell of cigar smoke and empty brandy bottles lingered on the air, Mirabelle felt herself sink into thick carpet and she stopped, giving her eyes a moment to pick out the unfamiliar shapes.

The room was circular, not much more than fifteen feet in diameter: likely cosy compared to most in this house. She was on the corner, she realised, in one of the towers with the copper domes that she'd picked out in the photograph in Fred's *Standard*. In the middle of the room, a table covered in thick green baize was set with a rack of mother-of-pearl gambling chips. There were four chairs placed in a square. This had been where George Highton spent his last hours playing backgammon. She touched the back of one of the chairs and tentatively sat down. If four men had played at this table, who were the other three?

Getting to her feet again, Mirabelle decided to examine the walls where shadowy shelves housed decanters and glasses, a few books, some plates and vases. Her eye stopped momentarily on a clock but on minimal examination, even no expert, she could confidently date it as later than one which would be opened and wound using the key she had retrieved from under Dougie Beaumont's mattress. 'What were you up to, George?' she murmured. What had Highton meant when he said he had come to protect his interests? Perhaps this place was a simply a better choice than drinking himself to oblivion in Soho? Had he found himself too short of company he could bear in town? Enid Crowe and her husband had been familiar, comforting even. Perhaps that was what Highton had really been looking for. Or had he stayed after the arrival of the car for another purpose?

Mirabelle was considering this when suddenly a sharp line of yellow light appeared beneath the door. Someone had snapped on the electric in the hallway. They turned it off again and there was a high-pitched giggle and a scuffling noise on the marble. Outside the window, Mirabelle made out a dark movement – the policeman taking in this development, no doubt trying to peer through a window and see what was going on. Mirabelle backed into the centre of the room, thinking that with so little furniture there wasn't much choice of where to hide. She panicked momentarily, her eyes darting, but there was nothing for it but to slip underneath the table. Just in time she fell to her hands and knees and rolled out of sight.

'Shhh.' It was a woman's voice.

The baize didn't quite reach the floor and Mirabelle could see the light of a torch directed at the carpet. The fools, she thought, the policeman would spot that immediately. It was far too dark to use a torch. The man was right outside.

'This is positively maudlin, Henny,' a male voice said. 'We aren't supposed to be in here.'

'Well I don't know why. He didn't die in the card room, did he?'

'Don't say that. Poor George.'

The woman walked over to the table. As the

light from the torch continued to dart over the carpet, all Mirabelle could see of her was a pair of expensive green satin evening shoes with elegant heels. She heard the girl pick up some gambling chips and click them together. Then there was a low giggle as the man's more traditional shoes approached. After that everything went too silent and then Henny said, 'Well who's maudlin now, Nigel, kissing me at the scene of the crime?'

'It's better than just standing here, having the creeps, don't you think?'

Henny must have pushed him away. The two pairs of shoes separated.

'Anyway this isn't a crime scene – George was hale and hearty when he left us, if a little worse for wear.'

'You're only sore because he beat you.'

'No he didn't.'

'You don't have to pretend. The maid told me what they found. The policemen were given tea in the kitchen and one of them told her there was a fortune in poor George's pocket along with that dreadful letter. One hundred and twenty pounds plus change.'

'Nonsense. I cleaned him out. He said so.'

'Oh, Nige. Don't you think the police know what they're doing? It's a matter of public record. It'll all come out in court. Georgie Porgie was loaded. You know what he was like. No one could spin a line quite like Dingo. If he said he was out of cash, I'm surprised you didn't frisk him to check.'

'The sneaky so-and-so. We only packed away the board because he said he was skint. I've a mind to write him a bloody letter myself. From beyond the grave.'

'Don't,' the girl gasped. 'You are terrible. Whoever sent him that letter is probably the killer.'

There was the sound of the front door opening and the policeman's steps echoing as he walked across the hallway. 'We're in trouble now,' Nigel hissed.

The door of the card room opened and the light snapped on.

'Sir. Miss. I'm sorry, but this room is out of bounds.'

'Really, Officer?' Henny sounded genuinely apologetic. 'Well, nobody told us.'

'That's why there's a cordon across it. I'm afraid you'll have to continue your conversation elsewhere. It's a murder investigation, see.'

Nigel took charge. 'Yes. Of course. We wouldn't want to be obstructive. We were friends of Mr Highton. Have you caught the blighter who killed him yet?'

'Not yet, sir. Now, if you don't mind.'

Mirabelle lay her head on the carpet and watched as the shoes walked away. From the hallway, with the door open, she heard the policeman say something about ongoing investigations. Then he pulled up a chair just beyond the threshold, and closed the card-room door. 'Oh bother,' Mirabelle mumbled under her breath. She could understand why the man had decided to stay inside – even with no heating, it was warmer here and significantly more comfortable than standing at the front door all night. She crawled out, the carpet brushing her knees as she considered what she'd heard. When he died, Highton had been carrying one hundred and twenty pounds and some kind of threatening or unpleasant letter. That cast new light on his trip out of town. Perhaps when he came here he thought he had been running away from danger rather than towards it.

There was a high-pitched squeak as the policeman shifted and the leg of his chair scraped against the marble. I'd better get out of here, Mirabelle thought. With the door effectively out of action, she didn't have many options but at least the carpet meant she could move around without being heard. There was only one way out.

She crossed to the window and unbolted the sash, hoping that it would move smoothly across its casing. Wood on wood could make a harsh noise. So slowly it almost made her ache, she eased the window open. After only eight inches, she felt the movement tighten and stopped it dead before it could squeak. It would be a tight squeeze but she could make it. Mirabelle took off her coat and threw it on to the ground outside and then carefully manoeuvred herself over the sill, falling the last few inches on to the gravel, grabbing her coat and backing into a bank of ivy to get out of the way, just in case. Inside, the door to the card room remained closed and, after a few seconds, she sneaked over to pull down the glass. There was no way to lock the window from the outside, but perhaps no one would notice the bolt had been moved.

After pulling on her coat, Mirabelle skirted the façade of the house hoping to stay out of sight as long as she could. Then she turned back down the drive. The money in Highton's possession ruled

169

out robbery as a motive, or even greed on the part of the murderer. The contents of the 'dreadful letter' Henny had mentioned were enticing. Had Dougie Beaumont received a threatening letter before he died too? If so, was it reasonable to assume it had been burned in the fire? Had this whole thing simply been a shabby attempt at blackmail made by somebody who'd found the men out? If so, it had gone badly wrong.

Casting a glance back at Goodwood House, Mirabelle caught a movement in one of the upstairs windows. She wondered if Henny and Nigel had taken themselves to the first floor to continue their flirtation. No matter. From such a distance, no one would be able to recognise her and, anyway, she told herself as she picked up her pace, it wasn't illegal to take a walk at night down a driveway. That wasn't illegal at all.

Chapter 13

Our life is frittered away by detail

Breakfast at the coaching inn was limited to bread and eggs with some weak tea and large sugar lumps so irregularly cut that there was a serious risk of making the tea undrinkably sweet. Two men on the table next to Mirabelle ordered beer from a blonde waitress with limpid blue eyes and milky skin. They enthusiastically made a meal of it, abandoning the food on their plates and placing their glasses square in front of them. Listening to their increasingly animated chatter, Mirabelle deduced they were buyers for a chain of furniture shops and had arrived on the estate to conduct business at the sawmill. Tempers already fraying, the men started to debate the durability of different woods. Some people will argue about anything, she thought.

The London papers were on the sideboard but Mirabelle asked if there was something local and the girl fetched a *Chichester Observer* from the kitchen as Mirabelle poured herself another cup of tea. The report of George Highton's death was brief and simply said that the police were investigating. In the *Daily Telegraph* there was a short obituary and Mirabelle noted that Highton had been an officer in the Loyals – a Lancashire regiment. Older than Dougie Beaumont by two years, he had seen active service in Italy towards the end of the war.

After making the best of the eggs, Mirabelle decided to take a look at Goodwood House from the other side. She had yet to ascertain exactly where George Highton had died or, for that matter, the details of how he had been killed. If he was an ex-officer in the Loyals, he would have been trained to defend himself, though, she thought, that wouldn't help him if the poor fellow had been shot. Like all the other papers, the *Daily Telegraph* had simply said that he had 'died in suspicious circumstances' and made no mention of either the money in his pockets or the mysterious letter. Mirabelle would be interested to know just how suspicious the circumstances

171

were, if a weapon was used, or if like Dougie Beaumont's killer, the man who did for George Highton had been hands-on.

That morning from her window, in the early light, Mirabelle had noticed there was a bunker and a green just beyond the inn. It was part of a golf course laid out around the perimeter of the main house – everything close by – and, as she left the table, she asked the direction of the clubhouse. The waitress pointed out the road to take and Mirabelle figured the course must have views of Goodwood House. The estate was certainly somewhere there was plenty to do, with its aerodrome, golf course and racing track. After checking her watch, she used the telephone at the bar and had the operator put her through to the office on Brills Lane.

'Hello,' she said.

'Mirabelle! How are you this morning?' Vesta always sounded delighted on the telephone, no matter the subject of the conversation.

'I'm down in the country' Mirabelle replied. 'I thought I'd take a long weekend.'

The girl made a noise that indicated her dubiety. Mirabelle rarely, if ever, took holidays and certainly not to the countryside. 'Are you all right?'

'Yes. I'm fine. I'm off to the golf course this morning.'

'Golf? I didn't know you played golf. Where on earth are you?'

'Goodwood.'

'Oh, I've heard it's lovely. Charlie's friend Jacko played there last year – a party at a big house. I think they thought that jazz was rather risqué.' Vesta's voice slowed and Mirabelle made out the sound of newspaper crinkling down the line. The tone of the girl's voice changed as she put two and two together. 'Was that Goodwood you said?' She sounded disapproving.

'Is what happened in the *Argus?*'

'Yes.'

'What does it say?'

'That some bloke was killed.'

'Read it out, Vesta.'

'George Highton. Twenty-nine. A racing journalist. Oh, really, Mirabelle!'

'Does it say how he died?'

'Murder. He was murdered. Well, suspicious circumstances anyway. I can't believe you won't touch divorce cases, but you'll dive into this sort of thing. I'm going to ring Superintendent McGregor.'

'Oh for heaven's sake. Goodwood is out of McGregor's jurisdiction. There's nothing he can do. That's the problem with the police. It takes different forces for ever to coordinate.' Down the phone line Mirabelle could feel Vesta's lips purse. 'Look, I can't just ignore this,' Mirabelle explained. 'This man was a friend of Dougie Beaumont's. I have a duty.'

'McGregor really ought to be told.'

'I'm going to find out what I can.'

'Mirabelle, you're impossible.'

'You can't complain that I don't tell you what I'm up to, and then complain anyway when I do. I'm perfectly safe, Vesta. I'm just going to look around.'

'All right,' the girl conceded. 'But be careful.'

As Mirabelle hung up and handed back the telephone, the waitress couldn't look her in the eye. 'I'm sorry,' Mirabelle said, 'I didn't mean to make you feel uncomfortable. Did you see Mr Highton when he was here the other day?'

The girl nodded. She looked as if she might cry.

'Had you seen him before?'

She nodded again. 'He stayed here when the racing was on.'

'It must be very busy then, but you remembered him?'

'He always tipped,' she said. 'Not all the gentlemen bother.'

'I imagine it was a terrible shock when they found his body. Did they bring him here after they found him?'

'The ambulance came to the big house. But the policeman wanted his things. You know, from his room. I packed it all up.'

'What had Mr Highton brought with him?'

'Just his razor, some clothes and his clubs, of course.'

'Clubs?'

'Golf clubs. He played yesterday afternoon. Oh, and he had a bottle of brandy on the bedside – he never had that before.'

'There wasn't a journal or letters or photographs?'

'No. Nothing like that.'

'A snuffbox?'

The girl shook her head.

'I wonder, did you find out how he died? I mean, how it happened?'

'Cook says it must've been a tramp. A vagrant, she called it. They pass through sometimes. Them and the gypsies.'

'Did anyone see a tramp?'

The girl shrugged. 'They come and go.'

This seemed unlikely, given the amount of money that it would appear had been left on Highton's body and the presence of a threatening letter in his possession, but Mirabelle didn't argue. 'Well,' she said, 'I'm sure the police will find who did it.'

'We ain't allowed out now. I mean once it's dark. We were told we ain't allowed on our own cos the man's still out there.'

'Quite right,' Mirabelle said. A vision of herself the night before, stumbling around the park in the pitch black came into her mind's eye. 'Well, I'll just go for a walk, I think.'

As she left the inn, she fell in with the perimeter of the golf course. The air was heavy this morning and the fallen leaves clustered in damp smears along the road. It must have rained just as it was getting light. The air smelled damp. Two women dressed in tweed were hacking their way around the fairway. How enlightened to allow women members, Mirabelle thought. She stopped to watch them tee off. Her mind wandered as she arced around the park and she found herself wondering where George Highton had hidden whatever personal items he took from Dougie Beaumont's top drawer and if they might now turn up. Then the irony struck her that, if that was the case, he might not have saved either himself or his lover from the censure of the police or the wider world. As she followed the road, she caught glimpses of Goodwood House across the fairway. She could just make out a policeman in uniform, still on duty at the front door. Then, as the house fell out of sight, she passed the estate farrier where three horses were tethered in the yard. She continued on. After almost an hour she came to a Georgian building – the clubhouse. A sign pronounced it was members only. At the front, three smart cars were parked to one side and, as Mirabelle approached, she realised that they were masking another sign that said THE KENNELS. The building seemed far too nice to house dogs.

Just inside the front door there was a scruffy reception desk and a man perched on a high stool behind it. He jumped to his feet as she came in.

'Miss.' He nodded towards a registration book, which was clearly used for signing in.

'I'm not a member,' Mirabelle admitted.

The man's eyes hardened. 'It's members only,' he said.

'I see.' She thought on her feet. 'The thing is, I'm staying at the coaching inn and I went for a walk and I seem to have hurt my ankle. The road is slippy, with all the leaves. When I spotted you ... I wonder if you might make an exception. I need to sit down, you see.'

The man cast his eyes towards Mirabelle's ankles. 'Right,' he said. 'I best put you in the bar.' He nodded in the direction of a doorway ahead. 'I'll get someone to come with the first aid kit.'

'Thank you,' Mirabelle said and tried to limp convincingly.

The bar was painted a neutral tone of green and

on the walls the club's tournament results were mounted on wooden display boards. This year's Women's Champion, Mrs Butler, had evidently just had her name added to the roll. The paint seemed brighter than previous years but it would no doubt tone down. Mirabelle dropped into a chair by the window, which afforded a view of Goodwood House beyond a ha-ha that was cut into the rolling fields. She wondered how many golf balls had been lost there. Behind the bar, an elderly woman, with her greying hair in a bun, was polishing glasses. She was dressed tidily in black. 'We don't serve the tables,' she said, noticing Mirabelle moving towards a chair. 'If you want something you'll have to come up.'

Mirabelle looked around. There was nobody else in the room. 'The thing is, I've hurt my ankle,' she said. 'But I'm fine. It's rather early. I don't need a drink.'

'Was it the seventh?' the woman enquired.

'Pardon me?'

'People get carried away with the view on the seventh. You can see right over the Downs. One gentleman let go his golf cart and it rolled right down the hill.'

'I slipped on the road. I wasn't playing this morning. I'm awfully glad to see you have women members though.'

'The Duke wouldn't have it otherwise,' the woman chimed enthusiastically. 'There's always been lady golfers at Goodwood.'

Mirabelle smiled and decided to try her luck. She stared out of the window. 'I see they've kept the police guard over at the house.'

'Terrible business.'

'He played here, didn't he? Mr Highton? The day he died.'

'I served him myself.'

'Did he seem...?'

The woman needed little encouragement. 'They cut short the round because of the rain and I said, "You're soaked, Mr Highton. You better be careful you'll catch your death." "I'm a hardy soul, don't worry about me," he said. Makes you shiver.'

'Who was he playing with?'

'The fella with the black caddy. That makes me shiver and all.'

'Mr Crowe?'

'Yes. That's him.'

'I bumped into his wife only yesterday.'

'I don't think she's a golfer, Mrs Crowe. No, I can't recall her ever coming to the club.'

'I think the Crowes had come down to sort out a car that was arriving over at Tangmere. Mr Highton too. It was Dougie Beaumont's car, you see. It's all such a shock, really, when this kind of thing happens and you know the people. One murder after another. It's so unexpected.'

'We got used to it in the war. The fellas from the airbase – here one day and gone the next. But not in peacetime. And not a murder, as you say.'

'Do you know where they found George Highton's body?'

The woman gesticulated towards the window but did not have time to answer, as the conversation was interrupted by a man appearing at the door.

'Are you the lady who is injured?'

Mirabelle silently cursed the fellow's timing but she nodded and he came in, holding a leather case.

'May I?' He knelt down and reached for her ankle. 'This one?'

She tried to remember which foot she had limped on when she walked in. Working in the field was not easy, she noted. You really had to be on the ball. 'Yes – here,' she said, indicating the left.

The man touched the joint gently and Mirabelle pretended to wince. 'I'll bind it up for you,' he offered. 'But the nearest doctor is over at the airfield. I can call him, if you like.'

'No. I don't think it's broken. It's only a strain. There's no need to trouble anyone else,' Mirabelle said lightly, imagining Dr Coughlan's face if she turned up again in his vicinity so soon after she'd fainted at the Bader Arms. 'I'm sure that if it's supported with a bandage it'll make all the difference.'

The woman behind the bar returned to sorting out stock on the shelf behind her, as the fellow wound the bandage tightly around Mirabelle's ankle. Then he sat back on his haunches to survey what he'd done. 'You should try walking.' He held out a hand to help Mirabelle get up. She did so, still affecting a limp, though only slightly now.

'That's much better,' she said. 'Thank you.'

'It'll just take rest and you'll be good as new.' The man packed up the first aid box and Mirabelle wondered if she ought to leave. But then the bar door opened once more and the women she had passed earlier came in from their round of

179

golf. One was wearing a fetching purple hat, which Mirabelle hadn't noticed from her vantage point beyond the hedgerow.

'Good morning, Iris.' They both made for the bar. 'Is tea too much to hope for?'

Iris made no promises. 'I'll see what I can do,' she said and disappeared into the back.

The women settled at a table near the bar. 'That looks painful,' one offered sympathetically.

'I went over on the road.' Mirabelle smiled, beginning to feel guilty about lying. 'I saw you playing earlier. Did you have a good round?'

'Not bad.'

'I imagine it feels rather grim round here today.'

'Quiet as the grave,' the woman admitted. 'Did you know the poor chap?'

'I had met George Highton. Yes. Iris said he was in here yesterday – only hours before he died.'

'Dreadful. They must be quite shaken in the big house.'

The man closed the first aid kit with a decisive click and got to his feet. 'Well, if that'll be all,' he said.

'Thank you,' Mirabelle smiled again. 'It's much better.' She turned her attention to the women. 'Mr Highton was playing with an acquaintance of mine. Mr Crowe. Well, I know his wife, really.'

'Enid?'

'You know the Crowes as well?'

'And that terrible business about the poor girl's brother. It's been a ghastly week. Quite gruesome.'

'Dougie Beaumont was a neighbour of mine.'

'In France?'

'No. Down on the coast. He was a wonderful

driver, as I understand it, though I only saw him race once.'

'We were at the race meeting last year and afterwards there were drinks. They've taken over the old traffic control tower for that kind of thing. It's quite fun actually. Dougie seemed to enjoy himself. They live life to the full these fellows. Quite right too. His parents were there – so proud the pair of them. And now, this week, Dougie Beaumont and George Highton, both of them dead within days. We were just saying on the fairway–'

'Now, now,' the woman in the purple hat cut in. 'Really, Angela, we shouldn't gossip.'

Mirabelle tried not to look downhearted. She'd far rather that they told her everything. 'I'm sure the police have it all in hand,' she chipped in.

Angela shook her head and, laying a palm on her friend's arm, she ignored the other woman's warning. 'That's why it's so quiet today,' she explained. 'I mean the police simply took down the club yesterday. They searched the whole place. Swarms of them. They stopped play and everything.' The woman in the purple hat looked on disapprovingly but that didn't stop Angela. 'And they didn't find it. Well, of course they didn't find it. As if a member here would...'

Mirabelle's forehead wrinkled. 'I'm sorry,' she said, 'I don't understand. What were they looking for?'

'The weapon.' Angela's tone was insistent. 'They think it was a golf club, or some such nonsense. As if anyone would leave their clubs just lying around the park. They had chaps all over the greens and down in the ha-ha searching for the

181

bally thing and two fellows in the captain's office checking the membership rolls. Honestly! What a hoo-ha.' She lowered her voice. 'The thing is, as far as we heard, Highton was being threatened. Blackmailed even, but what I say is, there must be more to it. What kind of blackmailer carries a golf club around with them at two in the morning? And blackmailers don't kill people, do they? I mean, how would the fellow get his money then? It's nonsensical.'

Mirabelle's eyes were drawn across the grass to Goodwood House. She'd bet there were golf clubs aplenty in there. And then there were Highton's own clubs, which had been back at the coaching inn.

'It must be a dreadful way to go,' the lady in the purple hat said. 'Just imagine. A nine iron out of the blue. And the idea of blackmail – it's too sordid. Please, let's not talk about it any more.'

'What do you mean, a nine iron?'

The women looked at Mirabelle as if the question was inexplicable. 'It's a kind of club used for chipping the ball,' Angela explained.

The woman in the purple hat grinned. 'We don't know it was a nine iron,' she said. 'I was speaking figuratively.'

'But a nine iron would do it,' Angela cut in. 'It'd be better than a wood. I mean, if the police are right and it was a club, which I doubt.'

'I don't know. If I was ever to decide to actually kill Jerry I'm sure any old club would be adequate. If I ever got up the nerve,' the other woman quipped.

'Oh don't!'

'A sand iron would be best. I mean, if you really wanted to stave in someone's head. The angle and so forth.'

There was a clinking sound and Iris returned to the room with a tray of tea things that she laid down solidly, clearly indicating that the table would not be served and all drinks should be picked up at the bar. 'Would you like to join us?' the woman in purple offered Mirabelle as she sprang to her feet to comply with Iris's unspoken dictat.

'No, thank you,' Mirabelle replied, thinking Jerry had best be careful. 'I'd probably better get along.'

Chapter 14

The world is but a canvas to our imagination

Out of sight of the clubhouse, Mirabelle removed the bandage from her ankle and continued her walk, arcing round the house. If the police were right, then someone had attacked George Highton head-on, though the darkness would have shrouded their approach. In which case, he might have had no chance to take defensive action against the blow. To batter a person to death with a golf club was an act of extreme violence and one that bore the hallmarks of a spur of the moment decision. You'd need to be furious, Mirabelle

183

thought, and, given that, your fury would need to be provoked. She wondered what had happened at Goodwood House that evening. What had Highton said or done to infuriate his killer? Or was it simply a matter of what he was? Many people were outraged by queers. It wouldn't be the first time.

As the facts emerged, Mirabelle found herself increasingly uncomfortable. Highton and Beaumont, initially golden boys, were becoming sullied, hour by hour. Still, she told herself, they were also becoming more real. Their affair was still the most likely subject of any blackmail attempt and a decent motive for both murders. There was something unjust about this that spurred Mirabelle on. After all, why did it matter who you wanted to be with? The arrangements one person made with another wasn't anyone else's business. Perhaps it was no wonder that Dougie Beaumont had kept a stash of drugs. It was an escape.

Along the road, only a couple of minutes from the clubhouse, she came upon a large wooden hut set back from the tarmac. There was no sign outside but she could hear someone whistling behind the door. In for a penny, she thought, and knocked. The hut was within walking distance of the scene of George Highton's death after all.

'Hello,' she called tentatively as she turned the handle.

Inside, it was gloomy and, if anything, colder than the open air. The place was laid out as a stockroom. Brown cardboard boxes were piled everywhere. At the sound of Mirabelle's voice, the whistling stopped and a boy appeared from behind one of the stacks. He was bundled in a blue, irregularly knitted hat and scarf and wearing padded gloves that were too large for him. He was probably in his late teens, but the outfit gave him a comical appearance, and made him look younger, like a child trying on his older brother's clothes.

'Miss,' he said. 'Can I help you?'

'I was just taking a walk and I have got rather lost, I'm afraid. There's a sawmill near here, isn't there? I mean, on the estate.'

'The sawmill is a couple of miles off, easy. This belongs to the golf club.'

'Ah. I see. So all this stuff...'

'Golf balls. Tees. That kind of thing,' he said cheerfully.

Mirabelle looked doubtfully at the boxes. They'd easily house a lifetime's supply of either of these commodities.

'And you look after it. You work for the club, do you?'

'Yes, miss. I can give you directions to the sawmill if you'd like.'

'Do you have golf clubs here? I mean, in stock?'

'You need to go to a proper shop to buy a set of clubs, miss. Lillywhites just up from St James's is where most of the members go. You're a player, are you?'

Mirabelle looked coy. 'I'm staying at the coaching inn but I'm rather taken with the area.'

'They'll look after you over there.' The boy grinned. 'My sister is a waitress at the inn. She works behind the bar a few days a week.'

'Oh, the blonde girl?' Mirabelle squinted to try

185

to make out the resemblance in the parts of the boy's face that were showing. He had the girl's beautiful blue eyes, or a version of them and, just like hers, his skin was very pale. If he wasn't so swamped by his clothes, the similarity might have been more obvious.

'That's right. Ella.'

'She was very helpful this morning. Everyone is in such a state with this business over Mr Highton.'

The boy's eyes hardened.

'Did you know Mr Highton?' Mirabelle enquired, trying to sound innocent.

'Yes, miss. I caddied for him.'

'Were you caddying for him yesterday? When he played Mr Crowe?'

The boy nodded. Mirabelle waited a moment to see if he would continue. When he didn't she tried to encourage him.

'The Crowes were here to pick up a car, I heard. But they must have been tempted to stay on, I suppose. A round of golf would do that, wouldn't it? I was there when the car came in.'

'Mr Beaumont's car?'

'It was flown in. Sounds so glamorous, doesn't it? Did you know Mr Beaumont too?'

'Yes. Him and all.'

'I think there was work to be done to the motor. Seems a shame now Mr Beaumont is ... well, you know.'

'The car'll win without him,' the boy said. 'That's what they was saying yesterday. They're going to ask one of the other drivers to drive it in the races that count and Mr Crowe is going to

186

manage it the rest of the time. I half fancy a punt on it myself. In memoriam, isn't that what they call it?'

'This whole business must've shaken you up. It's always strange when somebody dies out of the blue, never mind two people at almost the same time. Never mind murder.'

The boy half shrugged but the movement was indecisive.

'I heard Mr Highton was a good tipper. That's what Ella said.'

'Yeah. He was generous all right. What happened – it's a shame.'

'A shame?' It seemed an odd word to choose – more suited to losing a friendly match or missing a train.

'No one deserves that, do they?' the boy continued.

It hardly needed saying. What was the child getting at? 'I can't say George Highton wasn't difficult sometimes,' Mirabelle tried to draw him out.

'He knew what he wanted.'

Mirabelle stared. 'Did the police check here yesterday?'

'Yes, miss. They asked me for an alibi and all.'

'And did you have one?'

'I gave it to the policeman. 'Course, everyone was in bed that time of the morning, so no one's alibi is worth much. That's what we was saying afterwards. I mean, anyone on the estate could've got up and gone over to the big house and no one would have been the wiser. The truth is anyone could've done it. But my money's on someone just passing through – a tramp or something. That's

187

what everyone's saying. The police have got some job on. I mean, how do you find out a thing like that? In the middle of the night and no witnesses?'

'It'd need to be someone strong though, wouldn't it? And angry.'

'Yeah,' the boy said. 'Angry.'

'You don't seem terribly shocked, if you don't mind me saying.'

'I don't know who whacked Mr Highton, miss. No one does.'

Mirabelle held back from disagreeing with him. At the very least, one person knew. The person who had done it. She decided there was no more to be got out of the exchange. The boy gave her the directions she'd asked for and, walking away from the hut, she realised that he was the first person she'd met who hadn't liked George High-ton or Dougie Beaumont. Everyone else seemed charmed.

It was colder now but still a pleasant walk back to the inn and, if nothing else, the time afforded her some grace to think things through. Questions were forming. Had the Crowes also been invited to dinner at Goodwood the night George Highton was killed? Had Highton lied and said he was out of money to end the backgammon game? Did he simply want to stop playing or did he have an assignation planned when he left the house? Had he come to Goodwood to meet someone? Now, as Mirabelle turned down the last stretch of road, the low autumn sun seemed frozen in the sky. It was odd to be away from Brighton; the sea's constant movement and the brisk wind that whipped off it. The Goodwood estate was still by comparison. At the bar, the warmth from the fire was welcome. Mirabelle sat on a tall stool beside the pumps and ordered a half-pint of bitter and a cheese sandwich.

'I met your brother when I was out,' she chatted, as Ella bustled about her duties.

'Benji?'

'At the golf club. He caddied for Mr Highton the day he died.'

'Benji always caddies for that lot.'

'That lot?'

'The racing crowd.'

'Do they come often? Outside the races, I mean?'

'A couple of times a year, I suppose. There are parties at the house.'

'Of course. I wonder why Mr Highton came down this time, though? I mean there wasn't a party, was there?'

Ella shrugged. 'Well, he missed the hunt. That was the weekend before. Everything usually goes quiet after the hunt and the ball and that. There's nothing much right up till Christmas. I dunno what he'd come down for,' she said, as she placed Mirabelle's glass on the bar.

With a sigh, Mirabelle sipped. The ale was delicious – yeasty and sharp – she hadn't realised how hungry the country air had made her. The cheese sandwich she'd ordered appeared and, as Mirabelle tucked into it, Ella started to clean a shelf, moving glasses around. It struck Mirabelle that bartenders seemed to spend more time cleaning glasses than they did serving drinks. She wondered why she had never noticed before. Sitting there,

189

the scraps of information she'd gathered knocked against each other, like balls in a pinball machine in one of the arcades on the front. Secrets drew her in every time – the unsaid. Mirabelle knew her interests weren't normal but still, how could the others just lay things aside? People were so intriguing and, besides, over the last few years she'd figured out more than one crime that never would have been solved by the police on their own.

When she'd finished eating she picked up the *Daily Telegraph* and went to sit by the fire to leaf through the rest of the news. Reuben Vinestock had written an article about horse racing and there was a feature about how London's smog was damaging the fabric of the buildings. She was just about to put down the paper and ask whether an *Evening Standard* might be delivered, when a girl in a white apron appeared from the kitchen and whispered in Ella's ear. The two of them disappeared into the back. Mirabelle hesitated for a moment. There was nobody else in the bar, no one to see. It was an easy decision. Lithe on her feet, she slipped behind the servery and peeked down a short, dark corridor, which led to the kitchen. The smell of soup hung around the kitchen door and, inside, the second girl was alone, chopping vegetables at an old pine table. There was nowhere else for Ella to have gone, Mirabelle reasoned, and then, outside the barred window to the rear of the kitchen, she saw movement. Thinking on her feet, she sneaked back up the corridor, through the bar, out of the front door and past the crates of empty beer bottles piled against the flint wall. Peering around the corner, she could see Ella and her brother hovering at the back. The girl had her arms wrapped round her frame to keep warm.

'What do you reckon?' Benji asked.

'Just go over. It can't do no harm. I mean, if you reckon you're owed something...'

Benji kicked the ground.

'Go on,' Ella encouraged him.

'Easy for you to say.'

'You wanted the money. No one made you, Benji.'

'You wouldn't have done it.'

Ella looked bashful. 'Well, I wouldn't want to.'

Benji made a noise that Mirabelle interpreted as exasperation. 'Right,' he managed to get out. 'I will then. It's all quietened down since yesterday and it's only Mr Harrison. He ain't the worst of them by a long shot.'

Mirabelle fell back. She recalled the name immediately. Harrison was Dougie Beaumont's friend. The tinkerer, the girl in the Bader Arms had called him. She'd said that the men had fallen out. This was intriguing. Ella darted back inside and Benji stamped his feet to keep warm as the girl fetched something for him from the kitchen – a bread roll it looked like. Taking this as a sign that their exchange was over, Mirabelle sneaked back to the front, just in time as Benji strode on to the road and headed in the direction of Tangmere. Ella and Benji may or may not know about the blackmail letter found on George Highton's body, but it sounded as if Benji was about to instigate some blackmail of his own. Mirabelle fetched her coat from where she had left it by the fire. When she was a little girl, her mother used to warm her

191

winter coat before they went out. Now her senses prickled as she got close to the flames and it felt as if the fire was an enemy in waiting. She ignored the feeling, telling herself it would pass. Ella appeared behind the bar just as Mirabelle was pulling on her gloves.

'Are you off, Miss Bevan?'

'Yes. I thought I'd take advantage of the light. It's lovely walking in the countryside.'

'Are you staying tonight, miss?'

'Yes. I think I will. Would you see to it that the room's made up?' Mirabelle said over her shoulder, considering the possibilities as she made for the door.

Tangmere was less than an hour away, closer to Goodwood than when she'd walked there from Chichester. Mirabelle set off at a lick down the country lane. She was determined to catch up to Benji and see what he wanted from Mr Harrison. She chided herself that she mustn't be naive. Within such easy striking distance of London, Goodwood was a play park for the rich and those who wanted to be. The various sporting occupations on offer were a huge draw. Most were above board but no doubt there were others, private concerns. People thought that underground secrets were the preserve of Soho, but out here, in respectable county society, you could hide a certain kind of party. You could put people together who wouldn't be seen dead in their real lives. Highton and Beaumont, it appeared, had got caught up in something secret. Their world looked glamorous from the outside but scratching the moneyed veneer of racing cars and glamorous locations, what she'd found was both murky and nebulous – a potentially dirty cocktail of money, sex and drugs.

Wondering momentarily if it would be quicker to cut across the fields, Mirabelle decided against it. The autumn soil was thick and muddy and the layout of the farms was irregular so she would find it more difficult to navigate away from the road. After walking for half an hour, she made out the spire of Tangmere church over the treetops and picked up her pace. With Benji out of sight, she stopped at the shop on her way into the village. As she opened the door, a bell sounded. Inside, there were shelves floor to ceiling, which, she noticed, were stacked in no particular order. The place smelled faintly of stoneground flour with a hint of citrus. This exoticism was immediately explained by a wooden box propped against the counter, piled with oranges the size of Mirabelle's fist. Some were wrapped in squares of tissue and others were displayed bare skinned. This box was the most interesting thing in a random collection of tinned goods, sacks of flour and sugar, and cardboard containers of onions. From the back, a woman dressed in a claret-coloured tabard emerged with a sniff.

'Hello,' said Mirabelle. 'I'd like an orange, please.'

'Help yourself.' The woman sniffed again. She pulled a handkerchief from her pocket and blew her nose.

'The first of the winter,' Mirabelle commented, as she picked one wrapped in red and white with the word Jaffa crumpled across its surface. 'I wonder if you might help me. I'm looking for a friend's place. Mr Harrison?'

'Sixpence,' the woman said, holding out her hand.

Mirabelle scrambled in her handbag. 'I must say, they look delicious,' she commented, slightly shocked at the price.

The woman deposited the coin in a cashbox on the shelf behind her and did not answer the question.

'It's always rather difficult coming to a new place. Finding your way around,' Mirabelle tried.

'You were here the other day, weren't you? You're the lady who fainted.'

Mirabelle recalled the face at the shop window as she had walked into the village on her way to the Bader Arms. This kind of thing was precisely the reason why she didn't want to live in a small place where everyone knew everyone else's business. In the past, she'd been labelled nosey by people who didn't like her, but at least she had a purpose when she went sniffing around. This woman's observations were simply intrusive. Still, there was nothing for it but to confess, at least in part.

'Yes. I'm staying at the coaching inn at Goodwood,' she admitted. 'I didn't get the chance to drop into Mr Harrison's the other day because of what happened. I thought I'd walk over and see him now.'

The woman paused before she accepted this explanation. 'Well, he's not in Tangmere exactly, miss. He lives back out the way you've come. You must've passed the turn-off.'

194

Mirabelle cursed inwardly. This mistake would cost her time. 'Oh, I'm just hopeless with directions,' she said lightly.

'Back the way you came, out of the village and second on the right at the old oak with the branch down. It's a farmhouse, Mr Harrison's got.'

'Oh yes. I expect that garage of his used to be a barn.'

The woman sniffed again. She clearly felt no need to make helpful small talk.

'Well, thank you,' Mirabelle said and the bell chimed on her way out.

There was no sign on the main road, but seeing the old oak tree Mirabelle took the turn-off anyway. The hedgerows grew high on either side, enclosing the track so it felt as if she was being funnelled down it. There were no passing places and no view. This must have run for about half a mile before Mirabelle came across the first of the outhouses that skirted an old farmyard. Two cars were parked untidily outside – a Ford and a Jaguar. This meant that in all probability at least someone was in, she thought, as she cut off the side road and on to the uneven cobbled surface of an old yard. It struck her that the place might have been a steading originally. One length of the farmyard appeared inhabited but the other sides looked abandoned. Coral-pink paint peeled from the old doors and windows and, here and there, engine parts were piled up. They didn't look as if they had been left in any particular order. In the corner, there was a tower of old tyres. To the right, one of the doors was half open and a thin wash of light emanated from behind the oil cans. That must be the garage. Mirabelle peered inside and smiled. She was right and not only that: she recognised the car. It was the long motor with '26' on the side – the one she'd seen him race. The one that had been in both the photographs she'd seen on Dougie Beaumont's mantel and in the leather pouch he'd hidden under his bed. Like a patient on the operating table, the car was jacked up directly under a wide skylight with a scattering of tools spread around it. She squinted to see further in. 'Hello,' she said, her voice uncertain. There was no reply. If Mr Harrison had been tinkering he was perhaps finished for the day.

Coming back into the courtyard, Mirabelle peered towards the occupied part of the building – a low, two-storey house with a glossy black door banked by an array of geraniums in pots on the moss-strewn cobbles. She didn't like to approach the windows – after all, the yard was enclosed and she wanted to keep her options open. Instead, she went back on to the road and nipped down the side of the building to the rear. The courtyard might have been messy but at the back there was a well-tended garden. A row of apple trees scattered ripe fruit across the grass and from this side of the house she could see straight into what looked like a sitting room. Mirabelle smiled. Benji was standing at the fireplace. With his coat and scarf off, she noted he was a very good-looking young man. His hair was less blond than his sister's and his cheeks sported a few freckles. He was perhaps nineteen years of age at most. In his hand he held a bottle of beer, from which he was swigging repeatedly between holding forth.

Listening to him were two other men – Harrison must be the one at the drinks cabinet, she reasoned. He was pouring a tumbler of whisky or brandy – amber spirits. Mirabelle squinted. She put her head to one side as she realised that the second man was Michael Crowe, Enid's husband. He laughed so loudly at whatever was being said that it echoed through the glass. What on earth were they discussing? What did these men owe Benji?

Mirabelle sneaked across the lawn and took her place beneath the window. Though the sound carried from inside, it was indistinct and, even this close, she couldn't make out the words. It was frustrating but at least it gave her time to take in the details of the room. Her eyes were drawn to the low table in front of the sofa, on which there was a single florid Victorian tile, thinly dusted with the remains of a stack of white powder. Dougie Beaumont, it seemed, had not been the only person who had procured a supply of cocaine. That was another link between the men, she thought, leaning as close as she could to the glass. It was no good – the words were too indistinct and she realised that if she wanted to hear what they were saying she'd need to break in. She was just eyeing the bedroom window further along, when the doorbell sounded and the conversation in the sitting room came to a halt. Harrison left. The room fell silent for a moment and then she heard his voice. He must have been shouting if she could hear him from here, she thought. Then all of a sudden Crowe got up and, in one move, stuck the tile behind a cushion and

197

threw Benji's jacket at him. The French doors opened and the boy was slung on to the grass, his beer bottle still in his hand as he scrambled with his scarf and hat. He pulled up against the wall out of sight as he did up his coat buttons. Then, as he spotted Mirabelle, his forehead wrinkled.

'Shhh.' She put her finger to her lips.

Benji crawled towards her, low to the ground.

'What are you doing here?' he hissed.

'Why did they chuck you out?' Mirabelle hissed back. Answering a question with another question was the best she could think of.

'None of your business,' the boy retorted, his eyes blazing.

Tentatively, Mirabelle peeked above the sill. There were three men in the room now. She cocked her head to one side. The new fellow was wearing a mackintosh and his gait appeared familiar but she could only see him from behind. Harrison was pouring him a drink.

'You're nothing but a snoop,' the boy murmured, as he took a resentful swig of his beer.

'I'd bet you can trust me more than you can trust either of them.'

'Who says I trust them? Who says?' The boy was angry. 'You followed me here, didn't you?'

Mirabelle sank lower on to the cold grass. 'Look, I'm trying to figure out who murdered George Highton. And Dougie Beaumont for that matter.'

'Well, that's the man you need to speak to.' Benji gesticulated towards the window over his head. 'He's a copper. Not that anyone round here is going to spill their guts.'

'Why not? Don't you want the murderer to be brought to justice?'

Benji shrugged.

'What did they do to you?' Mirabelle could hear a slight shake in her voice. 'Did they hurt you, Benji?'

'I'd never let anyone hurt me.'

Mirabelle struggled with how to put it delicately. 'My guess is that there were parties down here. I don't mean the hunt ball or the kind of thing that went on at the big house, I mean other parties. Private ones. Places like this that are out of the way. There was drink and a bit of powder and lots of men. I wasn't born yesterday. It's not as shocking as you think it is. Being queer, I mean.'

'I'm not a poofter, all right?'

'But they are.'

'Mr Harrison's not queer. Mr Crowe neither.'

'George Highton and Dougie Beaumont were.'

The boy relented, nodding peremptorily, his head hardly moving. 'Well, I don't take the powders. Only now and then. It doesn't do any harm, does it? Not like, well, you know. The other stuff they got up to. Makes me sick to my stomach. Like you said, the men and that.'

'It must be difficult to talk about. My guess is that Mr Harrison didn't approve of what was going on, did he?'

'No.'

'He had a fight with Dougie Beaumont. He tried to stop it.'

'Mr Harrison is just like most of the blokes. He's in it for the motors. But you're right. There were parties. Some weekends it was like Piccadilly

Circus down here. That's what Mr Harrison said. He'd had enough of it. They had to listen to him cos, well, he's good with an engine.'

'Did they stop?'

'No. But it got quieter.'

'Apart from the two of them getting murdered, you mean.'

The boy swigged from the bottle. 'Mr Harrison and Mr Crowe aren't going to appreciate you poking your nose in, miss. That's for sure. I'd keep your enquiries quiet if I were you. You might like some help with keeping it quiet, if you see what I mean.'

Mirabelle couldn't help but smile. He was trying to shake her down. 'I think you might be confused, Benji,' she said.

'Me? Confused?'

'Yes. Between the people who are criminal or complicit with criminals. The people who are out to hurt you whether you let them or not. And the rest of us.'

At least the boy had the decency to look sheepish and Mirabelle decided to press her advantage. 'Who do you think killed Dougie Beaumont and George Highton?'

'I dunno. But I ain't going to pretend to be all dewy eyed about it when I'm not.'

'Understood,' Mirabelle said, as she peered back over the sill. The boy was admirably tough – a survivor. Through the glass she took in the men sitting in conversation, the new arrival was within easy sight. He had taken out his notebook. Mirabelle's heart sank but, she told herself, maybe it was for the best.

'I might just ask that policeman, you know. Once he's finished,' she whispered. 'I can get you a lift home if you like?'

'No. I'll stay here, thanks,' Benji said. 'They'll let me back in when he's gone.'

'How much do you think they'll give you?'

Benji shrugged. 'Gotta be worth a tenner, isn't it?'

'George Highton was being threatened. Blackmailed, I mean.'

'Really? I pity the bugger who tried that on with Mr Highton.' The boy was earnest.

'Not you, then?'

'Mr Highton was pleasant enough if you were doing what he wanted. But woe betide you if you refused him something. No, I'll stick with Mr Harrison any day. He's a softer touch.'

Mirabelle believed him. 'So when you get back inside, they'll give you a tenner to keep quiet, will they? Are you reckoning on adding me in?'

The boy took another gulp of beer. 'Well, like you said, they ain't going to be interested in you, are they, miss? I mean, a lady on her own is the last thing they have on their mind. The money's elsewhere, isn't it? Keeping stuff out of the papers and that. They just don't want the world to know about, you know, all them poofters.'

Mirabelle took a moment to take this in. 'Thanks.' She got to her feet, slipping up against the wall. She dug in her pocket and handed the boy the orange. He grinned widely.

'Cheers,' he said.

Around the front of the farm there was a new car parked next to the Jaguar – a familiar black

Maria. Mirabelle opened the door and slipped on to the front seat, the cold leather giving way with a creak. At least sitting here would keep her out of the breeze while she was waiting for McGregor to finish his inquiries. He'd arrived more quickly than she expected – not bad for a copper. Not bad at all.

Chapter 15

It is always necessary to be loved

He smiled when he spotted her – the wide, easy grin of a man with nothing to hide. As he ducked into the driving seat, Mirabelle caught a whiff of whisky and a fading smell of soap.

'Hello,' he said, as he started the engine. 'So this is where you got to. I might have known.'

'I didn't think you'd have coordinated your inquiries so soon. I mean with the local force.'

'I didn't,' McGregor admitted, as he turned the car around. 'Vesta phoned me and I put two and two together. She's a smart cookie, that girl.'

'Did she tell you I was here?'

He nodded. 'I wasn't sure where you'd turn up, of course. I just hoped that I'd bump into you.'

'So you think the two murders are connected?'

'We don't have so many murderers in England that two people who know each other dying in suspicious circumstances within a day or two doesn't make me want to investigate the links between them. They were lovers, obviously. Was Highton the man you met at Beaumont's flat the day after the fire?'

'Yes.'

'I'll take a closer look at his effects. To see what he might have taken from the scene. A memento, do you think? Though I'm not sure queers are quite so sentimental.'

'I don't think George Highton and Dougie Beaumont were exclusive, if that's what you mean.' Mirabelle blushed. 'They'd known each other for a long time though and they seem to have had a solid interest in common in racing. That made them a unit, I suppose, but I don't think they were really a couple in the way most people...'

'That's just how it works, isn't it?' McGregor cast a sideways glance at her as he set off down the road. 'There's no point being coy, Mirabelle.'

'What do you mean?'

'I've been thinking.' His tone sounded as if he was making an announcement. 'And I can't think of another woman who'd be able to talk about this kind of thing. Not just the murders, but the rest of it. There's no point in diving in and investigating and then trying to pretend that you're shocked by what you've found. We have to learn to speak about things. Not sidestep them.'

'That's unfair.'

'Is it? You always seem drawn to the worst. People are just a puzzle to be solved. One after another. It makes me wonder what you think of me.'

She paused. 'I like you,' she admitted. 'It's obvious that I like you.'

'But you don't ... you won't... You think that I'm beneath you. I mean, this kind of place, this kind of set-up is closer to your world than mine.'

'Homosexual racing drivers?'

'Country houses. Sporting events. I've seen you in Belgravia, remember? I was trying to figure it out the other evening when you'd gone. I mean, if we're all only a puzzle to you, why not turn the tables and try to figure you out?'

'And what did you come up with?'

'That the world is changing and you're only just becoming accustomed to it. That you're changing, I suppose. You've changed since I've known you.'

'How?'

'You've come more alive.'

Mirabelle thought of the first day she met Superintendent McGregor. It was four years ago, when Big Ben McGuigan went missing. McGregor had blundered into the office like a fool, asking questions. He wasn't a fool, though. She'd got that wrong. And he was right about this too – they came from different worlds, and she had come back to life a little, since they met.

She changed the subject. 'What did Mr Beaumont say when you spoke to him?'

McGregor turned down a country road. 'You mean the father?'

Mirabelle nodded.

'What do they ever say? I didn't broach his son's predilections, if that's what you're asking.'

'Do you think he knew?'

'The man's an MP, Mirabelle. He saw active service during both wars. My guess is that he must have suspected what was going on, but there's no

204

way to tell. People shield themselves. Strangely, he was most exercised about the car. He focused on making arrangements for it. They can't set a date for the funeral yet and it's something positive, I suppose.'

'The whole family seem concerned about the car. Beaumont's mother mentioned it when I called to give my condolences and his sister and brother-in-law came down here to receive the thing. Highton said that's why he came down as well. He had a share in it, it seems. It's parked in Harrison's garage, by the way, at the front of the house.'

'Right now? They didn't mention that.'

'Did you ask?'

'No. I asked about Highton.'

'Do you know where his body was found?'

'Yes. I called in at the local station in Chichester and spoke to the investigating officer. I got a little detail to be going on with. The body was found on the driveway, just where it turns away from the house.'

'The murderer was waiting for him then. Out of sight of the building.'

McGregor nodded. 'Seems that way.'

'And the threatening note?'

'More like a rant – unsigned, of course. Whoever wrote it was angry. They felt hard done by. Part of the text is missing. There was a shower of rain before dawn and it washed out some of the ink.'

'The letter got wet in his pocket?'

'It was in his hand.'

Mirabelle shuddered. The image of George

Highton clutching the piece of paper that ostensibly killed him was a strong one.

'Here.' McGregor handed over his notepad. 'You might as well read for yourself. I took it down.'

She flipped through the pages. McGregor's writing was abysmal.

'You didn't train as a doctor, did you?'

'Very funny.'

You can't just set me aside like this, without anything at all. Bleeding heart is not enough. Do you think you'll get away with it? Do you think I'll let you cut me out? Then McGregor had noted that two lines were missing, too smudged to read before it resumed. *I'll bring you down. I only want what you owe me. I don't have an axe to grind but I know everything – years of it. That might prove useful in settling this mess. It concerns all of us, but as usual it's down to you and I.* There was no date. McGregor had noted one word, which was smeared, looked as if it said *money* and another looked as if it might read *family.* The note was unsigned, or at least any indication of a signature had been washed away.

Mirabelle considered the words carefully. She closed the notebook.

'It was a frenzied attack,' McGregor said. 'It probably took a few blows to bring him down.'

Mirabelle didn't speak again until the Maria drew up smoothly at the coaching inn.

'This is where I'm staying. I booked in for the night,' he said.

'Me too. Alan, I should tell you that there's some kind of party circuit down here. Something organised. Boys. Drink. Drugs. A good bit of high society too.'

McGregor's eyes regarded her calmly. 'You think that's the reason Beaumont and Highton were killed?'

'It might have something to do with it.'

'Thanks for letting me know.'

They got out of the car and McGregor retrieved an overnight bag from the boot. He's more prepared than I am, she thought, though she couldn't deny that she was glad he was here. As he made to move past her, she reached out and caught the lapel of his coat. Without considering the consequences, she pulled him towards her and, as they kissed, she felt her heart lurch. Then McGregor slid his hand around her waist and pushed her against the bonnet of the car. When they broke apart both of them were out of breath. Mirabelle tried to ignore the sense of confusion that was engulfing her.

'Drink?' McGregor offered.

Inside, the place was filling up for the evening with several tables already taken. McGregor ordered at the bar, but Mirabelle hovered a little way off, spotting one of the women from the golf course. Angela was sitting in a corner next to the window. She was wearing a fetching red satin cocktail dress and smoking a cigarette in a long amber holder. You'd think you'd see less of people in the country, Mirabelle thought, but then there were fewer places to go. Next to her a man in a dinner suit puffed on a pipe. Glad of the distraction, Mirabelle waved and crossed the room.

'Hello.'

'Oh, hello. Are you staying in this old place?'

'Only for a couple of days.'

'This is my husband.'

The man got to his feet. 'Derek Waterman.' He held out his hand.

Mirabelle shook it. 'Mirabelle Bevan. How do you do?'

Angela's gaze slid towards the bar.

'That's my friend, Alan McGregor. I ran into him while I was out walking,' Mirabelle felt compelled to explain. Angela and her husband made no comment and Mirabelle was glad of that. She knew how it looked.

'We're fitting in a couple of drinks before we leave for dinner. We're eating at the big house tonight,' Angela said. 'We thought we'd start early.'

'Well, it's only next door. How nice.'

'I don't know about that. Everyone is terribly gloomy.'

Mr Waterman tutted. 'Sorry,' he said, drawing on his pipe. 'Angela can be rather frank.'

'The thing is that there will be Beaumont family members,' Angela admitted. 'And this whole business is just so grim. It's exactly as we were saying earlier. I met Miss Bevan at the golf club this morning, darling. She knows the whole Beaumont clan, it seems.'

'Yes. I saw Mr Crowe this afternoon, in fact.'

'You're getting around. Enid's gone up to be with her mother, I believe, but yes, Michael will be here for dinner. And poor Dougie's father too.'

'Elrick Beaumont? I wasn't aware of that.'

'Well, I suppose he's come to see to the car.'

The car again, Mirabelle thought, as McGregor appeared at her elbow. 'Won't you join us?' Derek Waterman offered. It struck Mirabelle this was the first time she and the superintendent had ever socialised like this – on equal terms. She wondered suddenly if perhaps that had been their problem – they had never had any real context. They went places together, but as a couple they were always alone. Though that hadn't been a problem when she was with Jack. Remembering her manners, she introduced everyone, then took a seat and sipped the gin and tonic McGregor had bought. 'Mrs Waterman was just saying that Dougie Beaumont's father has come up. They are having dinner with him tonight at Goodwood House.'

'Really? Terrible business.'

'Dreadful.'

'Do you know the Beaumonts too?'

'I only met them this week,' McGregor admitted without disclosing why.

'You're Scottish,' Angela enthused, stubbing out one cigarette and inserting another into the holder. 'Well, you must play a round at our golf course while you're here, Mr McGregor. Mirabelle was at the club today.'

'I haven't got my clubs with me.'

'I'm sure they'll have some spare. Though they're probably rationed now. Signed in and signed out after what happened. Do you play golf, Miss Bevan?'

'No,' Mirabelle admitted.

'Oh you should. As my father always used to say, "It gives one something to do whilst out for a walk."'

'I've heard the views are marvellous.'

'If you get a clear day you can see right across the Downs in one direction and the skyline of

Chichester in the other. There's nothing like it.' Angela lit her cigarette and breathed in deeply. 'And, of course, it's excellent for the health.'

'I noticed you ladies didn't use a caddy this morning,' Mirabelle continued.

'Well that way there are no witnesses.' Angela smiled. 'But the club can arrange one of the boys to caddy if you prefer.'

'No witnesses,' Mirabelle repeated, thinking of something else entirely.

McGregor cut in. 'My game's not what it used to be. The last boy who caddied for me was terrible. "You're the worst caddy I ever had," I told him. "Surely that would be too much of a coincidence," he came back at me, sharp as a tack.' Everybody laughed and Mirabelle felt herself relax. It was nice to feel that she and McGregor could do something like this. Drinks as a couple.

An hour later, the Watermans left. McGregor sat back in his seat.

'The house is only over there–' he gestured '– isn't it?'

Mirabelle nodded. 'We better wait until it gets completely dark.'

Dusk was drawing in. People arriving at the inn came in the door, stamped their feet and rubbed their hands before ordering at the bar. The temperature was clearly plummeting. McGregor fetched another gin and tonic and a whisky while, alone at the table, Mirabelle considered telling him about the bits and pieces she had found in Dougie Beaumont's mattress. She dismissed the possibility – they were in such a good mood, the two of them, and she didn't want to make the superintendent angry again. Until she knew how the key and the money fitted in, she'd keep it to herself. She'd told him about the parties and the drugs after all. That seemed far more relevant. And besides, there were plenty of other things to figure out.

'Dutch courage,' McGregor announced as he returned to the table. 'Not that you need it.'

Mirabelle clinked her glass against his. 'There's something missing, isn't there?'

McGregor made to look around. 'What do you mean?'

'The case.' Mirabelle's eyes were still. 'One man is murdered and the murderer tries to cover his tracks by making it look like suicide. He even starts a fire, presumably to obliterate evidence. Within days, the first victim's lover is killed and, it seems to me, that is a momentary decision. The man is attacked, his life ended violently and the body is left where it fell. His wallet isn't rifled and a note that presumably incriminates the murderer is left on his body.'

'I have considered there might be two murderers,' McGregor admitted. 'But it's entirely possible that Beaumont's murder was planned, as you say, and Highton's might have become necessary afterwards. I haven't settled yet on which scenario is most likely. It's all down to motive, really.'

Mirabelle's tone was earnest. 'Exactly. I feel as if there's something we don't know yet.'

'I'm sure there's more than one thing we don't know, Mirabelle.' McGregor's eyes danced. 'Still, the reason they died has to be connected to what the victims have in common, which is each other, a taste for sex with other men – this party scene you've come across – their family and social connections and a love of motor racing. I'm glad to see you're taking my advice to heart. You're opening up your thought process to scrutiny.'

Mirabelle's gaze flickered and she smiled. 'I hadn't really considered the family. Not as a motive. They seem to be terribly close.'

'Quite apart from that, Dougie Beaumont was a cash cow. I don't think anyone in the family would have knocked him off.'

'What do you mean?'

McGregor beamed. 'What? Something you don't know? Dougie revived the family fortunes. After the war the Beaumonts were skint. They were on the verge of having to sell up – that big London house was going to have to go. But Beaumont started racing, won some money and turned out to have quite an eye for the stock market. He bailed them out. Paid off his father's debts over a couple of years and set up the old man in parliament. Fixed up the house. Covered his mother in pearls. The lot. Hasn't stopped making money since day one.'

Mirabelle sat back. 'Really?' she said. Through the window the light was fading. McGregor finished the last of his whisky and stared pointedly at the door.

'Come on,' he said, 'let's see what we can find out.'

Outside, it seemed too quiet compared to the cosy atmosphere in the public bar. Pulling their coats around them, they set out. This evening the gates were open and a lamp was lit in the gatehouse. Inside, Mirabelle glimpsed a man sitting away from the window. He was reading a magazine with a glossy picture of Roy Salvadori next to a sleek-looking Maserati on the cover. He took no notice of either of them as they stepped on to the driveway, dark shadows in a black night.

'There was a policeman on duty earlier,' Mirabelle said.

'They'll have finished with the scene by now. If there's a man there, leave him to me. We just have to figure out how to get inside.'

'Oh, I know how to do that.'

At the bend in the road they stopped for a moment. The trees were evenly spaced and, with the leaves falling, there wasn't a huge amount of cover, but then the night Highton died it was very dark.

'Where do you think the murderer came at him?' Mirabelle stepped to one side.

McGregor positioned himself on what must have been Highton's route as he walked back towards the inn, with the house behind him. 'Here, just past the bend and from the victim's right side,' he pronounced. 'It'd be easier to hide on the right, don't you think? In that dip. The fellow must have waited for Highton and then assaulted him. It's very close, isn't it? Real violence.'

Mirabelle nodded. Ahead of them the house was lit up and, as they rounded the corner, it came fully into view. Several of the downstairs windows were illuminated with buttery light and flickering candle lamps had been hung along the portico. It was going to be more difficult to slip in unnoticed than it had been the night before when the place was all but deserted in the pitch black.

'We should be in white tie,' McGregor joked. 'What's your plan for entry?'

'Last night the front door was open,' Mirabelle admitted.

The superintendent laughed. 'Well, no one could accuse you of not being logical.'

'But our best bet if we don't want to be noticed, is the card-room window. I left it unlocked – that's how I got out of the place. Hopefully, nobody has noticed and slipped the bolt back over.'

'Which one is the card room?'

Mirabelle pointed it out. The window was not lit. 'That's where Highton was playing back-gammon the night he died,' she said. 'He said he'd been cleaned out, but that wasn't true.'

'Come on.' McGregor hurried her.

Past the ivy, Mirabelle carefully drew up the window. She took off her coat and slipped it over the sill and then McGregor gave her a leg up before he passed on his coat and hat and pulled himself inside. It was a tight squeeze. Inside, the room looked exactly the same as it had the night before.

'Where do the doors lead?' McGregor whispered.

'The left goes to the hallway, the right one I think opens on to the ballroom, which is now an office. It was locked yesterday.' She could just make out his eyebrows rising. 'These old places have got to pay their way these days,' she said softly. 'The estate is supported by a sawmill and a turnery. I think there's even a commercial nursery garden. I had a look around today. Well, as far as I could walk. It's not all upper-class diversions.'

McGregor cracked the door to the hallway just a fraction. 'Where do you expect they are?'

He peered as the footman emerged from the dining room, the soles of the man's shoes clicking as he entered another room. The hum of conversation briefly floated towards them – the party were enjoying drinks.

'Well that answers my question.'

'I expect it's now or never,' Mirabelle replied, her heart hammering. 'They'll be going in to dinner soon. Come on, we'd best be quick.'

They crept across the hallway. A housemaid appeared at the head of the backstairs and McGregor pushed Mirabelle out of the way, against the banisters. They were rammed together so close she could hear his heart. Then the girl disappeared again and they crept quickly past the room where drinks were underway. Mirabelle tentatively cracked the next door along.

Inside, it was dark. As their eyes got used to the gloom, it became clear that the room was a library. She could feel McGregor behind her as they slipped inside. She waited a moment or two as the shadowy furniture became visible. It struck her that this house was too well built. In some places you would be able to hear voices from one room to another, but here you would hardly dream there was a drinks party in progress next door.

Dodging desks and easy chairs, McGregor took his bearings and crossed to the door that connected the library to the drawing room. 'Ladies first,' he said. Resisting the urge to touch him,

215

even if only to hold his hand, Mirabelle peeked through the keyhole, trying to keep her mind on the job. The first thing she caught a glimpse of was Angela Waterman's red satin dress, the low light playing prettily across its surface. There were a dozen guests. Elrick Beaumont was sitting next to Angela on a sofa. Michael Crowe was standing by the fire, chatting to a man with a serious expression and a pretty woman in frothy green chiffon whose distinctive shoes betrayed her as Henny from the night before. The man, Mirabelle thought, must be Nigel. Silently Mirabelle turned the handle and slowly manoeuvred open the door – only a crack. McGregor squatted next to her on the carpet.

'The police have no idea, do they?' Nigel's voice was familiar. He had a tone that carried. 'I mean, it's our taxes that are paying for the investigation and they have no idea who did it.'

'The chaps on the Brighton force seem keen but I'm not holding out hope. We have to get on with things and let justice take its course,' Dougie Beaumont's father replied, ever the MP.

'If it was my son, Elrick, I'd just be so angry. I'd want to kill the damn murderer myself.'

'No point in that,' Mr Beaumont said stoutly, his tone ever practical, no doubt, the same as when he was in committee. 'My wife is grieving, although she's trying to get back in the swing of things. Enid's gone up to London to help. The main thing is that we pull together, get Dougie buried and George too, if it comes to that. We just have to get back to normal. You know what Winston says – when you're going through hell, just keep going.'

'Hear, hear,' his son-in-law cut in. 'And talking about it all the time is maudlin.'

'It's different for us. I mean, you don't live in this neck of the woods. Every time I come up the drive I'm going to think about poor George.' Nigel shuddered. 'And who's next? That's the question. I mean, who's to say two is the limit of this madman's ambition? Maybe he wants a bash at all of us.'

Angela Waterman took a sip of her drink. 'Really,' she said, 'I agree with you, Mr Crowe. Let's not talk about it any more.'

Mirabelle couldn't help but smile. Angela, after all, had talked about the murders more than anyone. A Dutch ormolu clock on the mantelpiece chimed the hour.

'Dinner is ready to be served.' The butler leaned in to tell one of the women, and she waved the party through with a brisk, 'Come along then. Shall we?'

The group stirred and began to make its way to the dining room. Mirabelle noticed Elrick Beaumont catch his son-in-law's eye as he turned to offer his arm to one of the women. The briefest of nods passed between them and a sly somehow serious-looking smile before Crowe downed the last of his glass and laid it on a silver tray. McGregor's face was still, his concentration totally focused on the people, but Mirabelle took in the room: the fire crackling in the grate and the gorgeous pictures on the walls – oil paintings of landscapes and long-dead family members. Goodwood was well appointed if a little shabby. Henny lingered beneath the likeness of a far more august-looking woman. She fiddled with the strap of her frothy green dress, waiting for Crowe to accompany her to dinner. She coughed as the last couple left, clearing her throat.

'I keep thinking that if Dougie had come to the Hunt Ball he might not have been at home that night. I mean, it might never have happened. And if the car hadn't been arriving, Highton wouldn't have come down either. It's all about chance, isn't it?'

This jolted Crowe from his private thoughts. 'Sometimes your number's just up, Hen,' he said dismissively. 'That's how I see it. Dougie knew that. George as well.'

Henny looked wistful. Her fingers moved from the strap to seek out an earring and she played with it momentarily, twisting it. 'It's just, Nigel is right, isn't he? There's a murderer on the loose.'

'If anyone ought to be worried about that, it's me, isn't it? I mean I was the third partner in the car.'

'And aren't you worried?'

'Certainly not. Everyone thought Dougie would die on the track, but you can't choose your time or your place. There'll be no more murders. Two is quite sufficient. Don't be a goose.'

He offered her his arm and they followed the others out. Mirabelle sat back. McGregor shrugged. 'Chance,' Mirabelle said under her breath, because Henny was wrong. It couldn't really be chance. They were about to get to their feet when the door to the drawing room opened again and two footmen came in to clear the glasses.

'At least they're in better spirits than last night,' one said, keeping his voice low.

'You can hardly blame them, Johnny. I was the one that saw Mr Highton to the door. That shook me all the next day, I can tell you, and I didn't even know the gentleman.'

'He was pretty drunk.'

''Course he was. That doesn't make killing the poor blighter all right, does it?'

The glasses clinked as the men gathered them.

'Well, they ain't found the golf club yet and I ain't surprised. Needle in a haystack round here,' Johnny observed as the first footman placed a guard in front of the fire.

'They'll find who did it. The police aren't as stupid as everyone thinks,' he said.

'Well, that's a relief.' McGregor grinned when the men had departed. 'We're not as stupid as everyone thinks.'

Mirabelle stood up. Her knee felt as if it might cramp. She shuffled over to the fireplace and leaned against the mantel as she stretched her leg.

'I didn't know it was Beaumont, Highton and Crowe who were partners in the car.'

'Yes.' McGregor clicked the door closed and followed her, sinking into a leather armchair. 'I can't quite believe I'm ahead of you for once. At first I wondered if that might be a motive, but, of course, they ideally wanted Beaumont to drive it. He was the ace.'

'I'm glad we saw him drive. Saw him win.'

'Me too.' He reached out to touch her lightly on the curve of her hip.

'And Highton?' Mirabelle called him back to work.

'The second death followed the first. That's my sense. Though you're right, Highton was more disposable.' McGregor lay his head back and squinted at the ceiling. 'Will they use this room later do you think?'

Mirabelle shrugged. 'I don't know. After dinner the gentlemen stay at the table and the ladies generally return to the drawing room. I suppose if they intended to use it they would have set a fire by now.'

'You were born to this, weren't you?'

'Well, you know what they say – it's not where you start, it's where you finish.' Mirabelle found it impossible to imagine herself getting dressed on a nightly basis for this kind of dinner – all lace and diamonds. There had seemed little enough point to it all when she was growing up and, now, none at all. Life was no longer a series of daily occasions.

'I'll interview Crowe tomorrow,' McGregor decided. 'Just to be on the safe side. I don't see there is any point in sitting around, hoping to overhear something the ladies might say.'

Mirabelle shrugged. He didn't see the movement, just got to his feet. In the hall, the butler was organising the delivery of the first course to the dining room when, from the rear, Kamari emerged holding some ironed shirts and a bag of golf clubs. The butler turned his ire on the poor man. He grabbed him by the ear and hauled him back to the servants' stairs. 'Back stairs, boy,' he snarled, as he pushed him through the door.

Kamari was still smiling as the baize slammed shut. 'Niggers,' the butler sneered. 'You can't teach them.'

'That's Mr Crowe's servant, Kamari. His valet, too, by the look of it,' Mirabelle mouthed. 'Poor fellow.'

They waited until the butler returned to his duties, order was restored and the line of footmen had disappeared into the dining room.

'How does Mr Crowe know there won't be another murder?' Mirabelle said suddenly under her breath. 'And what will happen to Beaumont's and Highton's share in the car, now they're gone?'

'Exactly.' McGregor took her hand and pulled her across the marble floor. 'Why do you think I want to speak to him?'

With only a single, quick backward glance, they slipped across the hallway and out on to the drive. Mirabelle looked over her shoulder. Behind them, the dinner party was underway. The scene through the window was almost baroque. McGregor was right – this was the kind of life her parents had foreseen for her. If it were possible would she swap her time in Brighton to have all this again? After the war lots of people simply wanted to go back to how things had been. They wanted to forget the nightly bombing and the terror of waiting for news about their loved ones. They wanted to settle back into domesticity. But she couldn't. Once you had been part of something worthwhile, it was impossible to imagine going back to just passing your time. A dinner party was one thing, but endless days of golf, cards, horse riding, cars and lunch – nothing that made a scrap of difference. She didn't understand how they could bear it.

'I don't want it, you know,' she said. 'I'd rather be normal. Like you.'

'I'm not normal.' McGregor turned away. 'I'm not that good. They wouldn't even let me fight, remember?'

She didn't reply as she fell into step, but she slipped her arm through his and that seemed a comfort.

'What do you say to dinner?' McGregor said. 'Let's see what they can rustle us up at the bar.'

Chapter 16

To expect the unexpected shows a thoroughly modern intellect

The eggs were no better the second morning at breakfast than they had been on the first, and Mirabelle wondered if she should substitute them for beer, as the salesmen had done. She decided she'd consider it when McGregor came down and in the meantime she applied herself to reading the newspaper as Ella periodically topped up her tea. Languid drops of rain peppered the window and Mirabelle found herself in no hurry to get on with the investigation. Being down here with McGregor felt part-holiday at least.

'The eggs aren't up to much,' she said without looking up as the seat opposite her was pulled out.

'Well,' said a familiar voice, 'it's just as well I had a snack on the train.'

'Vesta!' Mirabelle fumbled the newspaper into submission and laid it to one side. 'I'm so glad to see you.'

Ella hovered with the teapot.

'Yes, please,' Vesta said encouragingly, placing her capacious handbag beside the chair and un-buttoning her coat. 'I've been on the road since early.'

'Would you like anything for breakfast, ma'am?' Ella asked, as she poured a fresh cup.

'No thank you.'

The girl brought another chair to the table.

'Are you expecting someone else?' Vesta lifted the steaming tea to her lips and took a sip. Then she sighed. No one could make a cup of tea sound more satisfying than Vesta.

'The superintendent stayed here last night.'

The girl grinned. Mirabelle realised she was blushing.

'Nothing like that,' she said.

'Of course not.' Vesta's smile continued none-theless. She looked round. The breakfast room was almost empty, bar a middle-aged man with a shock of blond hair, who was wearing a burnt-orange tie. He was eating his eggs extraordinarily slowly over by the rain-splashed window. 'Have you made any progress?' Vesta kept her voice low.

Mirabelle nodded. 'But we still don't know who killed either of them. Highton had a threatening letter in his hand when he went down. We think he was being blackmailed.'

Vesta took this in. 'We,' she commented. 'That's

223

progress in itself.' That smile again. 'You must be wondering what on earth I'm doing here? I brought this. I might have posted it but, to be honest, I was worried about you just going off like that.'

Mirabelle's gaze didn't falter as Vesta withdrew a large brown envelope from her handbag and handed it over.

'You think the countryside will be idyllic, but on days like this there's nothing to do, is there? I mean, if it rains. At least in town you can go to the pictures or something.'

Mirabelle didn't reply. The trick with the countryside was to be dressed for it and neither of them were. Inside the envelope she found two sheaves of paper – the details of the estates of Douglas Elrick Beaumont and George Goodwin Highton.

'Have these been released already?'

'No. I called in a favour. I had to use our petty cash. Luckily, both men had the same solicitor – the office seems to deal with all things Beaumont. They handled the purchase of Dougie Beaumont's flat, that's how I tracked them down. Then it turned out one of Charlie's old GI friends is seeing a girl whose cousin works there. I don't know if you've noticed yet, but both wills are dated the same day.'

Mirabelle's eyes fell to the paper. 'Oh yes. Directly before the racing season started this year. How curious.'

'Young men seldom think to make a will. I mean, you just don't consider death a possibility, do you? Charlie doesn't have one. In fairness, I expect Dougie Beaumont had to think about his mortality more than most. After all, competitive driving is dangerous. But it looks as if he brought Highton along with him the day he went to the solicitor. Perhaps they were in for a penny, in for a pound kind of blokes.'

Mirabelle scanned the text. 'And he left everything to Mrs Beaumont? His mother?'

'They both did,' Vesta said, sounding satisfied. 'Actually, by instruction, the wills are more or less exactly the same.'

Mirabelle switched between the papers. She had been reading George Highton's will and hadn't realised. 'Now that is interesting. Mrs Beaumont. How odd. We wondered if Michael Crowe, Dougie Beaumont's brother-in-law, might have had a motive. He was the third partner in the car. But he isn't mentioned here. Not a sniff.'

Vesta's expression shifted only slightly at Mirabelle's continued use of the word 'we'. She decided not to dwell on it. Making a big deal might put Mirabelle off. Instead, she continued, indicating the papers in Mirabelle's hand. 'Highton's will doesn't mention the car. In fact, that's the other thing that's odd. Beaumont, it turns out, had a great deal to leave including two-thirds ownership of the famous racing car and what looks like an enticing portfolio of investments. He owned some valuable paintings and there's also an "any property subsequently acquired" clause–' Vesta leaned over and pointed to it '–which, I suppose, means his flat on the Lawns, which he didn't buy till later in the year. Highton, on the other hand, didn't leave anything much. His entire estate is composed of personal effects – a signet ring and a watch, that's about it.' She sipped her tea and let this sink in for a moment. 'Also,' she continued, 'they are both down as living at the same address. I looked it up in the *A–Z*. It's in Farringdon – Bleeding Heart Yard. Nice name.'

'Bleeding Heart?' Mirabelle remembered the phrase from the blackmail letter. *Bleeding heart is not enough,* it had said. Had the men made some kind of deal over a house? Did the letter refer to something between them or had someone else been involved? 'Farringdon would be handy for George Highton,' she said. 'It's close to the *Daily Telegraph*. But I'd have expected Dougie Beaumont would state his address as the family home, wouldn't you? This predates him buying the flat on the Lawns. I mean, even if only for appearances.'

'Hmm.' Vesta sounded dubious. 'And if the men were living together in London, why weren't they living together in Brighton?'

'Perhaps they didn't want it to seem…'

'What it was?'

Mirabelle nodded. She picked up George Highton's will. Vesta was right. He had left practically nothing. It made no sense. 'Highton was a partner in the car. They all seem to recognise that. And there was plenty of money discovered on his body. An impressive amount, in fact,' she murmured, as she read the clauses again carefully. Her lips pursed.

'What is it?' Vesta put down her cup and leaned forwards.

Mirabelle shook her head and stowed the sheaf of papers back in the envelope. 'Come along,' she

226

said, getting to her feet. 'We need to catch the next train from Chichester.' She checked her wristwatch and pulled on her coat, searching in the pockets for her gloves as Vesta gazed mournfully at the unfinished tea and the welcoming fireplace in front of which she had imagined spending much of the morning. She couldn't understand why Mirabelle hadn't chosen a table closer to it. 'But I only just got here,' she said. 'I was hoping for a day away from Brighton.'

'Brighton?' Mirabelle checked her hat was in place and removed her purse from her bag, motioning for Ella to bring her the bill. 'Why would we want to go back there?'

As Ella telephoned Chichester station to send a car, Mirabelle tipped the girl generously. The colour of Vesta's skin was so often an issue that she felt grateful the girl hadn't made a fuss. But then Goodwood was cosmopolitan in all sorts of ways. She carefully sealed the envelope containing the wills and left it behind the bar. 'Give this to Superintendent McGregor, when he comes down. It's important.'

'Superintendent?' the girl mouthed as Mirabelle scribbled a note to attach to it.

'That's right,' she said.

Meanwhile, Vesta checked her hair and powdered her nose. 'Will we have long to wait?'

'I shouldn't think so. Would you like to have a peek at Goodwood House, before the driver gets here? It's only next door.'

Vesta peered across the room, out of the window. The sky was flint grey but the rain had stopped. 'Is it far?' she asked doubtfully.

'Come along,' Mirabelle replied. 'We might as well.'

The gates were still open this morning. 'Highton died on the drive,' Mirabelle encouraged her and Vesta duly perked up and increased her pace. In the distance, about a mile away across the park, a woman galloped side-saddle on a bay, heading in the opposite direction. The horse's movement was so fluid that Mirabelle found it difficult to take her eyes off it.

'That's so old-fashioned.' Vesta smiled.

Mirabelle stopped at the bend. 'It was here,' she said. 'This is where they found the body.'

Vesta stepped back to consider the spot from the side of the road. 'It's odd, isn't it? I mean you expect to be able to feel something but you'd never know, would you?'

From the other side of the house a smart burgundy Rolls-Royce rolled almost silently across the façade. It would seem the occupants of Goodwood House were up and about early this morning and all in motion. As the car turned down the driveway, the women hovered, keeping out of the way. It slowed as it came close. Mirabelle could see Mr Beaumont and his son-in-law deep in conversation on the back seat. She raised a hand to Kamari, who was perched in the front next to the chauffeur, with a set of golf clubs on his lap – presumably Michael Crowe's. His face twitched in recognition, but he turned slightly inwards as if to protect himself from scrutiny. Perhaps the butler's unwarranted violence had made him self-conscious.

'Who's that?' Vesta asked.

'Mr Crowe's man. Dougie Beaumont's brother-in-law. That fellow is his valet.'

'The black guy?'

'Yes. Mr Crowe comes from Nairobi.'

Elrick Beaumont suddenly spotted the women through the side window as the car rolled past. He gestured as he issued an order to the driver, who halted the vehicle abruptly. Beaumont rolled down the window and leaned out, staring back at them. Mirabelle noticed that his eyes were pale hazel, exactly the colour of the leaves that peppered the driveway. They were also set hard.

'I say,' he said sharply, 'I'm sure you shouldn't be hanging about here, ladies. The police wouldn't like it. You know that what happened took place, well, exactly on this spot.'

Michael Crowe squinted at Mirabelle. He sat forwards. 'You're the woman from downstairs,' he said slowly. 'The one who fainted.'

'What woman?' Elrick Beaumont snapped.

Mirabelle immediately had the sense that he was a man who expected to be in charge and fully informed at all times. Here he was, after all, issuing orders about where she and Vesta were standing on a public drive.

'I'm Mirabelle Bevan, Mr Beaumont. I live in the flat underneath your son's in Brighton. I was there the night he died. This is Vesta Lewis, my business partner.'

'Business partner?'

In the front seat, Kamari shifted so he could have a better look.

'How do you do?' said Vesta with, Mirabelle noted, a good deal of grace.

'Mrs Lewis is one of your constituents,' she added, spuriously. 'She is an ardent Conservative.'

Beaumont did not look appeased. 'Well, I can't imagine what you're up to down here,' he batted back. 'It seems rather gruesome.'

'Not at all. We came to play golf.' Mirabelle's voice was smooth. She stared at the bag in Kamari's lap and the man moved again, twisting himself away. Was it the golf clubs or himself that he was uncomfortable about, she wondered once more. 'It's a wonderful course,' she went on. 'Angela Waterman invited us down. But poor Mr Highton's murder has rather put a damper on our plans. We thought we'd go up to London for the weekend instead. I'm so sorry for your loss. I know Mr Highton was a close family friend. He had known your son since they were children, hadn't he?'

'Yes. We adopted the boy, rather.'

'Adopted?'

'You know how it was during the war. Nothing official but we all did our bit and he needed somewhere to stay. It's a second blow.'

'Such a tragedy. Please extend my condolences to your wife.'

'Thank you. I shall. Back to London, eh? Back to life. I really don't think you should be here, Miss Bevan. Right here, I mean. You should move on.'

Mirabelle smiled. 'Mrs Lewis and I are just waiting for a driver to pick us up. We thought we'd take a short walk. Country air and so forth. We ought to be getting back. We mustn't keep you.' She stepped away from the car. Michael Crowe kept his eyes on her as Elrick Beaumont rolled up the

230

window and the driver pulled off.

'I am *not* an ardent Conservative,' Vesta spat.

'Well, I had to say something!'

'You could have told him it was you.'

'He knows where I live so he knows I'm not one of his constituents. Besides, I'm a lifelong liberal,' Mirabelle replied, as they watched the car pause at the gates before turning right.

'I wouldn't be the least bit surprised if he did it, you know.'

Mirabelle took Vesta's arm. 'I don't think Elrick Beaumont is a murderer, dear. He's used to having his way, but murder, well, that's something else. Especially his own son and a close family friend. Besides any personal tie, Dougie was funding his career.'

'Well, someone did it and he's a politician,' Vesta objected. 'A Tory. There's no saying what he might get up to.'

'I had no idea you were so vehement. I only found out the other day that Superintendent Mc-Gregor is a revolutionary and now you turn out to be a committed left-winger.' A smile played around Mirabelle's lips.

'And that black fellow was downright fishy.' Vesta ignored her friend's teasing.

'Yes. He was. Come along,' Mirabelle insisted. 'We had best get back to the pub if we want to make it up to town.'

At the door to the inn, the hired car's exhaust shot a thick plume into the autumn air. As the women approached, the driver scrambled to find his feet on the tarmac and held the door so they could take their seats.

'No luggage?' he checked.

'None,' Mirabelle confirmed.

'I don't trust that black man,' Vesta said under her breath as she settled. 'I've got an eye for coloured fellows. I know a lot of them. And there was something up with him.'

Mirabelle didn't respond. She wondered instead how the tinkerer felt this morning, on the other side of the fields. Was he already working on the car with '26' on the side, putting Dougie Beaumont's renovations into place? Through the bar window she saw the blond man with the orange tie take his place by the fire and open a copy of *The Times*. He looked set for the day. Then her eyes were drawn upwards to the bedroom floor. McGregor's curtains were still closed. To her surprise, she felt almost sorry to be leaving.

'Well.' Vesta motioned from the back seat. 'Come on.'

The service to London was regular and the women didn't have to wait long at Chichester railway station before a train pulled in and they bundled into a first-class carriage. Outside the window, the Sussex countryside whizzed past in a jumble of green and flaming orange until at last they pulled in at Victoria. Mirabelle noticed Vesta's heels clicking as they walked across the concourse. She really must buy a new pair of shoes, she thought. The flat ones Superintendent McGregor had provided weren't up to snuff and she missed the feeling of authority that went with well-made high heels. As they approached the taxi rank, the air in town was scented with the first of the autumn fires, as London kindled its first coals of the season.

Mirabelle shuddered as she slipped decisively into the hackney cab at the head of the rank. 'I've no idea if he'll be working today, but it might be wise to start at the office, I suppose,' she said.

'What office? Who are you talking about?'

'The only person I know who seems to know the truth about both Dougie Beaumont and George Highton. I just didn't get it out of him the last time I was here.' Mirabelle leaned forward and instructed the driver.

Vesta didn't ask more questions. It was always intriguing to be back in the capital and, as the West End flew past the cab window, she studied the fashions and the enormous buildings, landmarks from her childhood, when now and then she used to venture out of Bermondsey. The great Georgian edifices always seemed cosmopolitan compared to the warren of low brick buildings, lines of two-up two-down houses, factories and warehouses where she had passed her childhood. It still felt to her that central London was grand beyond the scale of its population, composed of columns, porticos, pristine white stucco and elaborately dressed stone. The cab took them across town, into the fringes of the City, depositing the women on Fleet Street, where Mirabelle paid the driver. Without a word, she swept inside the office of the *Daily Telegraph* with Vesta in her wake.

'I'd like to speak to Reuben Vinestock,' she announced.

'He's out to lunch,' the receptionist said smoothly, hardly looking up.

'Could you check, please?'

The girl looked as if she might be about to object, but when she raised her eyes Mirabelle's expression brooked her no opportunity. Recognising that she was beaten, she sighed and picked up a telephone that sported an array of buttons with carefully typed labels. Her elegantly manicured finger pressed one and a red bulb lit on the console. 'Is Mr Vinestock in the office?' she asked. 'Oh yes. All right.' The girl covered the mouthpiece. 'You're right. Seems he is up there. Sorry. I thought they'd all gone. Someone is fetching him now. Who shall I say?'

'Mirabelle Bevan.'

'Mirabelle Bevan,' the girl repeated into the mouthpiece. The groan from the other end was audible and the receptionist's cheeks coloured. 'But I already said you were here,' she hissed. Vesta grinned. Mirabelle pretended to examine a collection of framed front pages mounted over a bench to one side. The girl hung up.

'He's not there, actually,' she said, unconvincingly.

'Don't be ridiculous,' Mirabelle replied. 'Come along, Vesta.'

'No.' The girl got to her feet. 'Please.'

But the women had already passed into the stairwell. On the second floor, the newsroom was even more deserted than the last time Mirabelle had visited. She wondered how these people managed to produce a daily newspaper when it appeared the office was constantly understaffed. At a desk at the back of the room, Reuben Vinestock was engrossed writing shorthand into a spiral-bound notebook. He did not look up even when Mirabelle passed through the wooden swing gate between the glass panels. When she had almost reached him he finally noticed. Nervously, he ran his hand through his hair and the familiar scent of pomade rose on the air.

'Oh God,' he said.

'This is my business partner, Mrs Lewis,' Mirabelle introduced Vesta.

Reuben gave a half-nod. 'How do you do?' he sounded defeated – worse than that, resigned.

Vesta replied with a wide grin and decided that this was far more fun than staying in the office on Brills Lane.

'Look, Miss Bevan, I'm sorry but I'm just not up to talking about all this...' Reuben broke out. 'It was bad enough when Dougie died, but now George is gone too.'

'That's exactly why I want to talk to you, Mr Vinestock. Specifically, I want to ask you about George Highton's will.'

Reuben folded his arms across his chest. 'I don't know anything about George's will.'

'I do. Mrs Lewis procured a copy.'

'How?' Vinestock spluttered. 'Poor George's body can't even be cold yet. What you don't seem to understand is that Dougie was my friend, Miss Bevan. Actually George was too. We knew each other through work but still. I've lost two people this week. Have a bit of respect, won't you? I'm not your errand boy and I don't understand what your interest is. You're just being nosey. It's none of your business.'

'Two men have been murdered. One was killed

while I lay sleeping in the flat directly beneath him. My interest, as you put it, is that I want to understand what happened. Don't you?'

Reuben heaved a sigh. 'Of course.'

'I wondered if you might be able to shine a light on why Mr Highton left so few material goods compared to his friend. Dougie Beaumont's estate comprises a portfolio of stocks and part-ownership of his car. But the truth was Highton was a partner in the car too, along with Michael Crowe and yet his share isn't stated in his will. Officially, Mr Highton left practically nothing.'

Reuben shifted. His arms came down. 'That's none of your business,' he said. 'And none of mine either. Besides, I don't see what bearing it has.' Then, after only a moment's pause, he relented. 'How did you manage to get hold of George's will anyway?' he asked.

You could knock people, Mirabelle thought, but you couldn't change their basic nature. Reuben Vinestock was a journalist through and through and his gaze was fixed hard on them.

'Tell him,' Mirabelle said.

Vesta took a deep breath. She was, after all, admitting to breaking the law. 'I have a friend in the solicitor's office where Beaumont and Highton lodged the documents,' she admitted. 'I paid for the wills, or for copies of them.'

Reuben looked disapproving or, Mirabelle wondered, was that a look of admiration? It was difficult to tell. She continued. 'The wills state the same London address. They were signed on the same day earlier this year. Though Mr Highton stated he had significantly less to leave than he in fact did. That surprised me. Had he come into his money suddenly, Mr Vinestock? He had a substantial amount of cash on him the night that he died. When I met him, he didn't appear to me like someone who was on his uppers.'

'He wasn't. I mean, you're right he had a share in Dougie's car for a start.'

'And that was worth something?'

Reuben nodded. 'Yes. It cost a fortune to keep the thing on the road. It's not cheap to attend race meetings and tour the Grand Prix circuit, but Dougie placed regularly enough that there was prize money. Also, George made a fortune betting on him. He knew when Dougie was having a particularly good day and when track conditions favoured him. He was practically psychic about where he'd come in. More recently, the car had other backers too. Beyond the ownership. They were interested in...'

'The renovation to the steering column?'

'Yes. I mean if you patented something like that, if it worked, that is, there would be money. Pots of the stuff. They had high hopes.'

'So Highton should have had means?'

'George always had means. He was good with money. Ever since I met him.'

'Both wills also have the same beneficiary. They leave everything to Mrs Beaumont.'

'Dougie's mother?' Reuben sounded incredulous. 'Really?'

'Was Highton close to her?'

Reuben shrugged. 'George was part of the family. He was a grammar school boy. He didn't come from a wealthy background. But I suppose

Mrs Beaumont was as close as he had to a mother. His parents died in the Blitz – in 1941, I think. His dad was in the Home Guard. After they'd gone, the Beaumonts took him in until he got called up. Mr Beaumont pulled some strings to get George a commission in a decent regiment. We didn't talk about it much. To be honest, I try not to think about the war.'

Mirabelle paused. 'I'm sorry,' she said, gently, 'it's just these details are important. Did you ever see Dougie and George with Mrs Beaumont?'

'Now and then. They felt sorry for her, I think. I mean they cared for her, of course, but she was just so hopeless. If they left her everything, maybe it's some kind of joke.'

'A joke?'

'I don't mean that exactly.' Reuben leaned against the desk. 'It's only, they used to rag each other about how hopeless Mrs Beaumont was. She was proud of Dougie and she always looked the part, but she didn't have much ... self-confidence. She couldn't always follow what was going on. I mean, with his career. I never saw her make a single decision. She just turned up and floated along with whatever was happening. Mind you, it can't have been easy for her. He probably knocked any sense of competence out of the poor woman early on.'

'Who?'

'Elrick, of course. All families are different. I mean, from the outside, you'd think the Beaumonts had everything. But Elrick Beaumont is formidable – a real powerhouse. Anything going on, you could be sure he had a hand in it. He was a kind of tyrant, I suppose. Dougie hated the old man and worshipped him at the same time.'

'But I thought Dougie was the one who bailed the family out.'

'He did. But no matter how far he got, how much he did, he'd never abandon his mother and sister. I think he wanted his father to be proud of him too. It was tangled, I suppose, and he hated himself for it. I lost my father, Miss Bevan. It's difficult to imagine someone wishing theirs away...'

'But Dougie Beaumont did?'

Vinestock nodded. 'Maybe,' he said. 'He didn't say as much but the old man was hard on him. He was hard on everyone.'

'So he was a bully?'

'Yes.' Vinestock's shoulders rolled slightly. 'I know he beat the boys when they were younger. Dougie had a scar he was self-conscious about where the old man had had a go at him with a horsewhip. I think that's one reason they were away so much. If it wasn't France or Italy, it was Nairobi. I joked with Dougie that was why he had to be the fastest. To get away from his dad.'

'Sounds as if they were scared of him.'

Vinestock considered carefully before he replied. 'Fear is relative, isn't it?' he said slowly. Mirabelle wondered what Vinestock had seen. What he'd escaped from. 'On balance, I'd say they were scared. I hadn't thought of it like that.'

'I knew it,' Vesta cut in. 'You don't have to nudge a Tory far till you find a Fascist.'

Vinestock laughed. 'Politics is a bloody business, Mrs Lewis. And that being the case, Elrick Beau-

239

mont has certainly found himself suited to it. He went straight into the Commons in '45 and found his feet, even under Labour. But I wouldn't go quoting Mr Bevan on the subject of the Conservative Party in here.' He smiled at Vesta. 'This is the *Telegraph*. We're Tory through and through.'

Mirabelle was thinking out loud. 'Dougie saved the whole family,' she pondered.

Reuben's eyes lost their focus. He sighed. 'I didn't know them then. The first time I met George was in here a couple of years ago. The first time I was invited to the family house it was already renovated. Dougie said it was in a real state when they were kids. They used to have buckets in the nursery to catch the raindrops. It seems crazy, doesn't it? I mean, in Belgravia. But it's good when a family sticks together. I mean, that's what families are supposed to do. George said Dougie was buying himself a happy family. But he wasn't, really. It wasn't lack of money that was the real problem.'

'Was Elrick happy about his son's career?'

'He isn't a man I'd associated with the word "happy".'

Mirabelle tried to imagine what it would feel like for Dougie Beaumont – afraid of his father and trying to attain his approval while living a life between his respectable family home, the lights of the racing circuit and the grubby world she'd touched upon of seedy parties and secrets. To traverse so many roads, in so many different guises he must have been a good actor, she thought. Maybe they both were – Highton and Beaumont together. Perhaps the things they got up to were an escape. Increasingly, there was something sad about a life on the racing circuit. Something desperate. They must have held their secrets close, the two of them, thrust together.

'There aren't any women in here,' Vesta commented, looking around. 'I mean, apart from the girl on reception.'

Reuben Vinestock smiled. 'The *Telegraph* doesn't run an advice column, Mrs Lewis.'

Mirabelle felt Vesta stiffen. That wasn't going to help. She turned her attention back to the matter in hand.

'Mrs Lewis and I are interested in where they lived,' she said. 'I mean the address at Bleeding Heart Yard. Dougie and George lived there together, didn't they?'

'Yes. They had a lot of parties.'

'I'd like to see it. I wonder, might you be able to help?'

Reuben considered for only a moment. Then he went to a desk a couple along from the one he was occupying. He opened the drawer and took out a key on a piece of string. 'George kept a spare in his desk,' he said. 'I want to be clear – I'm doing this for Dougie and George. Not for you. Do you understand?'

It was a ten-minute walk to Bleeding Heart Yard or at least it was ten minutes given that Reuben kept up quite a pace. Mirabelle and Vesta fell in behind him, walking north towards Farringdon. As they got further away from the Thames, the streets bore fewer scars of being heavily bombed though in places there was still a strange mixture of tall, new buildings and vacant lots between the offices, shops and pubs. Mirabelle thought there were other areas of London where George Highton might have chosen to live, even if this part of town was convenient for the office. Still, journalists worked irregular hours, she reasoned, and it was cheaper around here than setting up home in Chelsea, Fitzrovia or Belgravia, where she might have placed Highton and Beaumont if she'd had to guess. It was also less visible. Did Elrick Beaumont know that his son and his lover kept a hideaway? Was this place another of their secrets?

Reuben turned down Ely Place – a grand stretch of Georgian buildings with an ancient church installed at the end. Beyond the church, the street was cut off by a high wall, but to one side there was a gate built into the brickwork. Reuben pushed it open and, as the women stepped over the threshold, the scale of the architecture became immediately more industrial. He took the key from his pocket and halted at a Georgian ware-house. From the roof there was a winch for hoisting heavy goods up to a large wooden door that looked perilous to open.

'Here?' Mirabelle checked.

'Doesn't look like anyone lives here, does it?'

'No.'

'The top floors are rented by Pastorelli and Rapkin, you know, the instrument makers. Compasses. That kind of thing. They have a workshop up there.'

'And Dougie and George lived in the bottom two floors?'

Vinestock nodded.

'Why?'

He shrugged. 'I don't know,' he said.

'How odd.' Mirabelle spoke under her breath as she took in the exterior of the building. An old-fashioned iron gaslight hung useless over the front door. The windows were shuttered on the inside, the place closed up. As Vinestock turned the key in the lock and pushed his way inside, the door caught on a scatter of letters that had accumulated on the mat. Reuben snapped on the light and picked up the mail, sorting the correspondence into a pile. Inside, the hallway was narrow and dark, lit only vaguely by a long dirty window at the head of the stairs. Reuben turned into the sitting room. 'I thought George owned this place,' he said, opening the shutters. 'But given what it said in his will, maybe he just rented it.'

'Wow.' Vesta breathed out audibly. The air felt heavy, the room long abandoned, though it was furnished exquisitely and far beyond what might be expected of the architecture. Hand-painted wallpaper set off ornate furniture. Over the mantelpiece, silver candelabra sported an array of beeswax candles in different stages of use. Shelves of leather-bound books covered an entire wall, most of them, Mirabelle noted, sporting titles – cricket and rugby. A pile of ash in the grate was only the start of the dilapidation. To one side, a table was shrouded in dark velvet cloth that had collected a cobweb down one side.

'He spent most of the year in France,' Reuben said by way of explanation, or perhaps excuse. 'I don't know if he had even come back here yet. What are we looking for?'

'I don't know,' Mirabelle admitted.

She walked out of the room and leafed through the letters that had arrived for George Highton – a few bills and a postcard from Monaco that simply said 'When you are next here we will drive up to the hills. M'. Along the hall she cut into a second, smaller room. It clearly served as a kitchen although there was only a tiny hotplate to indicate the room's function. On the oak table several opened bottles of red wine had turned to vinegar, releasing a tangy scent. There was no food – not even a tin of soup – although a trail of rock-hard breadcrumbs on the dresser betrayed that someone had once eaten here, albeit untidily. The air of dilapidation continued upstairs – an unmade bed framed by a wrought-iron bedstead with dull brass knobs, a pillow abandoned on the floor and a suit hung in a wardrobe with its door wide open. The shoulders of the pinstriped jacket were peppered with pale dust. Vesta shuddered. It was easy to imagine a ghost living here. She could almost feel one.

'I thought George Highton was in London last week,' she said.

'Well, it looks as if he didn't come home if he was,' Mirabelle chipped in.

'He was at work, though. I saw him. He came into the office after Dougie died,' Reuben insisted. 'Before he went on the tear.'

The last room was a makeshift bathroom. These warehouses must have originally had outdoor privies, but George Highton and Dougie Beaumont were perhaps fastidious in such matters. The bathroom had been fitted relatively recently – a modern suite in canary yellow ceramic was plumbed into a box room at the front. The contrast immediately reminded Mirabelle of the bright blue sofa in the front room at the Beaumonts' house – a splash of modern colour slightly out of place. A heavy, patterned curtain obscured the window overlooking the street. Mirabelle pulled it back. Beside the bath there was a plate piled high with unused bars of soap, as if to taunt the rest of the house with the spectre of cleanliness. Mirabelle picked one up. It smelled faintly of sandalwood. Beyond the bath there was a mahogany cabinet built into the wall. She opened the cupboard door. It creaked. Inside there was an array of treasures. Small icons, shimmering with gold paint interspersed with candlesticks and a carved burr snuffbox in the shape of a hedgehog. On the bottom shelf, in easy reach of the bath, there was a cut-crystal bottle of Italian aftershave and a cut-throat razor with a mother-of-pearl handle. Mirabelle's eye was drawn to a small clock in a leather case tucked into the corner.

'That's odd,' said Vesta. 'I wouldn't keep a clock anywhere near the bath.'

'There's nothing here. I'm not sure what I thought I'd find.' Mirabelle motioned the others out ahead of her. 'Does that suit in the bedroom belong to George?'

Reuben peeked back into the other room. 'Yes. I think so.'

'Can you pick out anything here that belonged to Dougie?'

Reuben paused at the head of the stairs. 'Nothing personal.'

Mirabelle paused. She faced him head-on. 'Had they fought, Reuben?'

Vinestock shifted. He took almost a full minute before he spoke. 'They had a blazing row at Le Mans. I don't know what it was about. Guys sometimes just fight with each other. Brothers fight, don't they?'

'Was that the last time you saw them together?'

'No. They headed up to a Grand Prix afterwards. That was quite something. After that they went back to France but I couldn't say if they were together, you know.'

'And they got on during the race?'

'Seemed to.'

'Did you see them together since?'

'No. I mean, I saw George when he came in the other day before he died. But I hadn't seen Dougie. I spent the summer in London. I covered the cricket and, of course, Ruth Ellis was hanged and I ended up doing a couple of pieces about that. It was holiday season so we have to fill in. What is it that you're getting at, Miss Bevan?'

Vesta's eyes blazed with the same question. 'Well, it's obvious. I mean, you've just confirmed that they fell out,' she said.

'And you think George would kill Dougie? You don't understand. There's no way George would do that. Whatever their differences.'

'Why?'

'He just wouldn't.' Reuben waited long enough to read Mirabelle's dubiety. 'But anyone can do anything, can't they? I mean, that's what you're thinking? You didn't know them, Miss Bevan.'

'I'm just reasoning things through.' Mirabelle

paused. 'Look, if you don't mind waiting, I'd like to use the facilities.'

She closed the bathroom door and switched on the tap to cover the noise of her investigation. Then she opened the mahogany cupboard and reached for the clock. She pulled it from the leather case as she felt inside her bag for the key she'd found under Dougie Beaumont's mattress. It fitted perfectly. Carefully, she turned the lock and the back opened. Inside there were no cogs or little wheels. The workings were gone and, instead, there was a bright yellow roll of Kodak film. Mirabelle weighed it in her hand. It was an interesting idea, she thought, using an old clock as a box, a hiding place that no one would think to open. What had Beaumont photographed? And why had he left it here – the only thing that seemed to belong to him in the whole house. Efficiently, she turned the key and slipped the clock back into place. Then she stowed the film in her handbag.

She stood back and looked at the shelf before picking up the burr snuffbox that lay next to the clock. In for a penny, she thought. It was empty, although telltale traces of white powder were caught in the hinges. Mirabelle leaned back against the toilet. Looking more carefully at the icons, she noted they were chipped at the edges and one had splintered so that part of the image was missing. There was a lot to consider. She'd need to have the roll of film developed for a start. Was this what they had fallen out over? The implied story felt biblical – had brother killed brother, lover killed lover? And if so, who had perpetrated the second killing? Or was Vesta right and Elrick Beaumont had found out about their secret life and taken action? That seemed insupportable given how important Dougie was to the family finances. She fumbled to flush the toilet and make her way back into the hallway. Vesta and Reuben were waiting downstairs.

'It's just not possible,' Reuben was hissing, his voice low. 'Whatever she thinks.'

'Who do you think killed Dougie, then?'

It seemed he had no reply. There was a short silence before Mirabelle let them hear her footsteps on the stair.

The three of them walked back to Fleet Street in silence. Reuben paused at the door of the office. Inside, the receptionist peered through the glass as if she was trying to divine what was going on. It must be a slow day.

'I suppose I ought to let Mrs Beaumont know,' Reuben said. 'I mean, the things in the house are hers now.'

'I'd wait a little, Reuben,' Mirabelle said kindly. 'We know what's in the will, but she might not yet.'

'Well, if you figure out who did it...' Reuben said.

'I'll let you know. It'd be a scoop, after all.' Mirabelle smiled.

'Not for that,' he objected. 'I suppose the police...'

'Or the red tops,' Vesta chipped in.

Reuben didn't answer. He looked dejected as he disappeared inside.

'I feel sorry for him,' Vesta commented. 'What are we going to do next?'

Mirabelle considered a moment. This was Fleet Street, so there were bound to be photographic studios nearby where she could have the film developed. But by the same reasoning the people who worked in those studios must have a maze of journalistic contacts. If she handed in the film here there was nothing to stop them selling whatever was contained in the images to the highest bidder. She made the decision to call on an old friend instead.

'We need to go west,' she said. 'We have work to do.'

Chapter 17

Women of good taste always come to terms with fashion

The bus stopped at Harrods and Mirabelle decided she couldn't stand the flat shoes any longer. Clothes rationing might have ceased but still, it could be difficult to find what you wanted and Harrods was not only a safe bet, it was on their way. The doorman swung the entrance open and the women slipped inside, squeezing past a gaggle of children no doubt bound for the school department for their annual outfitting. It was that time of year. Mirabelle and Vesta headed for the lift, where a sullen boy, wearing a gilt-strewn uniform, ran them up to the shoe lounge. Mirabelle had first visited this department with her mother when she left the nursery. It was here she had slipped on her first pair of heels and had realised that they felt right. During the war, she had visited Harrods only seldom, although now and again there wasn't an option and, if you had coupons, Harrods could generally get you what you wanted. These days the carpet in the shoe lounge was worn, although fetching plants had been strategically placed on side tables over the tattiest edges. The walls were decked with displays. A dowdy assistant hovered in attendance as, at the other end of the room, two women tried on stilettos and hobbled intermittently up and down in front of the mirrors.

'They make your ankles look simply marvellous, Rosemary,' one enthused.

Mirabelle called over an assistant and enquired after dark brown heels. 'Nothing too sensible,' she said as she gave her size and took a seat.

Vesta hovered with half an eye to a pair of red patent baby dolls on a revolving stand. Her face brightened every time they came around.

'They'd suit you,' Mirabelle encouraged her.

Vesta turned over the price tag the next time the baby dolls appeared. 'Italian,' she commented doubtfully. 'Well, perhaps in the summer.'

Mirabelle removed her flats and stood up, flexing her toes to feel the carpet beneath her stockinged feet.

'It all comes down to people, doesn't it?' she said.

Vesta cast her eyes over the display.

'Not the shoes, silly. I mean, any case we've ever solved. It always comes down to people. That's what I keep thinking. This time more than ever.'

Vesta sank into the seat next to Mirabelle. She put down her handbag on the carpet and looked thoughtful. 'You mean someone they knew did it?'

'Definitely. Whoever killed Dougie Beaumont knew him. George Highton too. It comes down to circles within circles. That's what I realised at Goodwood, and I realised it even more today, talking to Reuben. All of these people knew each other for different reasons. Like that revolving display over there. One lot knew each other because they were part of the smart set, another lot knew each other because of a shared interest. Racing cars is an obvious one but these men had illicit interests and lots of them. Beaumont's friend, Harrison, was right – that sleepy country estate is like Piccadilly Circus. Looking at their lives, Dougie Beaumont and George Highton had to fit into different worlds and they had to be whatever was expected of them. A loving son. A hard-nosed investor. A racing driver. A party person. A lover. A friend.'

'Don't we all have to do that? I mean, sometimes it feels I'm always trying to fit in.'

'Yes.' Mirabelle nodded, though it crossed her mind that she hadn't made an effort like that in a long time. 'But Beaumont and Highton were playing for high stakes. They couldn't fail at any of it. They had secrets. One slip and they might lose everything. I don't think we're even close to getting at the bottom of everything they were up to. And really, where does all the money come from? Normally, I'd look at their debts but both men were cash rich. I mean, if you follow the money, it just gets you nowhere...'

'What about the car?'

Vesta was about to press the point when the assistant returned with a stack of shoeboxes. Mirabelle stopped to peruse the options, picking one pair and inspecting the style from each side, before discarding it. Eventually, she settled on a pair of chocolate, crocodile-skin winkle-pickers with treacherous heels.

'Gosh, I've rather missed the height,' she admitted, strolling in a leisurely fashion down the carpet.

Vesta grinned. Mirabelle was far more elegant than the ladies with the stilettos, who were still trying on pair after pair in a flurry of indecision on the other side of the lounge. One looked as if she might tumble at any moment. By contrast, it was clear Mirabelle was born to high heels – nothing could topple her.

'Would you wrap the flats and send them on?' she asked. 'I wonder if you still have my account details? It's been a while. My name is Mirabelle Bevan. My address has changed since I last shopped in Harrods.'

'I'll look up the name, madam.' The girl disappeared towards the counter with the flats in tow.

Mirabelle stared out of the window. On the street below, a smart lady was walking a Highland terrier on a lead.

'That reminds me of you and Superintendent McGregor,' Vesta giggled.

'The cheek! Really, Vesta.'

As the woman stopped at the kerb the dog looked up at her as if to ask for permission to cross. Mirabelle and Vesta burst out laughing, guiltily.

'You just abandoned the poor man in the country.'

Mirabelle looked mildly troubled. 'I left a note,' she objected. 'The thing is that the superintendent can't go where we need to go. As a police officer he's far too conspicuous.'

'Isn't it his job?'

'He is bound by too many rules. And in this world people are more likely to talk to you or me than someone from the police. Anyway, he doesn't like it when we go anywhere he deems dangerous.'

'Is that what we're going to do?'

Mirabelle shrugged. 'If it's an inside job, we'll have to go inside, won't we? One circle or another.'

The sales assistant came back with a heavy ledger and scored out the address just west of Sloane Street where Mirabelle had lived with Jack.

'Brighton?' she said cheerily, as Mirabelle dictated the address on the Lawns. 'I've heard it's nice down on the coast.'

'It's nice in the summer,' Vesta cut in. 'At this time of year the wind can be vicious. One way or another.'

'One way or another,' Mirabelle repeated. 'Come along, Vesta. We really need to be getting along.'

The Beaumont residence wasn't far. Mirabelle wondered fleetingly why the family hadn't settled in St James's but the place she'd paid her respects to Mrs Beaumont had clearly been the family home for some time. Perhaps her forbears hadn't been as ambitious as her husband. Mirabelle deftly guided Vesta in the right direction, through the maze of Georgian and Victorian streets behind Harrods. Before they hit the main road, however, she stopped in front of a blue door and hesitated.

'Is this the Beaumont house?' Vesta asked.

'No. This is where we find out which of the circles these men dodged between was the most deadly.' Mirabelle shuffled on the pavement.

'What are we waiting for?'

'I haven't been here for a while,' Mirabelle admitted. 'It's a club.'

The girl squinted and Mirabelle realised that to Vesta the word meant something quite different. 'Not for music.' She shoved her fondly. 'There's no jazz.'

'Did you come here during the war?'

'Not really. Afterwards, mostly.'

'Well it looks posh.'

Mirabelle shrugged. 'The thing is that there's been no measure following the money. Maybe it's the other currency we should have been looking at.'

Vesta looked blank.

'Information,' Mirabelle said, rolling her eyes. 'Come along.'

Instead of knocking at the front door, she pushed open the gate and took the steps down to the basement, where she rang the bell. Within seconds a kitchen maid answered. The girl was clearly shocked to find a well-dressed lady on the doorstep. 'We thought you was the fishmonger,' she said.

'I wondered if William was in?'

'He's clearing lunch, miss. Up in the bar.'

'Can I come in?'

The girl hopped from foot to foot. 'We ain't allowed. The Colonel says. It's security. No one comes in this door. Not a soul. No matter what.'

'Well, I could wait here and you could fetch William.'

The girl thought about this and then nodded. The door clicked shut, leaving Mirabelle and Vesta on the mat. 'What does she mean about security?'

'This building is the safest place in London,' Mirabelle replied enigmatically. 'It's also the most dangerous.'

Vesta crossed her arms. 'I thought you were making progress,' she said. 'But I see I was mistaken. Let's try that again. What is this place?'

'It's the Blue Door. It's a club.'

'For...?'

'Ex-servicemen and women.'

Vesta had been to plenty of ex-servicemens' clubs. Charlie played them now and then. Once he had gone on a tour. Not one had been housed in a Georgian townhouse and no one had ever mentioned security. 'Aha,' she said.

'I have a membership here. It's for First Aid – nursing.'

This cut no more ice with Vesta than Mirabelle's last answer. 'The safest and the most dangerous,' she repeated back to her. 'A club for nurses?'

Mirabelle sighed. 'It's SOE,' she admitted. 'All the members are SOE.'

'And you?'

Mirabelle shook her head. 'First Aid Nursing Yeomanry.'

'You were a nurse?'

'No. Not really.'

Vesta felt her temper rising. 'Oh for heaven's sake,' she started, but she stopped as the door opened once more and a man with hair dyed an unnatural colour of brown stood before them. He was wearing livery. His face lit up.

'Miss Bevan!' he all but shouted in delight.

'William.'

'How nice to see you. How are you, for heaven's sake?'

'I'm fine, thank you. You look well. This old place obviously suits you.'

The man's gaze shifted towards Vesta.

'This is my business partner, Vesta Lewis.' Mirabelle smiled. 'We run a debt collection agency together.'

William made a strange move, almost as if he was bobbing a curtsy.

'How do you do?' Vesta said.

'Well, what can I do for you, Miss Bevan?'

Mirabelle produced the roll of film from her bag. 'I need this developed. It has to be done with a degree of...'

'I understand, miss.' He put out his hand.

'How long might it take?'

'I can have it for you later this afternoon. Two hours, perhaps.'

'Might I telephone?'

'Of course. Mr Golding is still in the office. I'll let him know when it's ready. I can have one of the runners deliver it to you.'

'I'm afraid the pictures might be shocking, William.'

The expression on William's face did not flicker on account of either curiosity or discomfort. It was as if every photograph he'd ever developed had been shocking.

'Is there anything else, miss?'

'No. Thank you.'

Back out on the street, Vesta regarded Mirabelle carefully. 'Where did that come from?'

'The house in Bleeding Heart Yard. I found it in the bathroom.'

'What do you think it contains?'

'I don't know. My guess is that Dougie Beaumont left it there and intended to pick it up later.'

'Not Highton?'

Mirabelle shook her head. 'It was locked in a box. Beaumont had the key.'

Vesta did not ask any more questions. Mirabelle was a locked box herself, she decided. It was infuriating. They walked on, turning on to Sloane Street and then continued in silence to Sloane Square where the lights from the theatre on the east side glowed neon as they crossed the road. Mirabelle couldn't help feeling it was good to be back in high heels, strolling along Eaton Gate. The private gardens in front of the townhouses were peppered with golden leaves like sovereigns strewn on the muddy ground. This area was unreservedly grand. As the women made their way along the pavement, they peered alternately between the huge first-floor windows and the near-black bark of the sycamores set against the last of the leaves. Mirabelle found herself feeling nostalgic.

'I used to live around here,' she admitted. 'During the war.'

'It looks nice.'

'It was. We were further over, towards Chelsea.'

She touched Vesta's arm to indicate that they should turn. 'The Beaumont house is this way,' she said.

'How are we going to get in?'

'We're not, just yet. I think surveillance would be a good idea.'

Vesta sighed. The last time Mirabelle had put somewhere under surveillance Vesta had fallen asleep in a stairwell and Mirabelle had abandoned her just when things had got interesting. Admittedly, it was a while ago, on a case that had taken them to Cambridge, but still. 'We're a little conspicuous, aren't we?' she pointed out.

'Yes. And it might take a while.' Mirabelle looked around. In the park at the end of the road there was a wooden bench. 'Come along,' she said. 'We'll be able to see the house from there and nobody will question two ladies taking the air. Not even in this weather.'

'It's residents only. We can't climb over the railings.' Vesta sounded shocked.

Mirabelle removed her lockpicks from her handbag. 'This won't take a moment,' she said. 'Keep an eye out.'

The lock sprung easily and the gate creaked. Vesta rubbed her hands together. The gloves she'd chosen today were a wonderful jade green but they weren't lined. 'If we'd had to climb over, the heels would have been an advantage, you know,' Mirabelle pointed out. 'But you're right – two women vaulting over a set of railings is far more noticeable than one fiddling with what most people would assume was a key.'

'What are we looking for?'

'Comings and goings. I'll stay here. I've plenty to think about and, in the meantime, you can check around the back. See if you can figure out who is in the house. Why don't you try to find Kamari – the fellow you don't like the look of?'

Mirabelle sat on the bench and placed her handbag on her lap.

'You'll be here?' Vesta checked.

'I'll be watching.'

It was, after all, a better option than sitting still in the freezing cold. Vesta nipped back on to the street, passing a footman walking two less than energetic black Labradors. She disappeared out of sight around the corner. The houses here might be grand but there were laneways that led to rows of mews to the rear, which nowadays formed garages and sometimes accommodation for the staff or even relations who were down on their luck. London was short of housing and people would move into places they might not have considered before the war. A well-dressed man in a silver Mercedes Benz drove sharply around the corner and cut past her rather closely. Vesta held her nerve despite the fact that the cobbled street was difficult to negotiate in heels. When the car had passed, she started to count the houses until she came to the rear of the Beaumont residence.

They had done a good job on it, she thought, she'd give them that. Other places had windows that were poxed with peeling paint, especially at the back, but the Beaumont place was shipshape all round. The mews door was open and the burgundy Rolls-Royce that had passed them on the driveway at Goodwood filled the garage with only a foot either side to spare. Vesta listened, but there was no indication of movement inside the garage. In fact, the mews felt curiously still. Turning sideways, Vesta edged past the car and slipped through the door that led on to the Beaumonts' garden. Mirabelle had nerves of steel, she thought, as she perused the arrangement of doors and windows. Mirabelle would just break in but Vesta simply couldn't. She never had. Instead, she loitered, peering through the windows that overlooked the garden. The light was on in the kitchen and inside, a woman in a white cap and apron was overseeing several pans on the range. Vesta wondered what was on the menu, but she wasn't close enough to make it out. The upstairs windows were still, but she could pick out a vase of fresh flowers on a dressing table. High above, the chimneys spewed smoke into the pale sky. At least she'd established the house was in use.

Next, she turned her attention towards the garage. First, she checked the car, but the luggage had been removed and there was nothing of interest in the boot or the glove compartment. Moving on to the rest of the mews, there was a small room off the garage that housed tins of oil, a deep white sink with a dripping brass tap and some gardening equipment. At the end there was a wooden staircase so steep that it was almost a ladder. When she climbed it, she saw that it opened into what must have been the old hayloft but now served as some kind of store. Ahead of her, battered suitcases were piled at one end. Two dressmakers' dummies propped each other up as if they were the worse for wear. Behind the cases there were three heavy leather trunks. These were embossed with initials: 'D.E.B.', 'E.B.' and 'D.G.H.' Vesta smiled. Crouching, she opened them one by one. It would seem they had been used to pack away old school clothes. Enid's contained a hockey stick and a small silver cup engraved with the words 'House prize: Drama' as well as several pieces of a navy uniform. Dougie's was mostly full of sporting whites, very much like George's. A few well-worn textbooks were stacked at the bottom. A cricket ball. A leather pencil case. A long out-of-date ticket stub for a Chelsea home game. Nothing of importance.

With a shrug, Vesta moved on to the filing cabinets, the contents of which were in disarray and certainly not filed according to her own exacting standards. The first contained a mass of unsorted papers that related to the work that had been undertaken on the house – roofing receipts, surveyors' reports, delivery chits for plumbing supplies, wallpaper cuttings and paint swatches. The renovation of the house had cost a small fortune, but then Vesta could have guessed that. Getting Mirabelle's flat back into shape came with a hefty price tag, so upgrading a whole house would be prohibitive for most people. Even at a cursory glance, the bills came to ten thousand pounds. She moved on. The second filing cabinet yielded riper fruit. Carefully, Vesta leafed through a thick sheaf of correspondence as she sat on the end of one of the school trunks. Contrary to Mirabelle's understanding of the men's finances, it looked as if George Highton was in considerable trouble. He was in hot water with the taxman. The letters claimed tax payments outstanding in the sum of over £2,500 in a dispute that had been ongoing since 1952. Vesta wondered how on earth George Highton might have run up such a huge bill. Two thousand five hundred pounds was more money than Vesta and Charlie had recently paid for their new house. 'How interesting,' she mumbled, recalling the terms of his will. If Highton had run into trouble perhaps he had signed away his assets with the intention of declaring himself bankrupt. People did it. They'd had cases like that in the office. It was a dishonourable way out of financial difficulty but perhaps Highton had chosen it. She was considering this when she was startled by the sound of movement downstairs. Moving slowly, she replaced the papers, closed the cabinet drawer and crept to the head of the staircase. With her heart pounding, she crouched to peer through the banister.

Downstairs, Kamari was whistling beside the sink as he polished a set of brasses with a filthy cloth. Vesta tutted, almost unconsciously. He'd never get them gleaming that way. The sound was out before she could stop herself. Kamari turned.

'Bobby? Is that you?'

Vesta froze. Kamari peered into the garage next door, but finding that the chauffeur wasn't there, he shrugged his shoulders and returned to his work. Vesta's hands were shaking. She clutched them together. Effectively, she was now trapped in the attic. Mirabelle was far more adept at this kind of thing. She could escape from practically anywhere. Vesta cursed silently. What on earth had she been thinking? Kamari finished the brasses and moved on to oiling Mr Crowe's hickory golf clubs and scrubbing a scatter of muddy tees and some grass-smeared golf balls in the sink. He was drying these with an old piece of towel when the chauffeur popped his head through the door.

'Are you almost done?'

'You need a hand?'

'Yes.'

Kamari propped the clubs to one side and disappeared into the garage. Vesta crept silently downstairs and peered around the door frame. The chauffeur was underneath the Rolls-Royce and Kamari was handing him a spanner.

'The boss is gonna love you even more for this, Bobby, boy.' Kamari's face was lit by a grin.

'It's my job, isn't it? Seeing to the car.'

'No, he's gonna love you.' Kamari's lips formed a smooch.

'And you've never been tempted? You want to get ahead, nigger? Well, you ain't got what they're looking for. Have you? You're just soft on Mrs Enid. You *love* her and she hardly gives a sniff in your direction. As if a lady like her would care about a nigger like you.'

Kamari's grin dropped away. His lip curled in an expression of contempt. When he spoke, his voice dripped with fury. It was quite a turnaround from the persona he presented normally – the wide grin that protected him. Vesta felt almost afraid.

'If you weren't so white, I'd say you were

Kikuyu,' Kamari spat. 'You can't trust a Kikuyu. And you got that look in your eyes.'

Bobby rolled out from under the car. 'You don't look in my eyes, darkie. You got it?'

'Big white man, big big.' Kamari was undaunted.

Bobby's temper frayed. He pushed Kamari against the wall with such force that a scatter of loose plaster crumbled on to the concrete floor. 'I dunno what they see in bleeding Kenya, anyway,' he said through gritted teeth.

'Well, you never will, cos they won't take you, will they?' Kamari grinned again though it was hardly easy-going. 'Don't think I don't hear you dropping those hints. Like doodle bombs.'

'At least I get something out of it, my way.' The chauffeur rubbed his fingers together in the internationally recognised sign for money.

Kamari turned away, rolling his eyes.

Vesta ducked back towards the sink. No love lost there, she thought. And still no safe way out of the mews. She crept back up the stairs as Kamari skulked through, picked up the brasses and left through the garden door. It was odd that the two men had been taunting each other about the Beaumonts and the Crowes. In that moment it had seemed as if everything about them revolved around the people they worked for – as if being here wasn't only a job. These people seemed so tangled up with each other. Still from what Vesta knew of Enid Crowe, she didn't seem like the kind of woman about to embark on a cross-race affair. That took guts. Charlie's friends who dated white girls were hounded even more than the black men who stuck to their own kind. It was the preserve of rebels and thrill-seekers, not a pampered upper-class girl who'd never done anything. And what about the chauffeur? How many men were involved in this ring that circled Beaumont and Highton and their particular tastes?

Sniffing, Vesta realised she could smell tobacco snaking through the bare boards – after the altercation, the chauffeur was having a cigarette. Her heart still pounding, she sneaked down to take a peek. The man was standing in the laneway watching another chauffeur further along who was washing a Bentley. While he had his back to the garage, she decided to try to get away. Pressing herself against the wall, she edged round the car and stepped smartly on the cobbles. Just at that moment the chauffeur swung round. Vesta's heart skipped a beat.

'Oy! What are you doing?'

With her mind racing, Vesta tried to remain nonchalant – that, after all, is what Mirabelle would do. There was no way that the man could know she had come from the garage. In fact to him it could look as if she had walked down the lane. Just say something, she chided herself. And then the words came. 'I'm looking for the black guy. You know the one? He works for the Beaumonts?'

The chauffeur drew on his cigarette in what could only be described as an aggressive fashion as he eyed Vesta up and down. 'Whatchya want him for?'

It crossed Vesta's mind this was a good question, just as she decided she might as well push the bloke's buttons. 'I wanted to talk to him about Kenya,' she said decisively.

'Bleeding Kenya!' The chauffeur practically exploded. 'Who cares?'

'Have you been?' Vesta asked.

'I wouldn't go if they paid me double.'

'Me neither,' she admitted. 'But the Beaumonts seem to like it.'

The man's face contorted into a sour expression. He threw down the butt of his cigarette and ground it out with his heel. 'It's all monkeys and malaria and all they go on about is the stunning views. Stunning bleeding views from the cockpit of the plane.'

'I have heard it's beautiful.'

'So you're not one of them, then? Kenyan, I mean?'

'No. I'm from Bermondsey.'

The man snorted with laughter. 'Bermondsey,' he repeated. 'Yeah. You look local.'

Vesta checked her watch. 'Well, if he's not here, I better be going,' she said.

'Oh, I can fetch Kamari, if you want? He'll be sniffing around inside. He's housebroken, see.' The man's eyes were cruel.

'I can't wait. I have to get back.'

She spun on her heel and stalked up the mews, picking up her pace as she rounded the corner. On the upside, she no longer felt the cold, she thought, as she strode down the pavement, heading for the safety of the park bench. Vesta's heart rate settled down but, she noted, having to hide had been thrilling. In the park, Mirabelle hadn't moved.

'Fruitful?' she enquired.

'Yes. George Highton owes a bundle of money

to the taxman. Over two thousand pounds. And there is some suggestion that the chauffeur might be involved in, well, you know. Indecent behaviour.'

'Gosh. One does begin to wonder if there are any traditionally orientated men left.'

A wisp of a smile crossed Vesta's face. She was about to say something about the terror she'd felt, about being caught in the hayloft and having to bluff to get away when Mirabelle straightened up, straining to see beyond the railings. Vesta followed her gaze just as a hackney cab pulled to a halt outside the Beaumonts' residence.

'Well, well,' Mirabelle said, watching keenly as Enid Crowe emerged and darted through the front door. The girl had a curious expression, which Mirabelle couldn't read – was it fury or determination, she wondered. Whichever, Enid had the gait of a sulky child, her smart hairdo bobbing beneath her hat.

No sooner had Enid disappeared into the house than a butler slipped down the front steps and paid the driver before helping Mrs Beaumont on to the pavement. The poor woman lingered a moment, looking at the house as if she was entirely defeated at the prospect of going inside. One hand darted to her pearl necklace, though this time she wasn't twisting it in distress, this time she clutched the pearls as if she was holding on to them for her life. Then the butler offered his arm. The door closed with a decisive click and Mirabelle immediately got to her feet and set off at a lick along the pavement.

'Where are you going?' Vesta demanded,

following two steps behind, but Mirabelle had no time to explain. She knocked smartly on the cab window before it could pull away.

'Excuse me,' she said.

'Where to, miss?'

The driver was surprisingly elderly and bundled up in at least two thick, home-knitted sweaters with a jacket on top and a tweed flat cap. Perfectly sprightly, he jumped on to the road and rounded the car to open the door, casting a frosty look over Vesta. Mirabelle checked over her shoulder to make sure that no one in the Beaumont house had spotted her. Then she ushered Vesta on to the back seat and slipped in next to her. The driver slammed the door, retook his seat and started the engine.

'Please,' she said, 'just drive, will you?'

The man glanced back at her, but he did as she asked. At the end of the street, he paused before deciding to turn right. 'Harder than you'd reckon, making your mind up which way to go.' He smiled. 'You trying to dodge somebody?'

'Quite the reverse,' Mirabelle assured him. 'I was hoping you might be able to help me.'

'Me? Help you?'

'It's my god-daughter, you see. I'm most dreadfully worried about her.'

Vesta looked back in the direction of the Beaumont residence. Then she stared at her friend. Mirabelle really was quite extraordinary. If only she'd had this kind of imagination in dealing with the chauffeur only a few minutes before. She was sure she'd appeared shaken but perhaps he was so furious after his fight with Kamari that he hadn't noticed. The cab driver was more on the ball.

'Whatever do you mean?' The man laughed.

Mirabelle reached into her purse and pulled out a five pound note. She unfolded it ostentatiously. 'I pay highly, you see,' she said.

'Well, you've got my attention, miss. I'll say that.'

Vesta sat back, waiting to see what Mirabelle would say. This was better than the wireless, she thought. Really.

'The thing is,' Mirabelle continued, 'the poor girl has been led astray and her mother is not dealing with it well.'

'Who's this?'

'My god-daughter. Her mother is a very dear friend.'

'Well, I don't see how...'

'You just dropped them off, driver.'

The man pulled into the kerb and turned in his seat. 'Them two?' He gestured in the direction of the Beaumonts' house.

'I want you to tell me about the argument they had. You'd be doing me the most enormous favour.'

'Who says they had an argument?'

'Her Majesty says so.' Mirabelle flicked the banknote. 'I'd be terribly grateful. You see, I want to help, but to do so I need to know more than is evident. It's a family situation, you understand.'

'I dunno.' The man considered a moment. 'I mean, I don't want you thinking I eavesdrop on ladies in the back of my cab.'

'Well, of course not, but the poor girl is dreadfully distressed. I'm sure she must have raised her voice. I mean, you might not have heard anything she said, in which case you can drop us here. Vesta, dear, do you have a shilling for the fare?' Mirabelle went to put away her money.

'And you're her godmother?'

'Oh yes. Lifelong. I just want to know what I shall be walking into later, if you see what I mean? Be prepared and all that.'

'Like the Girl Guides?' The man hooted, opening his mouth wide and revealing a pink-gummed grin. Mirabelle stared blankly and within seconds the driver regained his composure. 'All right, miss,' he said, 'but it wasn't anything much. They were only arguing about some fellow.' The man put on a voice, mimicking the women. '"Now he's gone things will never be the same." That's what the girl said. And your friend, the mother, said something about money and how she hadn't expected it. Something about being left something in a will. And the girl went quite potty at that. "It's not about the money. How could it be about money? You'll just do whatever Daddy wants anyway." Furious she was. She shouted that bit. And then your friend said that the girl had never lived without money, though it seemed to me that a lady like that, well, she probably hadn't lived without money either. And the girl said something about never getting over it and that she'd had enough. Very dramatic.'

'Gosh.'

'Well, you know what females are like when they say things in temper. And then the mother said it was just as well the girl was married cos she'd shown her true colours and they all had to live with that.'

'True colours? I see. Did they mention any names?'

The man thought for a moment. 'She said, "It's all down to Michael now." The mother, not the daughter. And the girl said, "He can't drive for toffee." And the mother said it didn't matter how well he could drive, he'd just have to do it cos they could find someone else for this and that, but mostly it had to be someone they trusted.'

'Tell me, where did you pick them up?'

'They were at the House of Commons. One of the policemen flagged me down.'

'And? Anything else?'

The driver considered a moment. 'No. That was it.'

'You've been very helpful. Thank you.'

Mirabelle handed over the five pound note and he grinned widely.

'Cheers,' he said. 'Nice doing business with you.'

'Will you take us back there?'

'To the house where I dropped them?'

'No. To the Commons.'

'But shouldn't we go back and see...' Vesta objected.

Mirabelle's eyes flashed. 'No,' she said. 'This hasn't been about the women, Vesta. Let's face it. Haven't you been listening? This whole thing is about the men.'

'I knew it was Elrick Beaumont. You can't trust a politician – not a Tory.'

Mirabelle shook her head. 'Well, I don't know how you came to that conclusion. Really.' She

271

kept her voice very low. 'Besides, for heaven's sake, haven't you just learned to never say anything of importance in the back of a taxi?'

Chapter 18

Know how to listen, and you will profit even from those who talk badly

It had been some years since Mirabelle had visited the House. During the war, occasionally, she had spent a morning sitting in the Strangers' Gallery, lulled by the speeches. It had felt comforting to be close to the pulse of decisions and to know that, in sharp contrast to the regime Britain had been fighting, the people on the green leather seats had been elected to represent their constituents and were accountable, because anyone could come and hear what they had to say. If it hadn't been rude, she'd have said that there was something soporific about the House of Commons. Something settled. The gothic grandeur of Pugin's design made it seem more ancient than it was. The statues, tapestries and paintings were soothing. The movement of the river outside the leaden panes of the committee rooms and offices felt perpetually tranquil. In fact, the old place resembled a church more than anything else, though it was far larger. Certainly in the dark days of wartime Mirabelle had been more likely to seek comfort at the Palace of Westminster than at the

272

cathedral over the road. Today, the deep chime of Big Ben from the Elizabeth Tower announced her arrival and immediately drew her back to wartime days, listening to Winston Churchill at the dispatch box.

Deposited on the pavement, Vesta drew herself up and checked her coat was properly buttoned. 'I've never been inside,' she admitted. 'I've only ever seen it from the bus.'

'There's no need to be nervous. This building belongs to you. It belongs to all of us,' Mirabelle reassured her.

'Did you used to work here?'

'No. I was a secretary in Whitehall, that's all,' Mirabelle replied sadly.

Vesta looked at her friend with dubiety. Whatever Mirabelle had done during the war, she couldn't believe it ought to end with the words 'that's all'. She stood a little straighter walking inside, as a policeman in a dark cape held open the door.

'Thank you, constable,' Mirabelle breathed and, as usual, Vesta wondered, How does she know?

Inside Westminster Hall, the faint smell of bleach mingled with the scent of printed paper. The summer recess had just passed and the House had reconvened. It was lunchtime and the hallway was almost deserted. A man in a pinstriped suit wearing a bowler hat, scurried out of the door, clutching a battered black briefcase, late for a meeting. A female secretary in a pale blue suit and a Baker Boy beret, hugged a buff file to her chest as she slipped inside with only the barest nod at the policeman on duty. In a rush, she overtook Mirabelle and Vesta as she made her way across the tiled floor, tipped a wink at the doorkeeper and tripped up the stone stairs.

'Well,' Vesta hissed, 'what do we do now?'

'Follow her.' Mirabelle fell into step. 'Come along.'

The women headed up the long hallway with the sound of their heels echoing, till they came to the foot of the stone stairs where the secretary had disappeared round the corner. The doorkeeper was a young man, freshly shaven. He had the air of someone who had just completed his National Service, his military haircut not yet grown out.

'Ladies?' he said. 'Visitors, are you?'

Mirabelle adopted a lofty air. 'We're here to give evidence to the committee.'

The man picked up a clipboard and consulted it only in passing. 'The Wolfenden?'

Mirabelle nodded. As if this was somehow amusing, the doorkeeper's face assumed a supercilious air and his manner became instantly more relaxed.

'Well, they've broken for lunch.' He smirked, eyeing the women up and down. His gaze lingered on Vesta's décolletage, where a slice of dark flesh showed beneath her tippet. From his leering expression you would think she was practically naked. He licked his lips.

'Well, really,' said Mirabelle. 'Can't we go up and wait?'

The man took his time before answering. He leaned against the table and checked over his shoulder to make sure he wasn't overheard.

'What's your hurry? All the lads are wondering

what the Wolfenden's going to come up with. Morals of the nation, and that. It's been a downward spiral since the war. And, whatever comes out of it, just remember, we know what they decide first, so we should get it first, right?' He gave an exaggerated wink.

'Oh dear.' The words escaped Mirabelle's lips as she recalled what she had read about the committee's business in the paper – an examination of the laws surrounding prostitution and homosexuality. There seemed little question of the matters in which the young man was assuming she and Vesta were expert. Casting her mind back to the column in *The Times,* she remembered that the evidence the committee was to hear was considered so repugnant that there had been some discussion about whether the female committee members would be up to the job of listening to it. Quickly, she scrambled to regain lost ground. In a way, she decided, this was the best assumption the boy could have made. It didn't take more than a couple of seconds before she rounded on him. 'You have misunderstood, young man. Mrs Lewis and I are from the Ladies' Christian League. I can't believe that you mistook us for Jezebels. That is to say, all I can do is point out that you've made my case about the cesspit our nation is wading into. Mrs Lewis and I are not prostitutes.'

As Mirabelle spat the words, the doorkeeper realised his mistake. His cheeks coloured and his gaze plummeted to his boots. 'Right,' he said. 'Sorry, ma'am. It's just some of the people in attendance at that committee, the ladies and the gentlemen, for that matter–'

'I don't want to know.' Mirabelle cut him off. 'Perhaps we could get a cup of tea in one of the dining rooms? I'm sure this dreadful assumption of yours won't come to light when we give evidence. But that's the problem, isn't it? I mean, were we to loosen moral constraints, men will have the right to make such assumptions. Why, if my husband could–'

The man fumbled with the clipboard. 'I'm sorry,' he cut in. 'I didn't mean to offend any-one...'

But Mirabelle was not to be stopped. 'You, sir, have offended God. Which is far more important. And worse, you have been so busy cavorting that you've succumbed to a dereliction of duty. Had you not been eyeing up Mrs Lewis perhaps you might have remembered to ask our names. This is the House of Commons, young man. You are in Her Majesty's service. I tell you, when I worked in Whitehall during the war ... well, we shan't go into it, but the men on duty here were spruce. Stand straight, won't you? Eyes ahead.'

The boy stood to attention, his expression now betraying his terror at this protracted onslaught.

'That's better.' Mirabelle raised her eyes heaven-wards and took Vesta's arm. 'Come along, dear. Let's try to settle ourselves before we have to go in.'

As they climbed the stairs, Mirabelle allowed herself the barest smirk. Then rounding the corner at the top, Vesta's eye was caught by the ornate tapestries and the huge stained glass windows. It seemed that there was no surface in this building that wasn't painted, gilded or carved. Ahead of them, St Stephen's Hall was skirted by a long row of statues that led into the central lobby.

'The Wolfenden Committee. Ladies' Christian League,' Mirabelle informed the next doorkeeper loftily. 'We're early, of course. It being lunch.'

This man was far older and more interested in his newspaper than testimony relating to the morals of the nation. He waved the women through with hardly a second glance. This lobby acted like a crossroads. Ornate offshoots headed in all directions.

'It's very grand,' Vesta hissed, peering towards the double doors to the Commons Chamber.

'Oh this is nothing. You should see inside the Lords. There's a golden ceiling. Honestly.'

The girl looked upwards. Even ungilded, the vaulted ceiling was impressive. It seemed impossible that it could get grander. 'Wow,' she said. 'What on earth is the Wolfenden Committee, anyway?' It seemed Vesta was taking things in slowly.

'It's examining gross indecency.'

'And that bloke thought we were...'

'He thought you were a prostitute. I'm not quite sure what he thought I was up to, at my age.'

'You're not so old. Perhaps he reckoned you for a madam,' Vesta rejoined. 'You've got some nerve, Mirabelle.'

'No more than he had.'

'Well, we're in now. So what is it that we're looking for?'

'Elrick Beaumont's office. Every member has an office. This way.' She pulled Vesta towards the corridor directly ahead.

Through the double doors another keeper

moved forwards solicitously. 'Madam?'

'We're giving evidence to the Wolfenden Committee but not for another hour. We were told we could find my constituency MP, Elrick Beaumont, in the members' dining room. He left a message to join him.'

'Of course. Shall I take you through?'

'No. There's no need. I know Mr Beaumont – he's a personal friend. I'm sure the staff in the dining room will help us. I've been here before.'

'Yes, I thought I recognised you.'

Mirabelle allowed herself an enigmatic smile. The smell of cigarette smoke and hot bread rose as they approached the first of the dining rooms, but now out of sight of the last doorkeeper, she didn't stop. 'The libraries are along here somewhere and the committee rooms are upstairs,' she whispered for Vesta's benefit.

'And the offices?'

'All over.'

'What's downstairs?' The girl's eyes were drawn to a dark and archaic-looking stairwell.

'The crypt. There's a chapel.'

'So...'

'Upwards. I think we want to go up.'

They took the first set of stairs. As they climbed higher, the windows became smaller but still, there was a view of the Thames and far below they could make out several members drinking brandy on the terrace, catching what might be had of the autumn sunshine. It was impossible to tell who was who, the men forming a collection of dark hats amid the wisps of cigarette smoke. Up here there was a warren of corridors. The carpets were thick and every so often a heavy leather chair had been placed outside one of the doors so that applicants could sit and wait.

'We'll never find it.'

'We'll ask when we bump into someone,' Mirabelle insisted.

Sure enough, as they continued, a man juggling a high stack of files rounded the corner ahead.

'Excuse me,' Mirabelle accosted him. 'I'm new here and I've to go to Elrick Beaumont's office.'

'New? What do you mean?'

'I'm a secretary. These corridors are rather labyrinthine. I got lost, I'm afraid.'

The man peered around the side of the files, his thick glasses shifting down the bridge of his nose. In his top pocket an ebony pipe balanced precariously as if it might tumble any minute. 'And who is this?' He tipped his chin at Vesta.

'Vesta Lewis,' Vesta introduced herself, holding out her hand. 'How do you do?'

'I can't shake.' The man swayed the files in her direction. 'Are you working for Beaumont too? I know he's fond of his African connections.'

Vesta was about to deliver her line about Bermondsey when Mirabelle cut in. 'Exactly,' she said. 'Mrs Lewis comes to us from Nairobi.'

'The Mau Mau,' the man replied. 'I mean, what to do about the uprising? It's going on too long, wouldn't you say. I'm just not sure how we should tackle it.'

Vesta bit her lip. 'More of what we're already doing, I'd say.' This transpired to be a good guess.

'Quite. I mean, we can't let them just overrun the whites, can we?' The man's tone was earnest.

'We have to put them down in the end, whatever it takes. We'll come out on top, of course.'

'Well,' Mirabelle cut in, 'that's certainly what Mr Beaumont is hoping. As you know, he has interests there.'

A strange look crossed the man's face. 'It's a shame about his son.'

'Yes.'

'You're on the wrong corridor, by the way,' he offered. 'Left and left again and you'll probably recognise it. Don't worry – everyone gets lost at the beginning. It took me ages to get used to the old place. I hope to meet you again.'

'Thank you.'

When they turned left the corridors began to look almost domestic, painted thickly in cream with a few watercolours of Victorian politicians mounted on the walls. Turning left once more, they passed a low bookcase housing leather-bound books on the subject of jurisprudence. The fourth door along bore Elrick Beaumont's name. Mirabelle paused before knocking. There was no reply. She tried the handle but the door was locked.

'Keep a lookout,' she instructed Vesta, as she withdrew her lockpicks. It took her only a few seconds to spring the door.

Inside, the room smelled of newspapers and dry leather. There were two windows, one either side of a small fireplace in which a single-bar electric fire was set. On Beaumont's desk there were pictures of his family – Mrs Beaumont reading a book, Dougie and Enid playing tennis and one of George Highton bent over the engine of a car, looking up with a smear of oil on his cheek.

'I didn't have Highton down as a mechanic.' Mirabelle showed Vesta as she rounded the desk and started to search the drawers, which yielded the usual array of pencils and rubber bands as well as a file of draft legislation. The papers were loosely bound and Mirabelle flicked through to find the titles: The first was called 'The National Health Service Act (1946)'. Reading what Beaumont had scribbled, she realised he had been questioning costs. 'Talk to Winston' was written next to one clause, which had been underlined, and then, further down, he had written 'Nothing but filthy Socialism' followed by 'We Must Change This'. The Tories had opposed the health service from the beginning. Mirabelle tried to stay calm – this was no time to get caught up in politics. She pursed her lips and moved on. Beneath the bill there were more papers relating to the Army Act upon which Elrick appeared to have written notes in the margins of a similar reactionary nature. Unsurprisingly, his main concern appeared to be to keep army action in British colonies as unregulated as possible. In another drawer there was a note inviting Beaumont for a drink with a fellow member, several cards expressing condolences on the death of his son, and a bill from a gentlemen's club.

'If Dougie Beaumont funded this for his father, I'm not sure he spent his money wisely. Look at this place,' Vesta tutted, running her finger along the dusty window ledge. 'The whole building feels like a filthy old boys' school.' Mirabelle was accustomed to such places. Vesta had noticed it again and again – she was at home in Cambridge or in a posh hotel in St James's or in the British Embassy in Paris. Just as she was at home here. Mirabelle did not comment, instead she sank into the leather chair behind Elrick Beaumont's desk.

'I'm still interested in how Dougie made his money,' she said. 'I mean the family owned the house already but he revived it. And paying for a parliamentary career, even if your office isn't very impressive, is costly too.'

'And Christmas in Kenya must lay them back a pretty penny.'

'I'm not buying this golden boy image. Winning races and gambling on the stock market.' Mirabelle felt in her handbag. 'Not entirely. They're hiding something. More than one thing.' She brought out the silver box she'd taken from under Dougie Beaumont's mattress. It had been on her mind. 'This belonged to Dougie Beaumont.' She flipped open the lid.

Vesta peered inside. 'What is it?'

'Cocaine.'

'The stuff the dentist prescribes?'

'Yes. I found traces of it at the place on Bleeding Heart Yard too. In a snuffbox in the bathroom.'

'You think Beaumont and Highton were selling drugs?'

'It's possible they might have been smuggling drugs. They travelled enough and it's potentially lucrative though I don't know if it would generate the kind of cash they needed. So far, it's the only thing I can think of.'

Vesta leaned against the desk and shook her

head. 'The boys like a smoke – Charlie's friends. Or opium pills – you can get the doctor to prescribe them. Cocaine, though, just isn't so popular. I don't see anyone getting killed over, well, something you can pick up at the chemist if you have a friendly dentist. I mean, if it was cigarettes. That would make more sense. You could make a fortune off bringing fags in. Besides, if you think about it – these men were hale and hearty right up to the moment they died – they definitely haven't spent a lot of time lounging around in opium dens.' Mirabelle shrugged and Vesta continued. 'In the taxi you said they'd cut out the women and you thought whatever is going on was between the men alone. Is this what you meant?'

'Not exactly. It's only the money seems to benefit the men most – they were living it up, weren't they? Beaumont and his flash career and Dougie and George and their international playboy lifestyle. The secrets belong to them. As far as I can see, Enid and her mother get a nice house to live in and that's about it. But that's not the only thing on my mind. The murders are very male. A woman wouldn't have been able to garrote Dougie Beaumont and then hoist him on his chandelier. At least, it doesn't strike me as a woman's way to murder someone. Does it strike you?'

Vesta shook her head.

'And smashing George Highton to death with a golf club? I mean, a woman could do that, but really, I can't see it in our players. These men were a tight team – a club, if you like. Dougie and George were more like brothers than anything else, even if they'd had a spat. And Elrick Beaumont might be a bully, but sometimes it takes a bully to hold things together. I think this whole thing was a family concern.'

'And where does Michael Crowe fit in?'

'I don't know yet, but he's as close to a son as Beaumont has left. And it looks as if they are expecting him to take up Dougie's mantle. Remember what Mrs Beaumont said to Enid: he'll have to drive. Even if he isn't any good at it. As if the driving, winning the races isn't the important thing. There's this sense of a family business to it all.' Mirabelle's eye fell on a framed print over the fireplace – an old political cartoon with Mr Punch peering from behind a mask – his own face even more grotesque than the one with which he was covering up. 'It's all about keeping up appearances. And you've got a point. Where on earth is Michael Crowe? The women are back at the house and Elrick Beaumont is here but where's the only foot soldier the Beaumonts have left? What's he up to?'

Vesta lifted the lid on Elrick Beaumont's leather-inlaid secretaire. 'Ooh,' she squealed enthusiastically, pulling out a book and laying it on the desktop. 'It's a diary.'

Mirabelle cast her eyes upwards. Vesta was easily distracted. Nonetheless, she turned the pages till she got to the beginning of September. The diary, it seemed, was for parliamentary business. The summer recess lay annoyingly blank but the months ahead looked busy. After the General Election that spring, the House had a lot of business to complete. Elrick Beaumont sat on several committees, though not, Mirabelle noted, Lord

Wolfenden's inquiry. Flipping forwards, she noticed that the following Friday was blanked out with 'FUNERAL?' in black capitals to which an 'S' had been added in blue. The family clearly hoped to bury both Dougie and George on the same day. Further on, on a date in mid-December, Beaumont had noted 'Heathrow to N' which Mirabelle took to mean 'Nairobi'. Busy people like the Beaumonts hadn't the time to travel by ship.

'What about last week?' Vesta peered over.

'The dates of the murders?'

She nodded. Mirabelle flipped the pages. 'Well, on the Sunday night when Dougie Beaumont died he was at a dinner at Boodles. The night of Highton's death there's nothing. But he has an alibi for Dougie's murder, depending on the time dinner ended.'

She sat back in Beaumont's chair to consider. Vesta flipped through more pages.

'Strange,' she commented. 'I mean a man like Beaumont must go out to dinner several times a week but it isn't noted. This month he's only put in that one dinner.'

The girl lay the diary to one side, checked the now-empty secretaire and moved on to a cabinet, which housed decanters of brandy and several packets of Brazil nuts, a smart leather case of cigars and a spare silk tie, lest Elrick Beaumont should need to change. Lastly, she searched Beaumont's overcoat, which was hanging on a peg behind the door. Smiling, she pulled out an *A–Z* from the inside pocket.

'That's an odd thing for a man who has a

285

driver,' she commented. 'Look, Mirabelle, this page is turned down at the corner.'

Mirabelle took the book and stared. The page included Fleet Street, Bleeding Heart Yard and all the streets nearby. 'So he knows about their hideaway,' she said. 'Well, that makes sense, I suppose. I mean Mrs Beaumont knows about the will.' She stared at the map, running her finger over the main road at Farringdon. 'And just that one dinner in the diary. Lord, it must have killed him.'

'What? What is it?'

'I've been an idiot, that's all,' Mirabelle said. 'Drugs! Honestly! What was I thinking? Beaumont wouldn't let his son be killed over something so tawdry. No. Whatever it is, it has to be much more important. We've been looking at all the wrong things. You're right – you come here and it's like an old school. You go to Goodwood and it feels as if everything happening there is important just because it's grand. But not everything deserves the gravitas it's accorded. It depends how you look at it, and we've been looking at it back to front. That little house most of all. I mean why is it there, Vesta?' Mirabelle jumped to her feet and stuffed the *A–Z* back into Elrick Beaumont's pocket. 'I've been a fool, but now I can see a way to follow the money. A real one.'

'How?' Vesta said. 'Tell me.'

But Mirabelle had already left the office and was heading back down the corridor. When she got in one of these moods there was nothing for it but to follow. Vesta sighed and, after casting a

286

glance back at Beaumont's office to make sure they'd left no trace of their visit, she hurried to follow her friend.

Chapter 19

We have the best government money can buy

Mirabelle didn't like to admit that she would be better off with McGregor's help. Back on the pavement, outside Westminster Hall, she silenced Vesta as she thought through the situation. She comforted herself that at least she'd left him the dead men's wills, so when she got in touch he ought to be in a good mood, no matter that she had abandoned him in the country. As she took Vesta's arm and crossed the road towards the Tube station, she slipped into a red telephone box, motioning Vesta to wait.

'The coaching inn at Goodwood,' she instructed the operator.

In due course, Ella's voice trilled down the wire. 'Oh hello, miss,' she said, when Mirabelle greeted her. 'Did you leave something behind?'

'Sort of.' Mirabelle smiled. 'Superintendent McGregor.'

'Oh, he left a while ago with the gentleman from customs.'

'Customs?' Mirabelle's mind raced. 'Did they leave their things?'

'No, miss. They settled up.'

'Do you know where they went, Ella? Did they leave together?'

'Superintendent McGregor gave the chap a lift in his car. They never said where to.'

'And what was the chap's name, please?'

'Hang on. I'll check in the register.' There was the sound of fumbling and then Ella's voice returned. 'Mr Mayhew. The signature looks like Charles.'

'I see. Thank you.'

The phone clicked. The tip she had given to Ella had been worth every penny. Mirabelle leaned against the glass panes and watched Vesta staring up at Elizabeth Tower at such an angle that she looked as if she might fall over. It struck Mirabelle that Elrick Beaumont had simply palmed everything off on the younger generation. He'd got them to do his dirty work. He didn't even own a share in the car. Not officially at any rate. She felt her temper rise. She had been looking at everything from the wrong direction and to get back on track it would be important to stay calm. Reuben was right – it was Beaumont who was in charge all right. She picked up the receiver again and asked for the excise service. Once she was connected she asked for Charles Mayhew.

'Mr Mayhew is out of the office.'

'Do you know where he went?'

'I can take a message.'

'No. Thank you.'

Mirabelle hung up. She had two choices and she weighed them carefully, feeling the chill as it seeped through the cold glass and into the fabric of her tweed coat. Then she picked up the phone again and asked the operator for the *Telegraph*. She visualised the receptionist on the front desk picking up the handset.

'Hello. I visited your office a couple of hours ago. I came to see Reuben Vinestock. Could you put me through to him, please?'

'I'm afraid he's out to lunch,' the girl trilled.

'Would you just check upstairs? At his desk?'

The girl's tone relaxed. 'Actually, miss, he really is out this time. He left only a few minutes after he'd come back to the office.'

'After I said goodbye to him?'

'Yes.'

'Alone?'

'Yes, miss.'

'And he hasn't been back since?'

'No. You're not the only person who has been looking for him either. He had a lunch appointment with a friend and the gentleman was none too pleased.'

'You mean someone came to pick him up?'

'Yes. Mr Crowe. He's often around the office.'

'Goodness. And he wasn't happy, you say? I do hope he wasn't rude.'

'Oh we get it all in here. He was difficult, that's all. I mean it's hardly my fault if Mr Vinestock leaves and doesn't say where he's going.'

'What did Mr Crowe do?'

'He shouted. Then he used the telephone to call for a car. He wasn't even pleased when that arrived. I wouldn't like to be his chauffeur, I can tell you that.'

'Was it a Rolls-Royce? A burgundy one?'

'Yes. Very smart. He sent it away. Berated the poor driver something terrible. Said he had no brain but at least he had muscle. Can you imagine?'

'Well, that's just unnecessary, isn't it? Thanks for your help.'

Mirabelle replaced the receiver and let the information sink in. Outside the phonebox, Vesta waved at her as if to say, *I'm here*. Mirabelle pushed open the door.

'Where exactly was the solicitor's office?' she checked.

'What?'

'The office that the Beaumonts used? Mrs Beaumont knew about the bequest when she came home in the taxi. Presumably she had been there.'

Vesta thought for a moment. 'Bell Yard. Near Lincoln's Inn.'

Mirabelle nodded and made her decision. 'We can walk there from Bleeding Heart Yard if we have to.'

'I suppose.' Vesta's forehead wrinkled.

'It's all within walking distance, in fact. I must have been a fool not to see it. And if McGregor is coming up to town with Mr Mayhew, which I assume he will, he is going to turn up at one of these places, at least.'

Vesta's eyebrows raised expectantly as Mirabelle ducked back into the phone box and raised a finger as if to say, *Just one minute*, and then dialled again for the Blue Door and was put through to Mr Golding.

'Ah, Miss Bevan,' he said, his tenor soothing. Mirabelle remembered how much comfort she had taken in Mr Golding's unflappable nature on the many occasions when she had called him in her earlier career. 'How nice to hear from you,' he said smoothly. 'Your package is ready. Where should I have it sent?'

'I'm heading for Farringdon. Is there somewhere you would recommend?'

'Let me see. There's a café on Greville Street. It's close to Farringdon Road. It's a discreet place – nothing fancy, just Formica tables. I can have it dropped to you there. About half an hour.'

'Thank you.' Mirabelle hung up.

As she stepped on to the pavement and raised her hand to hail the next passing taxi, Vesta fell in behind her.

'Well. Where are we going?'

'Lunch,' Mirabelle replied decisively, as the cab pulled up. 'But we can't talk about it until we're there.'

Vesta checked her watch. Lunch was indeed overdue. 'Couldn't we get a bus?' she suggested. 'I mean, if it meant we could discuss things on the way.'

'You can't talk about this kind of thing on a bus, Vesta,' Mirabelle said, as if the girl was completely mad.

'Well, where can we speak?'

Mirabelle leaned forward and gave the driver instructions to drop them at the end of Greville Street.

'In the park, if we're sure we're not being followed,' she said. 'Or over the telephone. Sometimes.'

Vesta turned, her eyes were hot with such fury

291

that Mirabelle laughed out loud. Vesta folded her arms across her ample chest. 'Well really.'

'Shh,' Mirabelle instructed with a nod towards the driver as the taxi set off along the river. 'We'll get there soon. I promise.'

The coffee shop on Greville Street was almost deserted as Mirabelle and Vesta took a table in the corner and a grumpy waitress with her hair tied in a pale purple scarf came to take their order. The walls were decorated with posters that were peeling at the edges but apart from this the place was spotlessly clean. The sound of a wireless at low volume was set to a music channel somewhere to the rear. At the other side of the room an old man, who looked as if he was a tramp, nursed a long-cold cup of coffee. At the table next to him, a woman dressed in black was reading a copy of *Bonjour Tristesse*. She sighed as she turned the pages.

'What do you want?' the waitress asked in an offhand manner.

'Tea,' Vesta started, 'and a filled roll.'

'What kind of roll?'

'Ham?'

The girl shook her head. 'We don't do ham cos of the Jews. The Yids don't come in otherwise. I've got egg or cheese.'

Mirabelle ordered one round of each and Vesta craned to look at the biscuits that were laid on a thick green plate on the counter. 'And one of those,' she added, pointing to an iced shortbread with half a glacé cherry on top. 'Unless you want one too?' she checked with Mirabelle.

Mirabelle declined and the girl walked back to the counter and disappeared behind a large urn from which there emanated copious amounts of steam as she made the tea.

'Well?' Vesta whispered, looking around. 'I think we're OK to speak here, don't you?'

Mirabelle paused. 'All right,' she replied. 'It's terribly complicated, though. The Beaumonts have a rather unusual family business. And they have a set-up that is predicated on misdirection.'

'Try me.'

'Well, you look at the family and you see a strong father but one kind enough to take in a Blitz orphan. You see new money ladled on top of old debts. The house in Belgravia is top class. Then there's the Rolls-Royce. Mrs Beaumont's jewellery and so on. After you've taken in the money, you see these hopelessly glamorous young men travelling the world with their passion – completely invested in racing cars. Groundbreakers, really, with smart ideas. But the men, well, most of that is only a front. They're just like Edith, really – the way she was when I first saw her. She seemed too small a person – an ordinary woman living inside a glamorous shell. Not a woman, really, more a child. I should have taken greater note of that.'

Mirabelle fell silent as the waitress served the food. Vesta poured the tea and regarded the cheese roll. 'Have you got any pickle?' she asked.

'You should've said.' The girl disappeared back to the counter.

Mirabelle picked up her egg roll and took a delicate bite. Vesta stirred a spoonful of sugar into her cup as the waitress returned with a smear of what looked like Branston pickle on a side plate.

'There,' she said.

Vesta scraped it into the roll. 'Go on.' She nodded.

'None of these people are the way they seem. You see, after the war, the Beaumonts solved a problem they'd had for a while. They were short of cash and Dougie made a very fortunate friendship in that regard. He sealed the deal by using his sister – he married her off to Michael Crowe, who is just as involved as the rest of them. His marriage to Enid tied him in. So they were a team, you see. The thing is that Dougie had found a way to make money. A gravy train. But all that happy family stuff. I mean it was only a cover. Elrick Beaumont is a bully. He needs people to dominate and he's dominated all of them. He got exactly what he wants.' Mirabelle stared at her cup of tea. 'That's why he took in George Highton. Highton was just someone else to bully. Someone he could bend to his will, if you want to be old-fashioned about it. All the members of the Beaumont clan had a difficult childhood, to put it mildly. And my guess is that it wasn't only beatings. There's a certain kind of man who needs to dominate absolutely. Do you know what I mean, Vesta?'

Vesta put down the cheese roll and swallowed. She felt sick. Mirabelle continued.

'What that meant was that the children stuck together – don't you see? I mean Dougie and George and Edith – they were united in their troubles at the mercy of this bully – this monster. They tried to protect each other and I suspect

294

they tried to protect Mrs Beaumont too. And that's why they stayed even after they were grown. I mean, she's their mother – hopeless but they love her.'

'And even now? I mean, they're old enough. If he did what you said...'

Mirabelle's eyes were limpid. 'I'm sure they talked about getting away. They may even have intended to. But they couldn't leave Mrs Beaumont and the truth is that now she is the only innocent party. Those situations, they're more difficult to leave than you'd think. Children from happy families grow up and make their own lives because the home is happy, but children from unhappy families ... haven't you noticed? They keep trying to work out their problems over and over. Even if they leave home, the unhappiness isn't over. It haunts them. Anyway, the boys got themselves out physically, if not financially. They were lovers and friends. A team. And Edith was their sidekick, really, and probably marrying Michael protected her to some degree. Elrick Beaumont may well have been holding their sexuality over them – after all the boys would end up behind bars if he gave evidence against them. Not that he would – not while they were all making money. So ostensibly they were having a glamorous life. Something most people dream of. And that was all fine until George and Dougie fell out.'

'You mean their lovers' tiff?'

'I don't think it was a lovers' tiff exactly.'

'You think George killed Dougie?'

'Oh no. He threatened Dougie and they fought, but he didn't kill him. He'd never do that. The problem was that Dougie had changed. He had a new interest, I expect, outside the world of parties and fast cars. He'd found something. Something of his own. Something he cared about, I guess. Whatever it was, that caused friction because their whole adult lives and even in late childhood they'd stuck together like glue, not a hair's breadth between them. There was trouble in paradise.'

Vesta put her head to one side. She was about to ask another question when the café door opened and a bell chimed. The young man who entered was unremarkable in every way. He headed straight for their table.

'Miss Bevan?'

'Yes.'

He reached into his pocket and slid an envelope on to the Formica tabletop. 'If you'd told me there was a sting on, ma'am, I'd have come the other way,' he said.

'A sting?' Mirabelle questioned him.

'Round the corner. I spotted at least four policemen.'

'In uniform?'

'No. Plain clothes, but obviously trained by the Met, rather than us. There's a van parked just off the main road with more men in it.'

Mirabelle's eyes darted. She gestured him to sit down. 'I better have a look.' She got to her feet. 'Would you stay with Mrs Lewis for a few moments?'

The man removed his hat and dropped into a chair.

'Would you like a cuppa?' Vesta offered.

'Actually, I'm parched.'

Out on the street, Mirabelle walked smartly to the corner and hovered, taking in the scene. Most people would hardly have noticed but there were men placed at various intervals. One was casually smoking a cigarette in a doorway, another stood in a first-floor window, just far enough away from the glass, half hidden by a curtain. Judging by the way they had positioned themselves, they seemed focused on a jewellery shop halfway up the street. Mirabelle walked towards it. She loitered at the window examining a tray of diamond and emerald brooches. Her mother had a fondness for emeralds. Through the window, behind the display, the shop appeared empty of customers. A young girl sat on a high stool brushing a velvet pad before she arranged half a dozen gold watches on it. Velvet, Mirabelle thought. That was it. Of course. The story was slowly coming together. Small clues. Things she'd noticed but not understood. She clicked open the door and the girl jumped to her feet.

'Good afternoon.'

'Yes, miss.' The girl came forward. 'Can I help you?'

'In the window there is an emerald and diamond brooch – might I look at it, please?'

'Of course.'

As the girl went to retrieve the pad, Mirabelle peered towards the back of the shop where an open archway revealed a safe crowned with a couple of decorative porcelain clocks, a Sèvres vase and a pile of papers. To the side there was a set of steep stairs.

'Is there more jewellery upstairs?'

297

'No, miss. That's just our workshop and the office.' The girl placed the pad of brooches on the counter. 'Which one was it?'

Mirabelle pointed to a modern geometric design. 'That's a beautiful emerald in the centre – nice colour,' the girl commented as she pulled it out. 'Would you like to try it on?'

Mirabelle was about to reach for the brooch when the door to the shop opened and McGregor strode in. 'Darling!' he sounded bluff. 'We were supposed to have a bite of lunch before we went shopping.'

'I couldn't help it. This caught my eye,' Mirabelle batted back.

'I'm starving. Positively ravenous.' The superintendent grinned. 'Buying something like this takes time – we want to consider it properly. Why don't we eat first and come back later?'

'Well, we're here now, Alan.' Mirabelle pinned the brooch to the tweed of her coat. She wanted to see how desperate he was to get her out of there. 'Of course, I'd probably only wear it in the evening,' she said casually.

McGregor put his arm around her waist firmly. 'I'm sure the lady will put it aside. Just for a couple of hours.'

Mirabelle handed back the jewellery. 'Oh all right.' She let him rush her out.

As the door closed, McGregor guided her sternly up the pavement, over the road and into a public house almost opposite. It was hardly the West End. Inside, there were no tables and the walls and ceiling were stained ochre with cigarette smoke. The barman sat sullenly smoking as he fidgeted with his pouch of tobacco and stared into the distance, only occasionally seeming to notice the policeman who was stationed behind the door.

'We don't serve women,' he said gruffly.

'She doesn't want to be served,' McGregor snapped, pushing Mirabelle into the snug. Inside, Charles Mayhew got to his feet.

'What are you doing here?' McGregor couldn't contain himself.

'Same as you. I'm on the trail of the Beaumonts. Or should that be Michael Crowe? When I realised there was a sting in place, I assumed it was you. I went into the shop because it seemed the easiest way to make contact. I didn't know where you were watching from. It's better we share information. Isn't that what we agreed?'

McGregor snorted angrily.

'Miss Bevan, isn't it?' Charles Mayhew offered his hand. Mirabelle shook it. 'I saw you at the inn in Goodwood,' he said. 'Superintendent McGregor assured me that you had no interest in this matter.'

'Did he? Gosh. I can't imagine why.'

Mayhew checked his watch. Behind him, the etched window of the snug overlooked the jeweller's. The shop could be easily viewed between the opaque strips of glass. 'I'm afraid we can't have you on-board,' he said. 'We're all set up. We've put in months of work. Eighteen months in fact. What you did was very dangerous, walking into the shop like that. You might have spoiled our whole operation. If Mr Crowe arrived, even had he seen you in the street, he would have been suspicious.'

Mirabelle ignored this point. 'When did the Beaumonts first come to your attention, Mr Mayhew?'

'Almost two years ago and quite by chance. The Mount Pleasant sorting office came across a package Mrs Crowe had sent from Nairobi.'

'Did it contain diamonds?'

'Very good. It happens now and then – an upper-class woman buys luxury goods on holiday and posts them home. Mostly the women don't even realise that there is tax due. We pick up the parcels coming in and bill them. In this case, it was careless of Mrs Crowe. When we realised how often the Beaumonts visited Kenya, we decided to keep an eye on them. The scale turned out to be rather astonishing. I still don't understand, given how many diamonds her brother and husband have smuggled into the country, why Mrs Crowe bothered with that paltry packet. I'm just glad that she did.'

'My suspicion is that she feels left out, Mr Mayhew. They don't appear to let either Mrs Crowe or her mother in on much.'

Mayhew shifted, his eyes darting to the street. He ran his hand through his shock of blond hair. 'Maybe,' he said.

'You'll be glad to get Crowe in custody. I imagine it was his idea in the first place. He's the one who is from Africa, after all.'

'Yes. When Michael Crowe met Dougie Beaumont during their National Service, he must have realised the possibilities. Diamonds are readily available in Uganda and easy to bring into British Kenya. Over there it's cheap, but here –

the stones are worth between fifteen and twenty times the going rate if you can get them into Europe. When Dougie established himself on the racing circuit they found a way to do that. It took us a while to figure out how they were doing it. We searched the car covertly on two occasions and didn't find anything.'

'How did they do it?'

'In the sump oil. They're clever, I'll give them that. And dangerous. Crowe in particular.'

'I'd say he met his match in Elrick Beaumont. He probably married Enid for good measure – to give him leverage.'

'It certainly made it all very tidy. I must say. Quite some racket.'

'It will be difficult for the ladies. Losing their men like this – at once. Beaumont and Highton dead and now you're going to arrest Crowe.'

'And Elrick Beaumont. Don't leave him out. I have men on the way to the Commons now. We've been following the Beaumont clan for a long time, both here and abroad. Elrick kept his hands relatively clean – let his boys do the dirty work but we can make something stick. Some of the places Mr Beaumont went, he'd have been hard pushed not to realise what his sons were up to.'

'Adopted son. Son. And son-in-law.'

'Quite.'

'When did you realise, Miss Bevan?'

'About the diamonds? Half an hour ago when I looked at the map. Hatton Garden, you see. I mean, what else would you be selling if you based yourself near here? And then I remembered

George Highton had a velvet tablecloth.'

'What?'

'Dark velvet – he'd have needed it to sort the stones.' Mirabelle cast her eyes towards the shop over the road. 'Is that where they make the sale?'

'Yes. They arrive twice a year, as far as we can make out. Spring and autumn. Regular as clockwork.'

'Do you have someone inside?'

'No. It's almost impossible. They're all Jewish, you see.'

'The dealers?'

'Some of them don't even speak English. It's like a foreign country in the back rooms. You wouldn't know you were in London.'

'Mr Crowe generally brings a translator, I imagine.'

Mayhew nodded.

'He has his chauffeur with him today, though. His regular guy seems to have let him down.'

'Lucky for him, given the circumstances.'

Mayhew leaned forwards as finally there was a movement on the street and Michael Crowe turned the corner with his driver beside him. They must have abandoned the Rolls somewhere and walked. Crowe was wearing dark glasses and carrying a tan briefcase with a large brass lock.

'They'll get away with the money, won't they? I mean the money they've spent?'

'There's no time to explain now, Miss Bevan. I'm sorry.' Mayhew flicked the light switch on and off in the snug and the man in the doorway across the road fell in ahead of Mr Crowe just as another fellow appeared from nowhere and fell in behind the driver. McGregor turned to leave.

'You're supposed to be investigating a murder, Alan. Two murders, in fact. And neither of those crimes were about this. I mean, the diamonds. All this is incidental – you do realise that? Crowe has an alibi, doesn't he? And so does Elrick Beaumont.'

'We'll get to that,' McGregor said, as he made for the door. 'Please, Mirabelle, just stay here.'

Mayhew followed him. She watched through the window as, across the road, Crowe paused at the entrance to the jewellery shop. The street was coming alive with plain-clothes policemen. One man grabbed the driver, who lashed out. Crowe realised what was happening too late and tried to run, but he was apprehended before he could make it as far as the other side of the street. Mirabelle leaned against the window as a police van rounded the corner and Mayhew grabbed Crowe's leather briefcase and sprang the lock with a penknife. From his expression it was clear that he found what he had expected – a large consignment of diamonds, sieved from the sump oil of Dougie Beaumont's car the day before in Harrison's garage. Plain-clothes policemen were now pouring into the jewellery shop, disappearing through the arch at the back and heading upstairs to apprehend whoever Crowe had intended to meet. On the pavement, Crowe looked furious. Mirabelle didn't like to think what he'd do if you crossed him – if you weren't a policeman, that is. 'They didn't kill Dougie because of this,' she said, low, under her breath. 'Nor George either. This is money – that's all.' But there was no one to hear

her. Outside, McGregor slipped handcuffs on to
Crowe's wrists, still miles away from solving either
of the murders. There was no point in waiting. As
Mirabelle left the snug, the barman looked up
with a sneer.

'Is there another way out of here?' she asked.

He gestured towards the rear. 'There's a lane
out there,' he said, 'past the outhouse.'

'Thanks,' said Mirabelle. 'I hope they're paying
you well.'

Chapter 20

*Give every man your ear
but few your voice*

It always amazed Mirabelle how contained
trouble could be. Something might happen on
one street and yet, round the corner it was business as usual, people unaware, going about their
business. Even when alarm bells set off, pedes-
trians merely looked up as if the sound was
falling from the sky. If they couldn't see anything,
they just carried on. Mirabelle slipped back into
the café where the woman was still reading her
book, the tramp was still nursing his cold coffee
and Vesta was sitting with tears streaming down
her face at the table with the man Mr Golding
had sent with the parcel. The poor fellow looked
embarrassed. In his line of work, people seldom
showed any kind of emotion. Mirabelle removed

a linen handkerchief from her bag and handed it to Vesta.

'You opened it, then?'

Vesta nodded but couldn't get out any words. A sob emanated from her lips. Mirabelle sat down and shuffled through the first few photographs. Her face betrayed nothing but she didn't want to continue.

'Thank you,' she said to the man. 'You better get on.'

He got to his feet gratefully and left, the bell attached to the door clanging behind him. Mirabelle deposited a few coins on the table to pay for the largely uneaten sandwiches. 'We better get on too,' she said gently.

'Where?' Vesta managed to get out with a sniff.

'It's not far.'

Back on the street, Vesta at least managed to stop sobbing. She followed as Mirabelle cut around the block and into Bleeding Heart Yard. The shutters on George Highton's place were open and the lights downstairs were on. Inside, they could make out movement and it appeared that several of the books on the shelves in the sitting room had been removed. Mirabelle knocked on the door and Vesta hovered behind her. The girl's fingers were quivering as she clung to the handkerchief, wrenching it between her fingers.

'I don't understand,' she said.

Mirabelle turned. There wasn't time to explain and besides she wasn't sure where to start. 'It's just as I said, Dougie Beaumont changed. He found something else. Something important.' She held up the envelope. 'These pictures shook up everything, you see.'

Vesta was about to ask a question but the door opened and Reuben Vinestock stood in the frame. 'Oh God,' he said. 'Not again.'

'You haven't found what you're looking for,' Mirabelle countered. 'Which is because I found it earlier.'

Reuben eyed her. 'Have you got it?'

'Can we come in?'

Vinestock stood back to allow them to enter. He closed the door behind them.

'Well?' he said, uneasily.

'I'm sorry,' Mirabelle replied. 'I didn't unravel things until now. I still don't understand it all. If I'd realised I'd have let you know straight away.'

Vinestock held out his hand and Mirabelle passed him the packet. He leafed through the photographs, the low sound of his exhalation punctuating the silence as he took in the images. 'Thank you,' he said, eventually.

'Did they do this? The Beaumonts? Was it them?' Vesta's tone was insistent – she sounded angry. The photographs had shocked her.

'The Beaumonts?' Vinestock was incredulous. 'No. The British Government is doing it. The British Army. This is what they are doing to Kenyans who want independence. These are con-centration camps, Mrs Lewis.' He pulled out one of the photographs. 'Ten years after everyone said "never again" and the gates of Auschwitz were blown open.' He proffered an image of a thin black woman, standing beside a barbed wire fence, her skin marked with wide sores. 'The British are sup-posed to be the good guys. And we're killing people. Starving the Mau Mau. Shooting them indiscriminately. Every day. Right now.'

'Well, we have to do something about it.' Vesta sniffed, trying not to look at the photograph.

'I am,' he said. 'I'm going to use these photographs as evidence. I'm going to write an exposé.'

'In the *Telegraph?*'

'Don't be ridiculous. The *Telegraph* is all for keeping the Mau Mau in their place. They think they're just *Untermensch*. Scratch a Tory get a Fascist, remember. No. I'll set up something under an assumed name with one of the left-wing papers. The *Daily Herald,* maybe. Someone will take it on. It's a big story and now I can prove it. If there are photographs, they'll have to run it.'

'It's evidence in the matter of Dougie Beaumont's murder too, isn't it?' Mirabelle cut in.

'Those bastards.' Vinestock's eyes blazed.

'I don't understand,' Vesta said again.

Mirabelle's eyebrows raised only a fraction as she deferred to Vinestock. His mouth was set hard.

'Dougie had no idea what was going on until last Christmas when he was back in Kenya and he flew over one of the camps. None of us knew. When he found out, it horrified him, and he immediately wanted to expose what was going on. He was a decent person. The trouble was, George wasn't. George didn't think this was any of their business. He reckoned it was too dangerous to get involved and given what's happened, maybe he was right. Anyway Dougie said if George didn't want anything to do with what was happening to the Mau Mau, then he didn't want anything to do with George. He'd made up his mind to go back to Nairobi and get evidence. These pictures. The two of them fought about it for weeks. Dougie said he'd changed. His old life wasn't enough any more. They spent weeks around Monaco and the South of France bickering. A sunny place for shady people, isn't that what they call it? The fighting went on and on. When they came back for Goodwood, Dougie moved out of here and then it really got vicious. I think he couldn't believe George didn't care, that he wouldn't help. The two of them had always been inseparable. Last time I spoke to him, Dougie said George didn't deserve the life he had, if he wouldn't take responsibility for people like this, people who were in real trouble. They are going to wipe out the Mau Mau. That's what they're going to do. The poor buggers don't stand a chance.'

'Do you mean, Dougie and George had never fought before?' Mirabelle's voice was calm.

Vinestock shook his head. 'Not seriously. It came out of the blue, I think – a surprise for both of them. I mean, they were totally fired up. Dougie had to do something. George felt he absolutely shouldn't. It got worse and worse. Dougie said George could start again from scratch for all he cared. That this place would be his only asset. They'd put together some kind of fiddle, I think, months before all this came up. Dougie had taken all of George's assets. He was supposed to hold them for him.'

'So George could avoid paying his tax bill?'

'I suppose so. George had made a fortune, quite separately from what the Beaumonts were up to.

He liked those icons, you know the ones with gold leaf – there are a few upstairs. He collected the ones that got damaged that he couldn't sell on. Mostly, he'd buy them on the sly from Russians on the lam. Then he'd hide them in his suitcase and bring them in. There's a lot of art on the Continent. George had a good eye. He sold several pieces to collectors for a small fortune and he never paid any tax, but the revenue service was on to him. The way it worked out, George and Dougie made it look as if Dougie owned almost everything – George's share of the car, for a start. They didn't want the taxman to seize that. They figured that if George couldn't pay up, then the taxman would have to go hang.' Vinestock faltered, blushing at his unfortunate analogy. 'I didn't mean... They just thought it'd make it easier to settle George's case.'

'That's why George was so keen to go down to Tangmere when the car came in. He was staking his claim to his share and he expected the rest of the Beaumonts to honour it.'

'I suppose. The Beaumonts must have known the two of them had been fighting. There was one family dinner, I heard, where the whole thing blew up over a hundred quid that George insisted Dougie owed him. The truth was, Dougie wasn't being fair. He was angry. But life isn't fair.' Vinestock brandished the sheaf of photographs in Mirabelle's direction.

'So Dougie took these photographs?'

'Yes. Three or four weeks ago. He went back to Nairobi on a flying visit. He intended to give them to me, so I could get them published. I said we had to keep it quiet until we could get the photos to press, but Dougie shot his mouth off a couple of times in France on the circuit. He'd drink and get angry. He couldn't understand why so many people he considered friends, didn't care about what was happening. It turns out they did care – just not in the way he expected. I don't know who killed him but this is why they did it. There are a lot of vested interests in Kenya – the Beaumonts aren't the only family that has a finger in the pie. There's a lobby to keep what's going on out of the public eye. Dougie was too upfront. Apart from anything else he had told his father and Michael that he intended to take action.'

'Do you think Elrick Beaumont killed him? His own son?' Vesta looked as if she wanted to punch someone.

'No. Tough as Elrick is, Dougie was the goose that laid the golden egg. I don't think he'd have knocked him off. But I'm not saying he didn't have a suspicion or just stand aside.'

'He knew,' Mirabelle cut in. 'He knew enough to give himself an alibi.'

Reuben stopped to take this in. Vesta was still trying to work out the story.

'So George? Might he have killed Dougie?' she said.

'George? No. He was genuinely beside himself when Dougie died. I didn't lie about that. After Miss Bevan came to the office the first time I asked him why he'd gone down to Brighton the day after the fire.'

'What did he say?'

'He cried. I think he'd gone because he

couldn't believe it. He thought they'd get over it. Make it up.'

'Did you find out what he removed from Dougie's bedroom?'

'He said it was a letter he'd written. I don't know what it said. Maybe I'd have found out if George hadn't died too.'

'Who do you think killed them, Reuben?'

Vinestock shrugged. 'I have no idea. Dougie died because of this, though. British Army? British Intelligence? Or maybe just a family friend who didn't want to lose the land he owned in Africa. With George, I mean, he could be difficult. He was tenacious. But the only person he'd had a fight with recently was Dougie, and Dougie was already gone. His death was a real bolt from the blue. It doesn't make sense. If I'm honest, I've been trying not to think about it. I've been trying to focus on these photographs. They're more important. The deaths were bad enough but losing the images too – I mean, Dougie died for them. When his flat was set on fire, I thought it was likely the film had been destroyed, I mean, that was why they'd done it. It wasn't until we came here earlier today that I realised there was a chance that Dougie might have left the film here, intending to drop it off after he'd sorted out his car.'

'But there's nothing of Dougie Beaumont's in the whole place.' Vesta sounded mystified. 'You said he'd moved out.'

'He did. I didn't expect to find Dougie's clothes. All that had gone months ago. But it was odd that there wasn't any mail for him. I mean, George

311

clearly hadn't been back – God knows where he was staying. But he had a pile of letters and there was nothing for Dougie. I figured someone had come in and picked up Dougie's mail. Dougie, as it turned out. And if that was the case he might have stashed the film, mightn't he? Where did he hide it, Miss Bevan?'

'Upstairs. In the bathroom. In a locked box – a carriage clock. Clever really.'

'Dougie was clever. I miss him.'

Mirabelle stared at the sitting-room shelves. Reuben Vinestock had been working his way through the stacks of books, hoping to find the film.

'I found their cocaine,' he said cheerfully, picking up a hardback copy of *The Weekend Cricketer* and opening it to reveal a recess that had been cut into the pages. 'But that isn't what I was looking for. Thanks for doing what you've done.'

'Please, be careful,' Mirabelle said. 'They have arrested Michael Crowe and the Beaumonts' chauffeur.'

'Arrested?'

'Just now. Only round the corner. The Beaumont family business has been under surveillance for some time. I wasn't the only person who realised they had been smuggling diamonds. And I realised rather late.' Mirabelle indicated the table shrouded in the dark velvet cloth. 'You helped, didn't you? It's how you got involved with them in the first place. Translating. Like you said – a clever Jew.'

Vinestock nodded. 'Do you think the police will pick me up?'

'I imagine they'll want to question you. They know you have translated for Michael Crowe in the past. He always does the deals, doesn't he?'

Vinestock nodded again.

'Well, you need to be careful all round then. If there are people who were prepared to kill Dougie Beaumont to suppress these photographs, they'd happily kill you for the same reason, Reuben.'

'I can't stand by while this is happening. Not if I can do something about it. During the war almost all my family...' His voice trailed.

Mirabelle touched his arm. 'You have to stay away from the police for long enough to write the article and sell in the pictures. Then your best bet will be to leave the country. You understand that?'

Vinestock looked touched. 'That will be the easy part. Well. Come on, then.' He picked up his coat and hat from the chair. 'I better get on with it.'

'You need to leave by the back. The window in the kitchen.'

'What?'

'It's a long story. Please, trust me. Go that way. It's safer.'

They helped him to open the sash and drop on to the laneway. 'Don't go home or to the *Telegraph*. Just do what you need to do,' Mirabelle instructed before closing the window.

Reuben hovered for a moment, staring through the grubby glass as if he was asking a question. Then he checked over his shoulder and was on his way.

'We should put back the books,' Mirabelle said. 'With our gloves on. At some point I'm sure the police will come and search for prints in here. We have to stay for a few minutes anyway, to give Reuben a head start.'

Vesta didn't say anything. She followed Mirabelle into the sitting room and started restocking the shelves. When she came to *The Weekend Cricketer* she held it up.

'What do you want me to do with this?'

'Just pop it back.' Mirabelle turned her attention to the last of the hardbacks – a set of three books about boxing – as Vesta slid the drugs into place and paused, leaning against the velvet-clad table as she perused the restored bookshelves. 'Thanks for not asking too many questions.'

Vesta shrugged. She wasn't tearful now. 'You're right about it being Piccadilly Circus.'

Mirabelle's face softened. 'Different people have different concerns. Most of the Beaumont clan only care about money. They have been smuggling diamonds since Dougie met Michael Crowe all those years ago. They found a way out of their predicament. They found a way to be rich.'

'And that's why Mr Crowe got arrested? That's what you said, didn't you?'

'It seems so unimportant compared to what Reuben Vinestock is about to attempt. But yes – Michael Crowe and his chauffeur, the pair of them. And Elrick Beaumont too.'

'Does this mean the two murders aren't linked, after all?'

'Really,' said Mirabelle, 'I'm beginning to think that killing George Highton was just a terrible mistake. And that would make sense except for the money.'

'Money?'

'Yes. He said he had no money to continue playing backgammon. But he died with over a hundred pounds in his pocket. At first I thought he'd lied about it, but now I wonder. And that note, as well.'

'The blackmail letter?'

'Yes. If Highton didn't have anything left, why blackmail him? I mean, there is no point in blackmailing somebody if they can't pay. He'd fallen out with Dougie and by extension with the rest of the family, so why would someone target him? I'd have thought Dougie himself, or Crowe or even Elrick Beaumont would be a better bet. He had nothing but this place.'

Vesta cut in. 'Do you want to go to the solicitor's office? We could ask some questions.'

Mirabelle considered. 'No. I think we need to go back to the Beaumonts' house. Enid and her mother will be there. They might not have heard the news yet. But there's one last thing we have to deal with before we go.'

Vesta followed Mirabelle's line of sight as she glanced only momentarily out of the window to the front of the house.

'Is there somebody out there?'

'I imagine so.' Mirabelle checked her watch and then reached for her handbag. 'I'd be surprised if there wasn't.'

Bleeding Heart Yard appeared deserted as they stepped on to the cobbles. Mirabelle strode confidently to a lock-up opposite George Highton's front door. The opening was a fraction askew. She pushed it further. Inside was the man who had dropped off the photographs and another fellow that Mirabelle hadn't seen before, though he must have been following them since they dropped in at the Blue Door Club.

'Reuben Vinestock is long gone,' Mirabelle announced. 'You can tell Mr Golding neither Mrs Lewis nor I will have any more to do with this. We just gave Mr Vinestock a decent start, that's all. And you might also tell Mr Golding that the Firm is on the wrong side in this matter. That's my opinion.'

The men shuffled uncomfortably.

Mirabelle turned on her heel and stalked towards the gate that led on to Ely Place. 'We can probably hail a cab on the main road.'

'We're never going to find out who killed Dougie Beaumont, are we?' Vesta glanced behind. She was almost sure they were no longer being followed but she still felt uneasy.

Mirabelle didn't answer. She didn't even break her stride.

'Are we in danger?' Vesta checked.

'I don't think so.'

'But they'll kill Vinestock if they can.'

'They'll try to get the photographs. They'll only kill him if they have to. If he won't give up.'

Vesta didn't know what to say. It was clear that Reuben Vinestock was determined not to quit. And those men. She wanted to ask how Mirabelle knew about them, but she was certain Mirabelle would never tell. She cast her mind back to the office on Brills Lane with its detailed ledgers, easy certainties and cosy cups of tea. It seemed like a different world. No wonder Mirabelle sometimes seemed so separate from everyone else. At the corner, Mirabelle raised a hand and a hackney cab pulled to a halt at the kerb. As she stepped inside, Vesta realised she was relieved that they couldn't discuss anything in the back seat. She decided she'd spend the journey thinking of what she would tell Charlie she'd been up to in London, because she definitely didn't want to admit what was really going on. Not by a long shot.

Chapter 21

Real knowledge is to know the extent of one's ignorance

The black Maria was parked outside when they got there. Mirabelle placed a gloved hand on the engine, which was still warm. McGregor must have left Mayhew to his interrogation and dispatched himself to Belgravia with the news of Michael Crowe's arrest. Perhaps he wasn't taking his eye entirely off the ball, after all. She rang the bell and the butler answered the door in short order.

'Mrs Beaumont is indisposed,' he said.

An English butler was a buffer between the family he worked for and the world – the post was an institution that stretched back for centuries. Mirabelle couldn't help think that the Beaumont's butler had the look of a man who would never say

317

yes to something if he could say no instead.

'I think Superintendent McGregor might be glad we have arrived,' Mirabelle replied smoothly. 'Do you think you could let him know that we are here?'

The man's face did not betray any recognition of the name Mirabelle had dropped. 'Please wait,' he said.

Mirabelle smiled. The truth, of course, was quite the reverse. McGregor most likely was cross with her. She'd embarrassed him in front of Charles Mayhew. Then he'd told her to stay in the pub on Hatton Garden and she'd left at the first opportunity. Still, at least the butler would have to announce that she and Vesta had arrived and Mrs Beaumont might be glad of the company. She could not be having an easy day.

Mirabelle shifted. A buffer of warm air lingered on the doorstep from the long radiators that were concealed behind covers running the length of the Beaumont's hallway. It was cold outside.

'Well,' said Vesta, 'it's terribly rude of him to leave us here, don't you think?'

Mirabelle was about to remark that she was sure he wouldn't be long when the door opened smartly and the butler reappeared. 'Mrs Beaumont is engaged, I'm afraid. Would you like to leave a card, Miss Bevan?'

It was a long time since Mirabelle had carried calling cards. 'No. Thank you.'

The door closed and Vesta let out an exasperated sigh. She stepped back on to the pavement and looked up at the house as if inspiration might come from one of the long windows that loomed above. Then her eyes lighted on something further up the street. 'Mirabelle,' she said, 'they arrested the chauffeur, didn't they?'

'Yes.' Mirabelle sounded distracted.

'So–' Vesta could hardly contain herself. '–who's driving the Rolls?' She pointed along the road just as the long burgundy car turned into the lane.

Vesta led the way. She was the one who had visited the garage before, after all. Mirabelle noted that you could tell the girl was furious from the way she walked. She had a sudden vision of Vesta not bothering to ask any questions, just punching whoever it was she found in the garage. The photographs had clearly shocked her. It was difficult, she remembered, when you first realised what evil there was in the world. Not only a murderer – something domestic – but cold hard evil. There was a worse revelation that Vesta hadn't come to yet – that evil like that required evil to take it on.

The Rolls-Royce was parked untidily outside the garage and they had to squeeze past it to get in.

'Hello,' Vesta called.

The sound of movement carried from the utility room next door and Kamari appeared in the connecting doorway. He squinted towards the women as if he couldn't quite make them out. The light, after all, was low. Still, the pretence was affected. They were quite recognisable, the two of them.

'Couldn't you get the car in?' Vesta said, pointedly. 'It's a tight turn.'

Kamari glared. He had given up smiling, it

seemed, and from his expression it looked as if he was angry too, although Mirabelle wasn't sure exactly what he was angry about. 'You're the one who came earlier right? The black girl? What is it? Why are you sniffing around, following me?'

To her credit, Vesta kept her voice smooth. 'We're trying to find out what's going on,' she said. 'To help.'

The man's eyes strayed in the direction of the main house. 'Help,' he said contemptuously. 'We don't need help. Not from two women. Go away. I have things to do.'

Vesta caught Mirabelle's eye, as if she wasn't sure what to say next. 'Don't you want to know who killed Dougie Beaumont?' Mirabelle stepped in.

Kamari's eyes widened. His voice lowered and, given what she had said, he stayed unnaturally still. 'The authorities will find out who perpetrated this terrible crime,' he said coldly. It seemed rather formal. Mirabelle let the silence lie. People gave themselves away every time, you just had to give them long enough. After four or five seconds, Kamari smirked, almost imperceptibly, but not quite, as if he had got away with something.

'You know who killed him,' she said. 'You know why, as well, don't you?'

The man's tone switched to outrage. 'How can you say that? As if I would know anything about Mr Beaumont's death and say nothing of it.'

'They were warned, weren't they? Elrick Beaumont and Michael Crowe. They knew what was going to happen and they covered themselves. And you too, Kamari.'

Kamari let this pass, only for a beat. Then he burst out, 'He was going to free them. He was going to let the Mau Mau go. It was weakness. Stupidity. He deserved to die.'

Mirabelle bit her tongue. Telling Kamari that she thought Dougie Beaumont had displayed both empathy and bravery would not help. 'What about George Highton? You were at Goodwood with your master the night he died. Do you know who killed him?'

'Get out!' Kamari stepped forward, gesturing ahead of him, as if he was herding sheep desperately along a track. 'You've no right to come here and ask stupid questions.'

'So you know that too.' Mirabelle didn't flinch.

Vesta couldn't contain herself any longer. 'It's one of Michael Crowe's golf clubs, isn't it? That's the murder weapon. One of the clubs you were practically wrapped around in the car. Which club was it? Which club did he use?'

'Mr Crowe is a gentleman,' Kamari spat. 'And he has an alibi. Go away.'

'Mr Crowe is in custody and will probably go to jail. But you're right, I don't think he killed George Highton,' Mirabelle snapped back.

Vesta swung round. 'Why?'

'Kamari knows why, don't you, Kamari?'

They waited. Kamari raised his eyes. He seemed panicked. 'I did it,' he said in a rush. 'I killed him. I waited till he left the house, I took one of Mr Crowe's clubs and I hit him hard.'

'Ha! I'll fetch the superintendent,' Vesta sounded triumphant. 'He'll have to let us in now. You hold him here, Mirabelle.'

She turned and stalked on to the paving stones as if she had achieved something. Mirabelle waited. She had more experience.

'Which club?' she asked.

'I cleaned them. There is no proof.'

'How many times did you strike him?'

Kamari's eyes danced as he thought about it. He couldn't answer.

Mirabelle pushed him further. 'What did you do after you'd killed Mr Highton, Kamari?'

'After?' It took him a moment. 'I cleaned the golf clubs. Then someone found him. I knew they couldn't prove it was me.'

She raised an eyebrow. He was the worst liar she had encountered in a long time. Still, it couldn't be easy in his second language. She continued to humour him. 'All right. Why did you do it? If you killed Mr Highton, you must have had a reason. He wasn't interested in exposing what the British were doing in Kenya. So what was your motive? Why did you kill him?'

Kamari stuttered. Then he managed to get out, 'He was a bad man.'

'What do you mean?'

'He was very bad.'

Kamari backed away. From his vantage point at the door on to the garden he could see the house. A flicker of distress crossed his face. He glanced past Mirabelle, but discounted that as an escape route. Then he took off in the only direction open to him – down the lawn. Mirabelle followed, clattering through the back door and past a maze of laundries and pantries and the kitchen. A scullery maid, who couldn't be more than fourteen, collided with Mirabelle in the corridor. The poor girl apologised, curtsying as Mirabelle rushed ahead. She clattered up the service stairs and at the top came out into the hallway. Up here, the house was silent. She looked left and right. Behind her, the stairs stretched to the upper floors. The building was huge and he could have gone in any direction. Then the doorbell rang and she spun round. Through a long pane of glass beside the entrance, Mirabelle caught a glimpse of Vesta hovering on the doorstep. She momentarily considered letting her in but Vesta would make a lot of noise and, no doubt, require an explanation. She didn't have long to make a decision. The butler would be coming.

Casting her eyes around the hallway, she counted seven doors. The ones to the left were closed, and, she guessed, at least two of them must lead to the drawing room where Mrs Beaumont was being interviewed by the superintendent under the glassy gaze of the stuffed heads over the mantel. Her instinct led her to the right, past the stairway. Then she heard a noise – a creak – almost as if the house had shifted in confirmation. She followed the sound. At the front, the door to the first room had been left ajar but it was unoccupied. Next along, however, the second door opened on to a study lined with leather-bound books. An oil painting of a family member was mounted in a wide gilt frame over the fireplace. Kamari wasn't here. It took Mirabelle a moment to realise what was out of place, what had made the noise. It was a fire. But it wasn't in the grate – instead someone had stacked a few logs on a tiger-skin rug in front of the mantelpiece. Under-pinning the little tower was a stack of papers that were kindling. Already flames were licking their way from the papers to the wood.

As if in a nightmare, Mirabelle grabbed a velvet cushion from one of the chairs and began to beat out the nascent flames, but the material must have been highly flammable and the cushion began to emit smoke as it caught alight. She dropped it in horror, her heart racing in panic. Then, as she spun round, trying to decide what to do, she noticed Enid Crowe sitting perfectly still at the desk. She had changed out of the clothes she'd worn earlier and now wore a large diamond pen-dant over a dark green blouse. The stone was huge and looked faintly ridiculous. Enid smiled and, as she moved her head, Mirabelle spotted diamond earrings too, glinting in the light from the window. She wondered how she had missed the fact that Enid was there – perhaps she had sat so still that she hadn't stood out. Mirabelle wondered if that was the problem. Enid had never stood out.

'Miss Bevan,' she said, putting down the fountain pen with which she had been writing before she froze. 'Can I help you?'

'I am looking for Kamari.' Mirabelle's eyes darted towards the fire.

'Kamari?'

'Yes.'

'I haven't seen him. He's usually in the garage or the kitchen. Cook spoils him rather. Dough-nuts and so forth.'

'Mrs Crowe, this fire.' Mirabelle felt her palms becoming sticky. The smoke was beginning to cloud and she coughed as she struggled to think straight. 'I'm sure we should put it out.' She stamped on the cushion.

'Do you think it will damage this house? This precious house? The house it turns out we've all been selling ourselves for. This house that is so important my father will let my brother die rather than lose the money it takes to keep this bloody house on the right side of the bottom line.'

Mirabelle's mouth was dry. 'I was rescued from the fire,' she said.

Enid stood up and banged her fist on the leather desktop. 'And nobody told me, of course. My own husband. My father. Nobody told me because I don't matter.' A tear trailed down her face.

'I think I'd be angry, just as angry as you must be,' Mirabelle tried. She wondered if she might be able to rouse the butler. The fire hadn't spread on to the tiger skin and there was still time, if they caught it now, to put it out without too much fuss. She cast around and strode over to a drinks tray. She picked up a soda siphon and emptied it on to the glowing heart of the little blaze.

'I can't believe what they made of me,' Enid spat, ignoring what Mirabelle was doing. She picked up a piece of paper from the desk and inserted it into an envelope. 'You know, when we were little we had a nanny. I don't know how they paid for her but she was lovely. We called her "Ina". Nug was terrible at talking. He only ever used short words right up until he left for school. I suppose she might have been Georgina or something. Regina, maybe. Nanny used to sit me on her knee and we'd look out of the nursery window and she'd say "Right over there is Buckingham Palace, can you see it over the rooftops? Now you tell me, how could everything not be well?"'

'Buckingham Palace,' Mirabelle repeated as the soda dribbled out. The fire was burning in a ring now. She had succeeded in quenching the flames at its centre but the burning papers had spread outwards to the edges of the pelt. The hairs were starting to singe. Mirabelle stepped back. She wasn't sure if she had done the right thing. After all, the fire appeared to be getting larger. Her heart was hammering ten to the dozen.

'When we went to the park, she always told us, "We didn't see anyone today we liked better than ourselves." Sweet, that, isn't it?' Enid sniffed. 'Except I don't like us any longer, you see. Why did you want Kamari?'

Mirabelle struggled to control the fact she was shaking. Enid seemed so nonchalant.

'Kamari confessed,' she managed. 'He said he killed George Highton.'

'That was sweet of him. But it isn't true. It would never do to have a whipping boy.'

Mirabelle's eyes met Enid's. 'But... Do you mean, you killed George Highton?'

Enid couldn't speak for a moment. Tears welled up and she struggled. 'Poor Dingo,' she said. 'I thought he'd done it. I thought he killed Dougie, you see. That stupid letter...'

Momentarily, Mirabelle's attention was diverted from the fire at her feet. 'You mean the blackmail letter?'

'Yes. I found it in his jacket pocket that afternoon. Well, you were there, weren't you? When I lifted his jacket. When he first arrived. I read it straight after that and I just assumed. God, never assume. That's good advice, isn't it? Well, I assumed George had sent the letter to Dougie – they were having a spat you see, and the stupid fools kept threatening each other. He wanted a hundred and twenty pounds he said Dougie owed him. Or else. I really thought he'd done it.'

'So you picked up one of your husband's golf clubs.'

'Yes. That night. After dinner. I waited on the driveway. I knew George would end up stumbling back to the hotel. I said I'd never forgive him and he had time to say "What for?" before I hit him. I didn't see how awful it was. It was dark and I was in such a state. Afterwards, when they brought his body inside, I saw what I'd done.'

'And you put a hundred and twenty pounds in his pocket.'

'Yes. Money in his pocket and the stupid letter in his hand. I thought that was why he'd killed Nuggie. For a hundred and twenty pounds. How ridiculous. What the hell was I thinking?'

'But your father and your husband covered for you?'

'It was the first time ever that I was important, as it happens. They didn't tell me, of course.'

'Tell you what?'

'That I was completely wrong. I couldn't have been more wrong. George had that letter cos he'd taken it from Dougie's things – he hadn't wanted the police to find it. He knew it made him a suspect. But he didn't kill Nuggie.'

'Do you know who did?'

'No. But they knew it was going to happen. That's what I can't get over. I mean, Michael took me out for dinner and we went dancing and I couldn't understand why because normally he never spends any time with me unless he has to, but he knew Nuggie was going to be killed and he wanted an alibi. If I'd have known, I'd have driven straight down there and helped him fight the bastards off, whoever they were.'

'You wouldn't have succeeded, Mrs Crowe, if you don't mind me saying.'

'How do you know? Turns out I'm a murderer. And you wouldn't have expected that.'

The burning logs shifted slightly at Mirabelle's feet and one tumbled to the side, landing against the leg of a table.

'Well,' Enid said, 'I hope you find Kamari. Tell him I appreciate what he said, but it really isn't necessary.'

'But...' Mirabelle watched as Enid stalked out of the room. 'Mrs Crowe,' she tried to call her back, but then she was distracted as another log tumbled and there was a shower of sparks. She almost tripped over herself in the scramble to get out of the way. Shaking, she bravely picked up the edge of the tiger skin and rolled it over on itself, kicking it to put out the flames. 'Help,' she shouted. 'Fire!' But no one arrived and she just kept going, frantic with terror. Eventually, exhausted, she fell to her knees, her stockings smudged with smoke. Tears wet her cheeks. It felt like the night of the fire over again, though this time she had stamped it out to a smoulder. She'd saved herself. The poor tiger was a soggy mess. The papers that Enid had decided to burn were all but unreadable. Recovering her composure, Mirabelle leaned against a deep leather chair, gasping. She wondered if she might faint but it wasn't like it had been at Tangmere. She felt herself rally as she crossed to the window that overlooked the garden and opened it to let out the smoke. Too late to help, there was the sound of footsteps and the butler appeared and, behind him, Vesta.

'Madam.' He sounded bemused. 'There is smoke in the hallway.'

'Yes. I put out a fire,' Mirabelle explained. 'Mrs Crowe set one, you see.'

She was about to ask for Superintendent Mc-Gregor, when there was a shriek from outside and, in front of the window, the flash of Enid's form fell past, only a couple of feet in front of her. The sound of the girl's body landing on the grass made Mirabelle flinch. Vesta rushed forwards. For a moment everything was too still, not least Enid Crowe's broken body. A smear of blood spattered the large diamond at her throat. Her legs were splayed.

Mirabelle thought she might vomit. 'Oh God. I should have stopped her,' she whispered. Her eyes moved to the desk. Had Enid been writing a confession? Before she could gather herself to say anything, McGregor and Mrs Beaumont rushed into the study.

'I said not to let them in,' McGregor snapped at the butler and then, as he moved forward and saw the body on the grass, he turned and tried to shield Mrs Beaumont. He was too late. The poor woman put her hand over her mouth.

'Enid,' she said blankly.

Mirabelle had a sudden sense of Mrs Beaumont being entirely alone in this grand house. Everyone had been taken from her – her son and daughter were dead, her husband and son-in-law were in custody. And George was gone. She was the last Beaumont left at liberty. It seemed there was always a woman who had to pick up the pieces. The butler moved forward and tried to guide her to one of the chairs but Mrs Beaumont waved him off.

'Borman, I shall need to speak to his Grace at Chichester,' she got out with barely a sniff. Then she turned towards Mirabelle. 'At least I know what to do this time,' she said.

Epilogue

Change in all things is sweet

Six weeks later

Mirabelle stared at the slate grey sea out of her long window. Behind her, the flat was all but perfect. Vesta had even replaced the paperbacks in the hallway. The air still smelled of fresh paint. Mirabelle wished she could be as easily renovated as these few rooms. She pulled a mohair wrap around her shoulders – it was cold today, but she didn't want to light the fire.

Beside the sofa there was a newspaper – the *Daily Herald* – not her usual choice. She had been buying it every day, but Reuben Vinestock's article had not appeared on its pages nor had his regular column turned up in the *Daily Telegraph*. His absence felt eerie. After a fortnight, she had phoned his office only to be told that Vinestock no longer worked at the paper and that they had no forwarding address. Still, she had continued to buy the *Herald*. Not to do so felt like giving up on him, but she knew she would, soon. She would have to.

Today's headline was about Elrick Beaumont's constituency where a by-election had been called. It looked as if the Labour candidate might win – the poor Conservative who was standing in Beaumont's place must have found it an uphill struggle to counter the accusations of Tory corruption, which had been levelled by the *Herald's* political correspondent. Mirabelle read the articles at a remove. That was how she felt about everything these last weeks. Removed. The day she had returned from London she had written an anonymous letter to the editor of *The Times* but she had no proof about the Mau Mau or for that matter about Reuben, and the letter had not been published or even acknowledged.

As the light faded from the sky, there was a rap at the door. She snapped on one of the side lamps and went to answer it. McGregor stood on the doorstep holding a bunch of lilies. Mirabelle shuddered. Lilies reminded her of death – the smell of them.

'House-warming,' he said.

She gave a smile, just a small one, and put the bouquet on the table by the door, motioning him to come in.

'Vesta did a good job,' he said, looking around as he took off his coat and hat. 'It's nice here. You'd hardly know, would you?'

Mirabelle did not reply. Instead, she motioned towards the tantalus of whisky on the drinks trolley. McGregor nodded. She poured them both a dram and added a splash of water. McGregor held up his glass in a silent toast and she clicked hers against it.

'I wish you'd left it to me,' he said. 'I hate to see you like this.'

Mirabelle savoured the peaty taste. 'I dream about her almost every night, Alan. Falling like that. The terrible noise of her landing.'

It was the most she'd admitted to anyone. Vesta and she had come to an uneasy agreement to say nothing about what had happened. The office had been uncharacteristically silent since they got back, the tension of checking the *Herald* the worst part of the day. They had failed to help anyone. That was the worst of it.

McGregor said nothing. Instead, he put his arms around her and Mirabelle sank into him. She had no idea how long they stood there. It was good that he was a patient man, sometimes, at least. When she pulled away he took her hand and kissed it.

'I'm sorry,' he said.

She moved forwards and pressed her lips to his.

The taste of the whisky was familiar and it felt comforting. She pulled him closer, clinging on tightly.

'I want you to stay with me,' she said.

McGregor didn't hesitate. He lifted her into his arms, carried her to the bedroom and laid her on the icy quilted satin. Mirabelle pulled him down towards her as he undid the buttons on her blouse and took in the brassiere that Madame Vergisson had sent only the week before. Ivory silk, tailored to fit. He looked at her as if to check that this was really what she wanted. Mirabelle nodded. She didn't want to think about it any more. She didn't want to think about anything. Even if it was only for this evening. Slowly, she wriggled out of the blouse. His eyes danced across her skin as it emerged. She took off her skirt too. It had been a long time. Too long. McGregor loosened his tie and leaned in to kiss her again. Then he slowly removed his jacket and trousers. Lying down beside her, his skin smelled familiar, the brush of his five o'clock shadow was comforting on her cheek. Mirabelle ran her foot down his leg as they kissed, wrapping herself around him and giggling that he still had his shoes on. She kicked lightly to flick one heavy brogue on to the floor. McGregor pulled back. She stroked his chest.

'I like to keep my shoes on,' he said.

She laughed. 'Would you like me to put mine back on too?'

He shook his head. 'Is it too odd?'

'Well, a little strange, perhaps.' Mirabelle glanced at his arms. He was more muscular than she had expected. She pulled him towards her again.

'Whatever you like,' she whispered. They started to move together. It felt like disappearing. This is exactly what I need, she thought. And outside, high above them, the moon rose over the surf.

Author's Postscript

I didn't know anything about the Mau Mau uprising until I bumped into Richard Lewis at the Central Library in Edinburgh and told him I was writing about the 1950s. He suggested I take a look at what was going on in Kenya and I was shocked by what I found. The history of Colonial and Empirical Britain often does not cover us in glory. Between 1952 and 1960 a conflict rose between the British Army in Kenya and an anti-Colonial, economically deprived, mostly Kikuyu tribal group who (quite rightly in my view) wanted land rights and more freedom. The British did not take kindly to their economic and social grievances and the conflict escalated quickly into violence after the Mau Mau killed a British woman in 1952. The openly racist British Establishment effected swift reprisals including confiscating livestock and land and imposing collective fines as well as declaring a State of Emergency and suspending civil liberties. They also began rounding up the Mau Mau into internment camps, where widespread malnutrition and illness quickly developed. In *Operation Goodwood* it's pictures of these internment camps that Dougie Beaumont smuggles out of Nairobi and Reuben Vinestock risks his life to try to publish in the end. In post-war Britain, the conflict was covered scantily in the press and always with a highly anti-Mau Mau bias so my fictional characters were brave in trying to expose the camps. They were horrible places and thousands of Kenyans interned in them died. At the time of writing the British Government is in negotiation with the last of the survivors over compensation.

Acknowledgements

This book is dedicated to the wonderful Jenny Brown, but there's more! Thanks so much to the many people who helped me – from Richard Lewis who brought the Mau Mau to my attention, to readers who made suggestions about locations, characters and subjects, to people I contacted along the way to help me with their specialist knowledge. A big thank you goes out to everyone at Goodwood who hosted me twice while I made my investigations. From the staff at the Goodwood Hotel and at The Kennels to James Peill, the curator of Goodwood House, and, of course, Lord March himself, who kindly agreed to the book's title and also invited me to a very glorious day out at the racecourse. Your generosity was just so kind. Doug Nye, who is a wonderful expert on vintage racing and all things CAR (I am Mirabelle, not Vesta, when it comes to matters of the motor), kindly shared his expert knowledge as did Euan Grant and the Goodwins, who helped with all things Diamond. In the case of making mistakes – the facts are yours, the errors mine. A big shout out is also due to the new publication team at Constable and Robinson who steered me through the ins and outs of a different kind of publication – so thanks to you too. Rebecca at VHA keeps me on track when it comes to matters of broadcast and what to expect. We have excellent phone calls (and occasionally a drink). Chin, chin. And, last of all, big love to my family who put up with me typing in the middle of the night, being distracted at meals and even on holiday and wait patiently while I trawl vintage shops and market stalls because Mirabelle or Vesta might have left something behind... Thank you, thank you, thank you. There, I've said it.

The publishers hope that this book has given you enjoyable reading. Large Print Books are especially designed to be as easy to see and hold as possible. If you wish a complete list of our books please ask at your local library or write directly to:

Magna Large Print Books
Magna House, Long Preston,
Skipton, North Yorkshire.
BD23 4ND

This Large Print Book for the partially sighted, who cannot read normal print, is published under the auspices of

THE ULVERSCROFT FOUNDATION